FULL SCOOP

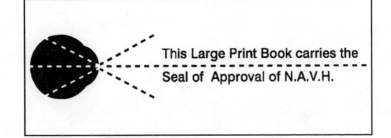

This Large Print Book carries the
Seal of Approval of N.A.V.H.

FULL SCOOP

JANET EVANOVICH AND CHARLOTTE HUGHES

THORNDIKE PRESS

An imprint of Thomson Gale, a part of The Thomson Corporation

THOMSON

GALE

Detroit • New York • San Francisco • New Haven, Conn. • Waterville, Maine • London

LIBRARY OF CONGRESS CATALOGING-IN-PUBLICATION DATA

Evanovich, Janet.
    Full scoop / by Janet Evanovich and Charlotte Hughes.
        p. cm. — (Full series ; #6) (Thorndike Press large print Americana)
    Includes bibliographical references and index.
    ISBN 0-7862-8711-X (lg. print : alk. paper) 1. Holt, Max (Fictitious character) — Fiction. 2. Large type books. I. Hughes, Charlotte, 1954–
II. Title.
PS3555.V2126F847 2006
813'.54—dc22   2006023810

U.S. Hardcover:
ISBN 13: 978-0-7862-8711-6
ISBN 10: 0-7862-8711-X

Published in 2006 by arrangement with St. Martin's Press, LLC

Printed in the United States of America on permanent paper
10 9 8 7 6 5 4 3 2 1

FULL SCOOP

CHAPTER ONE

"Maggie, what in the world are you doing up there!"

Standing on her swivel desk chair, Dr. Maggie Davenport jumped at the sound of her nurse's voice. The chair pivoted, swung to the right in a half circle. Maggie said, *"Eek!,"* and grabbed one of the shelves of the built-in bookcase, knocking off several medical books, including *Gray's Anatomy.* The tome bounced off her head. "Ugh!" Maggie winced as tiny dots blinked back at her like fireflies. The chair rolled several inches.

Nurse Queenie Cloud stood motionless, her mouth forming a perfect O. "You're going to kill yourself!"

Maggie tried to get the chair under control, but it refused to cooperate, twisting back and forth as though trying to dance to an old Chubby Checker tune. "Holy crap!" Queenie bolted forward and Maggie reached out blindly, accidentally sinking her fingers into the other woman's cap of tightly wound white curls. "Let go of my hair!" Queenie cried. She caught the back of the chair and steadied it. "Get down from there before we both end up going to the ER!"

"It's not my fault you came in here and scared me half to death while I was searching for a reference book," Maggie said. She managed to climb from the chair without further injury, but her head was already beginning to throb.

"What reference book?" Queenie asked.

Maggie finger-combed her dark hair from her face, squared her shoulders, and tried to appear as professional as she could under the circumstances. "My, um, *Encyclopedia of Rare Illnesses.* If you must know," she added in her best physician's voice.

"Don't you go batting those baby-blue eyes at me," Queenie said, "and don't think for one minute I don't know what you were looking for. You were trying to find your stash, that's what you were doing." She gave a grunt. "You haven't even been clean for twenty-four hours."

Maggie should have known better than to try to pull a fast one on Queenie. At seventy, the woman was as sharp as the day she'd gone to work for Maggie's grandfather. Six-year-old Maggie had shaken the black woman's hand and promptly announced that she knew how babies were made. Queenie still treated her as though she were six even though Maggie had a medical degree and a thirteen-year-old daughter.

Maggie slumped. "Hey, I've been listening to crying babies and grumpy children for almost two hours straight without a break. I'm going through withdrawal here. You can't expect me to go cold turkey."

Queenie gave a huge sigh. "I knew this would happen. Okay, you can have *one.*" The woman reached into the pocket of her white uniform, pulled out a Hershey's Kiss, and slapped it into Maggie's open palm like a surgical instrument. "Eat fast. We have a situation in X-ray and you've got patients waiting." She hurried out.

Maggie pulled the foil wrap off the piece of chocolate and tossed it in her mouth. She held it on her tongue and felt the chocolate soften and melt. She closed her eyes and waited for her endorphins to kick in. Endorphins were good things. Exercise and sex raised endorphins, too, but she hadn't exercised lately, and she certainly hadn't had sex. She thought about it a lot; boy oh boy, did she think about it. Too bad she didn't know anybody she wanted to climb beneath the sheets with even though she often went through her mental list of the men she'd dated since returning to Beaumont. Too bad she had to count on chocolate to do the trick. Maybe if she ate less chocolate the men on her list would look better.

"Dr. Davenport?"

Maggie opened her eyes and found Alice, her X-ray technician, standing in the doorway, peering at her from beneath chestnut-colored bangs that needed trimming and reminded Maggie of a sheepdog. "I'm on my way."

A moment later, Maggie stepped into the X-ray room where a tearful six-year-old Bobby Carmichael sat on the stainless steel table, still holding a wad of tissue to his nose that he'd bloodied after falling from a piece of playground equipment at school. Maggie had ordered the X-ray in case he had a fracture. In a chair nearby, his mother was giving him a pep talk.

Alice held a ten-by-ten undeveloped X-ray. "Bobby doesn't want an X-ray."

Maggie smiled at him. "What's wrong, Bobby? X-rays don't hurt. Have you ever had one?"

"At the dentist," he managed. "But —"

The three women waited.

"It's going to hurt if she tries to stick that big thing in my mouth." He pointed to the X-ray.

"Oh, honey, Alice isn't going to put it in your mouth," Maggie said. She turned to Alice. "You might want to carefully explain the procedure to Bobby."

Queenie stood just outside the door and motioned for Maggie, who joined her once Bobby had been reassured.

"Our all-time favorite patient, Henry Filbert, stepped on a rusty nail," Queenie said. "He's in Room One. Susie O'Neal has a bad cold in Room Two and Dee Dee Fontana is in Room Three. She brought the baby in for his six-month checkup."

"I hope Dee Dee took my advice and talked to her ob-gyn about her hormone imbalance," Maggie whispered.

"Jamie Swift-Holt is with her," Queenie said. "They're early so don't knock yourself out rushing."

"I'll see Henry first; then Susie." Maggie stepped inside the exam room and found eleven-year-old Henry playing a handheld game. He didn't look up. Nor did his mother, whose nose was buried in a *People* magazine. "What happened to your foot, Henry?" Maggie asked as she checked the wound.

"I stepped on a rusty nail," he mumbled, pushing buttons on his game as fast as he could.

"Now, why would you go and do something like that?" Maggie teased.

He looked up and regarded her through the lens of clunky tortoiseshell glasses. His blond bangs formed a precise line across his forehead. "What? You think I did it on purpose?"

Mrs. Filbert looked up. "It was an accident, Dr. Davenport," she said, giving Maggie a funny look.

The boy frowned. "I'm not stupid, you know." He went back to his game.

Maggie didn't bother to clear up the misunderstanding as she cleaned and treated the wound and wrote out a prescription. Henry might not be stupid, but he was spoiled and downright rude, thanks to wealthy parents who pandered to him. She looked through his file. "I see Henry had his last DPT at age four. I usually give my patients an adult tetanus booster after age twelve, so we can go ahead and give Henry his now just to be on the safe side."

"Uh-huh." Mrs. Filbert's gaze was once again fixed on the magazine.

"Okay, we'll get him all set up," Maggie said. When neither acknowledged her, she shrugged and left the room.

Queenie was in the hall attaching a sticky note to a file. "I have never seen the likes," she said. "Two weeks into the school year and half the kids in town have a cold."

"Henry needs a tetanus shot," Maggie said.

Queenie sighed and muttered, "And I was counting on this being a good day."

Maggie checked her wristwatch. Ten-thirty, and she still had a waiting room full of patients. And on Friday, to boot, when she closed early for the weekend.

Susie O'Neal was a second-grader with dimples and pigtails and pinafores that her mother often sewed for her. Maggie found the two staring at the wall mural Maggie's daughter had painted; puppies tumbling playfully on a floor, one stub-tailed and spotted fellow grasping a bedroom slipper between his teeth. Mel was an amazing young artist who'd taught herself to draw almost from the moment she'd learned to hold a pencil.

Maggie examined Susie, wrote out a prescription for her cough, and offered the usual instructions on treating the common cold. Unlike Henry's mother, Mrs. O'Neal listened carefully and asked pertinent questions. The woman was not demanding; it

13

was obvious she was respectful of Maggie's time. Maggie never failed to give Susie's pigtails a gentle tug before she left the room, if for no other reason than to see her cheeks pucker with a smile.

Jamie was playing peekaboo with her six-month-old nephew, Frankie Jr., when Maggie entered the room. The baby was all smiles and drool, and it was obvious Jamie adored him. Maggie was glad they'd rekindled their high school friendship; she and Jamie often lunched and shopped together. After swearing Maggie to secrecy, Jamie told her she was trying to get pregnant, but two months of negative pregnancy tests had prompted her to buy an ovulation kit. Unfortunately, she and Max were finding it difficult to do the deed since the antebellum mansion they'd purchased after their honeymoon was in renovation and crawling with contractors.

"That can't be Frankie Jr.," Maggie said. "It has only been two months since I last saw him, and he has doubled in size!"

Dee Dee and Jamie smiled so proudly it would have been difficult to figure out which of them was the baby's mother had Maggie not already known. They were both gorgeous, as usual, former beauty queen Dee Dee in a kelly-green dress that brought

est accomplishments.

"I'm pretty sure I'm right about everything," she said, reaching into her purse for an envelope and handing it to Maggie. "But I double-checked with his nannies to make sure," she added.

Maggie nodded. Because Dee Dee had become pregnant late in life her husband had hired three nannies to help out. They each worked an eight-hour shift. "Good thinking. By the way, how are those hormones of yours?"

Dee Dee looked at Jamie. "I think I'm doing better."

Jamie nodded. She and Dee Dee had been good friends long before Max Holt had come into the picture and swept Jamie off her feet, and now the two women were sisters-in-law and closer than ever. "Most of the crying jags ended once Dee Dee got back to her normal weight," she told Maggie. "You would *not* believe what a one-pound gain can do to this woman."

Dee Dee shrugged. "It's true that I'm a little sensitive about my weight."

"Yeah, just a tad," Jamie added with an eye-roll. "But crying seems to work to Dee Dee's advantage because her poor husband can't bear to see her cry. Check out what

Frankie gave her during the last mood swing."

Dee Dee held up her hand so Maggie could admire her new diamond.

Maggie arched both brows. "Whoa, that sucker is bigger than the paperweight on my desk!"

"You have to know how to work a man," Dee Dee said proudly.

"You should give lessons," Maggie told her. She began dressing the baby, something she enjoyed doing, and she made silly faces that had not been taught in med school. She waved her hand over his head as though performing a magic act. "I now pronounce your son adorable and perfectly healthy," she said, drawing big smiles from both women. "He's going to need his six-month shots."

"Uh-oh," Jamie replied.

"I won't cry like last time," Dee Dee promised, even as her green eyes grew watery.

Someone knocked on the door and Maggie opened it, expecting Queenie to look in. Destiny Moultrie stood on the other side. Maggie could see that she was deeply troubled; she didn't much look like the smiling photo that accompanied her column as the Divine Love Goddess Advisor for the *Gazette.*

"Hello, Destiny. If you're here to witness Frankie Jr.'s physical, you just missed it."

"No, I —" She looked frantic. "Is Jamie in there?" She peeked around the partially open door. "Thank goodness I found you! You wouldn't believe the lies I told Vera so she'd tell me where you were. I have to talk to you!"

Jamie looked surprised. "You mean right this minute?"

"Yes! It's *urgent* and *life-altering.*"

"Oh, boy," Jamie said, wondering what Destiny had come up with this time. She didn't have to wait long; Destiny squeezed past Maggie and stepped inside.

"There's going to be a full moon tonight!"

Jamie waited. "Is that it?"

Destiny shook her head. "It gets worse. Planet Mercury is going into retrograde, and Venus is moving into the seventh house. There is going to be trouble. *Big* trouble!"

All three women gave Destiny their full attention. "How big?" Jamie asked. "Big like in 'biblical proportion' or big like in 'people need to look both ways before crossing the street'?"

"It's going to affect communication; people are going to be fighting like cats and dogs. Husbands and wives will stop talking to each other, road rage will run rampant, and there will be one car accident after another." She paused and sucked in air. She looked at Maggie. "Do you have a boyfriend who wears Hawaiian shirts? Or maybe a beard?"

Maggie shook her head. She wasn't about to admit she didn't have a boyfriend at the moment. Or in the recent past. Or even the distant past.

Destiny went on with her predictions. "Because Venus is involved, Cupid will run amok, so to speak. People are going to be having a lot of sex. That's about the only good news I have." She paused and took a deep breath. "This is the scary part. I'm supposed to get married."

"Huh?" Jamie wasn't sure she'd heard correctly.

"It gets *much* worse. Freddy Baylor, the new guy in town who bought that bait shop, is hot for me. He doesn't look as though he has had a haircut or shave in months, and he —" She paused and shuddered. "He holds fishing worms and crickets and live minnows and heaven only knows what else. I can't possibly marry him."

Queenie opened the door and stepped inside. She was breathing heavily. "Henry

19

Filbert is gone."

Maggie looked at her. "Gone where?"

"Soon as I showed up with that booster injection you ordered, he shot out the door like a bottle rocket. *After* he gave me the finger and called me an ugly black witch doctor."

"Oh, gur-reat!" Maggie said. "Did you happen to see which way he went?"

"In the direction of that little strip shopping center," Queenie said. "I chased that boy for two blocks before I gave up. Just look what the humidity did to my new perm." She pointed to her hair. The once-tight curls had come unsprung and jutted from her head like tiny mattress springs. "Mrs. Filbert is having a conniption fit out front. Somebody needs to put that woman on Valium."

Maggie looked at Dee Dee. "Would you excuse me for a minute?" She opened the door and started down the hall. She could hear Henry's mother wailing from the reception room. "Hurry, Queenie! We have to find him."

Even as tall and lanky as she was, Queenie could not keep up with Maggie. "Hurry, hell," she muttered. "I'm too old for this nonsense. I should be sitting home watching the Shopping Network and collecting

Social Security. I ought to put the root on that boy. I ought to —"

Maggie skidded to a stop and Queenie slammed into her. They both gave a giant *ugh.* "Quiet!" Maggie whispered. "His mother might hear you."

"Yeah? The way I see it, she owes me a hundred dollars for *not* bringing him back."

Maggie threw open the door to the reception room where Ann Filbert was in the throes of hysteria and frantically punching numbers on her cell phone. She gave Maggie a dark look and pointed at Queenie. "That woman frightened my son. I demand that you fire her immediately."

"Everything is going to be okay, Mrs. Filbert," Maggie said, noting the open-mouthed stares coming from the other parents. A toddler in a pink dress yowled and reached for her mother.

"What if he gets lost or falls into a drainage sewer?" the woman cried, flailing her arms. "He's just a little boy. He has his whole life ahead of him. He has never been to a prom or fallen in love. He doesn't even have a 401K." She put the phone to her ear. "Hello? Is anybody there? Hellooo!" she shouted. She looked at Maggie. "Just wait until I tell my husband. We'll sue. We'll own this building before it's over."

Maggie glanced at her fresh-out-of-business-college receptionist, who was in the process of repairing a fingernail and seemed oblivious to the situation. "Fran, please take Mrs. Filbert into my office and offer her something to drink," Maggie said, wishing she had straight whiskey on hand.

" 'Kay," the girl said without looking up.

Maggie opened the front door, stepped out, and tried to decide where she and Queenie should start looking. She blinked at the sight of a small, caramel-colored goat tethered to a tree and feeding on Maggie's azalea bushes. She turned to Queenie.

The woman shrugged. "I forgot to tell you. Joe Higgins stopped by to pay on his daughter's bill just as I was returning from chasing Henry. Her name is Butterbean. She's a little cockeyed."

Maggie just stood there for a minute. Joe was a down-and-out farmer who insisted on paying his account with beast and fowl. He was not a man to take handouts, he'd told her proudly. Which was why Maggie had a dozen laying hens in an outbuilding at the back of her property that she'd turned into a henhouse. Not to mention a cage of floppy-eared rabbits, she reminded herself. Her daughter, Mel, referred to her as Mrs. Old McDonald and her farm.

"On second thought," Maggie said, realizing Queenie had no business running about in the heat. "Please hide the goat so our patients don't see her."

"Mind telling me *where* to hide her?" Queenie asked.

"Take her around back. Be sure to give her water. And Frankie Jr. needs his DPT."

"Okay."

"I'll be back as soon as I find Henry."

"Oh, yeah, don't be surprised if you run into people dressed like Elvis," Queenie said. "That convention is in town."

Maggie had no time to worry about men in Elvis suits. She hit the pavement at a dead run, heading toward the strip mall. Ten minutes later she spied Henry sitting at a table inside the Full Scoop ice-cream parlor. She threw open the door and marched in, unable to miss the two men sitting at the back. They were black-haired with long sideburns, and wore white rhinestone-laden jumpsuits and capes.

She turned to Henry, giving him her most menacing look. "Excuse me?"

"I'm not taking that stupid tetanus shot, and you can't make me." He scraped the bottom of the dessert dish, obviously determined to get the very last bite.

"I told him he could get lockjaw and die,"

Abby Bradley, the owner, called out from behind the counter.

Maggie shot her a look of disbelief. Abby was a busybody and a gossip. "I would appreciate it if you'd try not to traumatize my patient," she said coolly.

"I was just trying to help." Abby gave a huff and disappeared into a back room.

Chocolate fudge dribbled from Henry's chin. "And I'm not going to let that voodoo woman touch me," he said. "My dad thinks she's wacko."

Maggie put her hands on her hips. "Tell you what, Henry," she said, trying to keep her anger in check. "You don't want to take the shot, that's fine with me. But I'm going to have to insist you come back to my office and sign a waiver."

He blinked. "What's that?"

Maggie arched one brow. "Your daddy is an attorney, and you've never heard of a waiver?"

"Good grief, I'm only in sixth grade!"

"It's a document releasing me of any and all responsibility in case you get sick from not following my medical instructions." Maggie smiled. "In other words, your daddy can't sue me." She started for the door.

"Wait."

Maggie turned and smiled. "Yes, Henry?"

He stood. "Okay, I'll come back to your stupid office and take the stupid shot, but it better not hurt. If it hurts I'm going to tell my dad I want another doctor."

She opened the glass door and made a sweeping motion. "After you, Henry."

Zack Madden tried to ignore the doorbell. He ached all over just lying there motionless; he dreaded the moment when he'd actually have to move. The cast on his arm felt heavy and cumbersome, and his ribs were sore. He touched his forehead. The swelling had gone down, but the stitches were tight and they itched. His beard itched.

Finally, when it was obvious his visitor wasn't going anywhere, Zack climbed from the bed, grabbed his wrinkled jeans and T-shirt from the back of a chair, and pulled them on. He made his way through the dark condo, trying to steer clear of the furniture. If he so much as stubbed his toe at this point, he would just stick his revolver in his mouth and be done with it. He paused at the door and checked the peephole before unlocking it.

FBI Director Thomas Helms walked through the door, peering at him through wire-rimmed glasses. He carried a Starbucks sack. "I heard you got roughed up. Heard out her red hair and milky complexion; Jamie in navy, her blond hair cut in a sassy new style.

"He's going to be big like his daddy," Dee Dee said.

"You might just have another world-famous wrestler on your hands," Maggie told her. She took the baby and noted right away how alert he was.

Dee Dee shook her head emphatically. "No way am I letting him *close* to a wrestling ring. He's going to be a great scientist who will find cures for all sorts of terrible diseases. Or maybe president of our country one day," she added.

"Wow!" Maggie smiled at the goofy grin on the baby's face and tried to imagine an older version of him sitting in the oval office.

"Or maybe a famous male model or Chippendale dancer," Dee Dee said. "He could do butter commercials on the side."

Maggie cut her gaze to Jamie and noted her amusement. "It's always good to have a backup plan," she told Dee Dee. She measured and weighed Frankie Jr., checked his reflexes and motor skills, all the while asking Dee Dee about his eating and sleeping habits. Dee Dee answered each question carefully; then bragged about her son's lat-

15

they found the wire," he added.

"Yeah. After I've been dealing with those goons for almost a year they finally decide to frisk me. Luckily the good guys showed up before I was shot and mounted over somebody's fireplace."

"Any permanent damage?"

Zack shook his head. "I'll still be able to have children."

Helms chuckled. "You need anything?"

Zack closed the door. "A morphine drip, maybe?"

"How about a cup of coffee instead?" The older man handed Zack a tall cardboard cup from the bag. "It's black."

"Thanks." Zack took the cup and peeled off the plastic lid. "Have a seat." He checked his watch. Eleven o'clock.

Helms sat on the camel-colored leather sofa that faced a large plasma TV screen, a serious sound system, and every other toy a man could wish for. Zack took the chair opposite him. He took cautious sips of the coffee as Helms pulled out a second cup.

"I see you have a lot of signatures on your cast."

Zack grinned. "The nurses insisted on signing it." He pointed to the cast that ran from his wrist to just below his elbow. "It's a real babe magnet."

"And the beard?" Helms asked.

"Colombian women love beards. Unfortunately, most of the ones I know were recently jailed. I just haven't had the energy to shave."

Helms set down his cup. "Nobody knew it was going to be this big, Zack. More than two thousand pounds of pure coke," he added, shaking his head as though he still couldn't believe it. "Do you know what that is worth on the street?"

"I did the math. I could buy Rhode Island."

"One of the guys is already begging to turn state's evidence. He can give us names and addresses."

Zack nodded. "That's what we wanted."

Helms grinned. "Hey, you played one hell of a mob boss, my friend. We're going to use the videos in training."

"I miss being Tony Renaldo," Zack said. "I miss the Miami Beach penthouse and the yacht and the fancy cars and Italian suits. It never gets cold in Miami. Not like here in Richmond. Women in Miami don't wear much. A thin coat of suntan oil and a bikini, and they've got a full summer wardrobe." Zack sighed. "I miss the smell of suntan lotion."

"I feel your pain, Zack."

"I want to be a *real* mob boss when I grow up, Thomas."

Helms looked amused. "Right now you'll have to settle for being a hero. CNN is all over this thing. Everybody from Larry King to Anderson Cooper and Paula Zahn want an exclusive. They want *you,* Madden."

"I want Paula Zahn."

"They've sworn to protect your cover if you'd grant an interview."

"Not interested," Zack said, "but hey, I'd still like to have Paula sign my cast."

Helms leaned forward, clasping his hands together. "Look, I know this is bad timing, but the bureau could use some good publicity. Maybe we could work a deal. You agree to go on TV and make us look like heroes, and we give you something in return. We'll even let you have yours first since time is of the essence."

"I can't think of anything I want bad enough to agree to an interview where I'd have to sit in the dark and have my voice distorted so I sound like Darth Vader."

"Have you seen the news?"

"I've been sacked out. I'm on medical leave, remember?"

"Does the name Carl Lee Stanton ring a bell?"

Zack gave Helms his full attention. "What

about him?"

"He's on the run, and we suspect he's headed to Beaumont, South Carolina, to pick up the stolen money. Plus, there's the old girlfriend who rejected him. I feel sure he'll pay her a visit, so she and her daughter could probably use some protection. I'd like to have an agent inside her house waiting."

Zack looked thoughtful. "Any other agents involved?" he asked.

"Not at the moment. The police are on it, of course," he added, "but I don't have a lot of confidence in those sworn to protect and serve in Beaumont. I plan to keep close tabs on the situation and pass on information as I get it." He paused. "I also have a close friend in Beaumont. He can get anything on anybody at any time because he doesn't have to jump through hoops and deal with red tape like we do."

Helms produced a folded sheet of paper from within his jacket and passed it to Zack. "This printout has all the facts. And this —" He handed Zack a business card. "My friend can be reached at this number. He can be trusted."

"Max Holt." Zack was impressed.

"There's a jet waiting at the airport, and a rental car in Beaumont, South Carolina. If you're interested," he added.

"I can be ready in an hour," Zack said.

It was coming up to one o'clock by the time Jamie returned to the office, having gone by the convention center after leaving Maggie's office so she could cover the Elvis convention. She found her receptionist/assistant editor/bossy office manager, Vera Bankhead, staring at a sheet of paper. Vera looked up, and the expression on her face stopped Jamie dead in her tracks. "What's wrong?"

"Bad news," Vera said. "From the Associated Press," she added. "Carl Lee Stanton has escaped."

"What!"

"Here's the printout."

Jamie took the sheet of paper and quickly read the article. She looked at Vera. "What are we going to do?"

"Somebody has to warn her," Vera said. "You're her friend."

Jamie reread the article. Carl Lee Stanton had been bad news long before he'd robbed an ATM van and wounded the driver, then, two days later while on the run, killed an FBI agent. She could only imagine how dangerous he was after serving thirteen years of a life sentence at a Texas prison.

"Authorities think he's headed back to

Beaumont where they suspect he hid the money before he was captured," Jamie read out loud, her expression deeply troubled.

Vera met her gaze. "We both know that's not the only thing he's after."

The front door opened and Maggie Davenport stepped inside the reception area of the *Gazette*. She found Jamie and Vera deep in conversation. They were clearly surprised to see her, and even though they gave her the usual smile, Maggie felt as though something were amiss.

"Am I interrupting anything?" she asked.

"Um, no," Jamie said, and Vera agreed.

"I need to run an ad," Maggie said. "I have to unload a goat."

"Goat?" Jamie repeated.

Maggie explained how she'd ended up with Butterbean. "The best part is she's free."

"Well, you've certainly come to the right place," Jamie said, trying to maintain a casual attitude. "Our specialty is finding homes for goats."

Vera nodded. "Like I always say, you can never have too many goats." The phone rang. "Why don't you take Maggie into your office and discuss the ad," Vera suggested. "That way you won't be disturbed."

Jamie nodded. "Good idea."

Maggie followed Jamie inside her office. She chuckled at the sight of Fleas, Jamie's lanky bloodhound, lying on his back in front of a window where light pooled from a partially raised Roman shade. Skin sagged from every body part, as though someone had zipped him up in an oversized doggy suit.

"He wouldn't sleep like that if he knew how bad he looked," Jamie said.

Maggie checked her wristwatch. "I can only stay a minute. I have to get my goat home in time to pick up Mel at school." She rolled her eyes. " 'Get my goat home'? That sounds too weird."

"I have a weird life too," Jamie said, "so I can relate." She motioned for Maggie to take a seat in her small sitting area. "Okay, here's the deal. I didn't call you in here to discuss the ad. Vera came across an article from the Associated Press," she said, indicating the printout she held. "I can't think of a way to make this easier on you, so I'll just blurt it out. Carl Lee Stanton has escaped."

Maggie's smile vanished, wiped away by a look of astonishment and disbelief. "How?" she asked.

"He got away as he was being rushed to the emergency room near Texas Federal

Prison complaining of chest pains. He had all the symptoms of a heart attack. I suppose the prison isn't equipped to handle that kind of emergency?" she asked.

"Not if they needed to do a catheterization or a CAT scan, or in some cases a cardiac MRI," Maggie mumbled.

"Guards were leading him, handcuffed and shackled, toward the back entrance when two men drove up in a red Jeep Cherokee and started firing. One of the men, dressed as a clown, pulled Carl Lee into the Jeep, and they took off."

Maggie swallowed. "Was anyone killed?"

"Two guards are in critical condition. A witness thinks the clown got hit, but he couldn't be certain. People were diving behind cars and bushes." Jamie paused. "Authorities suspect Carl Lee is on his way back to Beaumont for the money," she said finally.

Maggie tried to take it in. Of course he would want his money. The police had never found the two hundred and fifty thousand dollars that Carl Lee had stolen from the ATM van when the driver and only occupant had broken company policy and stepped outside the vehicle for a cigarette. Carl Lee had been waiting.

"You and Mel need protection," Jamie said.

Maggie was suddenly hit with the enormousness of it. Her face went numb; the air felt thin, as though she were in a tight space and couldn't get enough oxygen. "Like the police are going to care what happens to Carl Lee Stanton's old girlfriend," she said.

"Hey, wait a minute. You were a victim, too."

A sudden thought chilled Maggie. "Mel," she whispered. "I need to make sure she's okay."

"Carl Lee has only been out for a few hours," Jamie said. "It's going to take him and his buddies a while to get from Texas to South Carolina."

"What if he somehow managed to catch a plane? What if he was provided with a disguise and fake identification? What if —"

"Anything is possible," Jamie cut in, "but it's highly unlikely that Carl Lee Stanton would take such a risk. That's the first place police are going to look. He's a cop killer, for Pete's sake! It was sheer luck that the ATM driver lived because you can bet Carl Lee meant to kill him." Jamie paused to catch her breath. "Every news station in this country is probably flashing his picture as we speak. Plus, his buddies aren't going to let him out of their sight. They expect to be paid for their trouble, and it doesn't take a genius to figure out how Carl Lee plans to come up with the money."

It made sense, Maggie thought. She met Jamie's gaze. "It's all going to come out."

"Not all of it. We covered our bases."

Maggie was thankful her parents were away and would be spared the news, if only temporarily. They had flown out two days ago for the trip Maggie's mother, a retired geography teacher, had always dreamed of taking. She wanted to see an actual Egyptian pyramid and visit the royal tombs that she'd read about and watched on the Discovery Channel. Maggie's father had surprised her with a two-week vacation package for their thirty-fifth wedding anniversary.

"Everybody in town knows I went out with him. I'm amazed it never got back to Mel." Maggie sighed. "I should have told her the truth a long time ago."

"We all talked about it, remember? We thought it would be better to wait until she was older, more mature. I can be there with you if you feel it's time."

Maggie blinked back sudden tears. "How do you tell your daughter something like that?" she asked, the dread and remorse hitting her like a huge wave. "Oh, by the way,

Mel, that handsome man in the framed photo on your night table is not your father. Your *real* father is a cold-blooded killer who escaped prison today, and when he gets here there is going to be hell to pay."

CHAPTER TWO

"What do you mean you don't have a rental car?" Zack demanded, setting his olive-green duffel bag down, as well as a narrow, oblong suitcase and an oversized shoulder bag containing the latest technology in laptops and what he referred to as his FBI toys. "Someone named Helms arranged it hours ago."

The man sitting across the desk at Dan and Don's Clean Car Rentals took off his baseball cap and fanned himself with it. Sweat beaded his upper lip, and his forehead glistened. "Well, sir, he must've talked to my brother, Don," he said, getting up to check the air conditioner. "Reason I say that is because I *know* he didn't talk to me. And the reason I know that is because it's Friday. And on Friday I bowl in a morning league so I didn't take the call." He held one hand in front of the droning unit. "Blasted thing isn't worth junking," he muttered.

"Okay," Zack said. "So it was Don who screwed up the reservation. I still need a car. How about you get on the phone and check with one of the other rental agencies and see if they have something."

"They don't. The reason I know that is because they've called me asking the same thing. We've got an Elvis convention going on. The reason I know that is because we've had one Elvis after another come through that door the last couple of days."

Zack gave an enormous sigh of frustration. He paced for a minute. "Hell, I guess I'll have to buy a used car."

"You don't want to buy a used car in this town. The guy who owns Beaumont Used Cars is a shyster. Name's Larry Johnson. Not only will he rip you off on the car, he'll want to sleep with your sister."

Zack glanced at his watch. One-thirty. He gave an impatient sigh. "Look, Don —"

"Dan. My brother is Don."

"Okay. Dan. I have important business."

The other man looked thoughtful. "Well, I don't know if you'd be interested, but my old van is out back. Mind you, it's not a spring chicken, but it runs like a charm. I've had two engines put in over the years. Got a full tank of gas in it to boot," he added. "I'll rent it to you for half what I charge for my other cars."

"That'll work," Zack said. It beat walking.

"Just fill out this card. Oh, and I'll need to make a copy of your driver's license."

Zack handed him the license, grabbed a pen from a chipped coffee cup on the desk, and went to work.

Dan copied the license and returned it.

The door opened, and a tall, stocky man with black hair and chin-length sideburns stepped in. Zack did a double take at the sight of his shiny, royal-blue jumpsuit and matching cape. The cape had been lined with silver lamé and rhinestone-studded stars adorned the outfit. He carried an old Samsonite suitcase that had seen better days.

"Your name must be Elvis!" Dan said with a hearty laugh. "My wife has a velvet painting of you in our dining room." Dan winked at Zack.

The man suddenly whipped a silver cell phone from inside the cape and, using it as an imaginary microphone, began singing "Jailhouse Rock," complete with swiveling hips.

Zack watched in silence. He'd landed in hell.

"I need a rental car," the Elvis twin said, once he finished his song. "The Holiday Inn is having a big whoop-de-do for us in half an hour. Don't want to miss out on free food and cocktails." He stepped up to the desk next to Zack.

Dan repeated the same spiel he'd given Zack. "You can use my phone here to call a cab if you like. The number is taped to the side."

"Appreciate it, pard-ner." He dialed the number and ordered a cab. "That long, huh? Well, I'll bet you can do better than that if I throw a big tip your way. I got a crisp ten-dollar bill; it's all yours if you can get me a ride sooner. *And,* I'll do one of my Elvis impersonations right here over the phone as an added bonus." He paused. "Oh. Well, okay then. My name? Lonnie Renfro." When he hung up he looked disappointed. "It's going to take an hour for the cab to get here," he said. "Guy said his drivers have been picking up Elvis impersonators all day, and everybody is sick of hearing Elvis impressions."

"Make yourself comfortable," Dan told him. He searched through a rack of keys and pulled a set from one of the hooks. "I'll be right back."

Zack followed Dan outside and to the back of the building. He arched one brow at the sight of a sixties-model van with fluorescent peace signs and big flowers on the side. "That's *it?*" he asked.

Dan smiled. "It's a classic, m'friend. It's got a lot of miles on it, but the new engine is only five years old. I know the exact date it was put in, and the reason I know is because that's when my ex-wife ran off with my brother-in-law."

Zack gave the man a sympathetic nod and opened the door on the driver's side.

"You can see it has the original green shag carpeting," Dan said. "And these beads hanging from the roof behind the seats can be pushed to one side so you can see out the back. They're just for privacy." He winked as he handed Zack the keys. "That's why I keep putting engines in it. Memories, you know?"

Zack stowed his luggage in the back. The two shook hands, and Zack climbed in and started the engine. He put the gear into drive and started forward, just as the man in the Elvis suit hurried toward him lugging his suitcase.

"Hey, could you give me a lift to my hotel so I don't have to sit around all afternoon waiting on a cab?" he asked.

Zack had already studied a map of the town and knew the Holiday Inn was on his way to Maggie Davenport's house. "Put

41

your stuff in the back," he said.

Carl Lee Stanton opened his eyes and blinked several times from behind the thick lenses of a pair of fake glasses that made up his disguise. He resembled Jerry Lewis in the *Absentminded Professor,* hair greased and slicked back, white shirt and bright red bow tie, and black slacks that were a good three inches too short. In his shirt pocket, he'd tucked a mouth appliance that fit over his top teeth for a bucktoothed look. He yawned. "Where are we?"

"Just outside Tyler," the man at the wheel said.

Carl Lee looked at the clock on the dashboard. "This is bullshit! We've been on the road four hours. We should be halfway to Shreveport, Louisiana, by now."

The man gave Carl Lee a quick glance. He'd been nicknamed Cook during his long stay at Texas Federal for "cooking the books" and skimming money at a federal savings and loan company he'd worked for. That his mistakes had been glaring proved he was not as smart an accountant as he thought. "It takes longer driving the back roads," he said. He adjusted the oversized cowboy hat he wore that had a habit of slipping forward. His country-western shirt, faded jeans, and boots made him look like a cattle rustler.

"I don't see why we can't drive the interstate," Carl Lee said. "Who the hell is going to recognize us in these getups?"

"You can go right back to sleep if you're going to start complaining again about that outfit. I think I did a damn good job putting it together." He paused. "It wouldn't hurt for you to show a little gratitude, you know?"

Carl Lee gave a grunt of annoyance. "I don't have to be grateful. I'm paying you a lot of money for your services once we get to Beaumont. If we ever arrive," he added.

"Hey, I'll drive the interstate," Cook said, his voice filled with sarcasm. "Hell, yeah! And if we get pulled over you can explain the clown in the backseat with a bullet in his gut."

"If he knew how stupid he looked in that clown outfit he would welcome death."

"People like clowns. Nobody would suspect a clown of doing anything wrong, which is why people were caught off guard when we showed up. And Loopy makes a perfect clown on account of he's got such a goofy-looking face."

"That's because he's crazy," Carl Lee said. "Everybody at Tex Fed knew he was crazy.

Why would you hire a crazy person to do this kind of a job?"

"I can't do anything to please you," Cook said. "All you do is criticize and nag. You don't appreciate my sacrifices and hard work."

"You're not going to pout again, are you?"

Cook started to answer, but the man in the back moaned. "It wouldn't hurt you to check on Loopy, you know. I should probably change his bandage. I'm afraid he's lost too much blood."

Carl Lee turned in the seat. Cook had unzipped the front of the clown suit when he'd tried to stop the bleeding with an old T-shirt that was now saturated with blood. "I can't tell if he has stopped bleeding or not," Carl Lee said, turning around once more. "There's nothing we can do. If he dies, he dies."

Cook shook his head. "You're a cold man, Carl Lee. I don't know how you sleep at night."

Maggie closed her eyes and counted to ten as Butterbean paused to chew on a paper cup. "Hey, goat," Maggie said, giving a gentle tug on the chain, "how many times do I have to tell you I'm in a hurry?" The animal raised her head and looked at Maggie through skewed brown eyes, even as she continued eating. Horns blew and people called out to Maggie, but she ignored them. By car, her house was a mere five-minute drive, but the goat was plodding along at turtle speed even as Maggie's mind raced a gazillion miles a minute.

How to tell Mel. How to tell Mel. How to tell Mel.

I need to tell you about your father, Mel.

Um, Mel, about your father . . .

By the way, Mel, did I mention that your real father is a convicted killer? No?

Damn. How many times had she rehearsed the speech in her mind, only to have it die before it reached her lips?

Suddenly, the goat came to another dead halt. Maggie turned. "What *now?*" she said.

Butterbean just stood there. Maggie wished she knew something about goats. She had been raised on a cattle farm but there had been no goats. She'd never even *been* around goats.

Maggie decided to try a different approach. She smiled and stroked Butterbean just above her nose. "I know you're scared and confused and probably miss your goat friends," she said softly, "but my life has gone to hell 'cause there's this really bad guy I used to know, and he might be com-

45

ing after me. I'm trying to deal with that right now," she added. "So, if you could just work with me, okay?"

In response, the goat began expelling marble-sized goat poop. Maggie stared. "Wait! You can't do that *here.*"

Butterbean proved her wrong. "Oh, great," Maggie mumbled. "Now what am I going to do?" There was nothing she *could* do at the moment but hope nobody was looking. The thought had barely left her mind before she spied Herman Bates, owner of Bates' Furniture and a city council member, cruising by slowly in his new Town Car. His eyes fixed on the goat; Maggie gave a weak smile.

Finally, Butterbean finished her business, and they trudged on. Maggie's feet hurt by the time she reached her house. Of all days to try to break in a pair of new shoes, she thought. She spied her neighbors across the street, Ben and Lydia Green, working in their flower beds.

They looked up. "Nice little pygmy goat you got there," Ben called out, as if it were an everyday occurrence to find Maggie leading a goat up their street. Of course, he probably wasn't surprised since he'd helped her build a chicken coop. Lydia just stared.

"Thanks." Maggie felt their eyes on her as she coaxed the animal up her driveway and to her backyard. The lightweight, twenty-foot chain was a tangled ball that Maggie had to undo before she hooked it around a shade tree. "I'm sorry to have to leave you like this, but it's only for a little while," she said, checking to make sure Butterbean had enough room to walk around. She filled a bucket with fresh water and grabbed a bag of carrots from her refrigerator. "This should tide you over until dinnertime," she said, shaking the carrots from the bag. Butterbean wasted no time chomping down.

Maggie entered the simple farmhouse that had belonged to her grandparents. She filled a glass with water and sipped slowly, trying to cool off. She was in dire need of a shower; her white skirt and melon-colored jacket were damp with perspiration, and her dark hair felt like a woolen shawl against the back of her neck and shoulders. The temperatures had soared all summer, and even though September had brought some relief, humidity still weighted the air.

Her mind went back to Carl Lee Stanton. Her gut told her he was headed her way. What would she do? She needed to grab her daughter and leave town. Yes, that was the answer.

Maggie sighed. If only she didn't have a ton of patients scheduled for next week:

checkups, new mothers coming in for the first time with their babies, and a young boy in the hospital undergoing a myriad of tests for his weakened immune system. That didn't include her walk-in patients; it seemed half the kids in town had colds.

And now she had a goat to worry about.

Damn.

She would send Mel away, she decided. Maggie opened a drawer that her daughter referred to as the junk drawer. It was the catchall, the keeper of all things they never used but couldn't throw away because one never knew. At the very back, beneath a tangled wad of lime-green yarn and a package of pipe cleaners, was her stash of miniature candy bars. She needed her endorphin, serotonin, dopamine lift. How could she be expected to deal with this kind of stress without a chocolate fix now and then? She finished off the bar in two bites, only to reach for another. She put it back.

She was absolutely *not* going to use chocolate as a crutch to get through this.

She was strong.

She was brave.

"Yeah, right," she muttered, and snatched the candy from the drawer once more before she could change her mind. She was scared to smithereens; that's what she was.

The wall clock snapped her to attention. Twenty minutes, and the bell would ring at Mel's school.

Maggie hurried into her bedroom, stripped off her office clothes, and dressed in jeans and a T-shirt that read YES, I AM THE CENTER OF THE UNIVERSE, a gift from Mel on Maggie's last birthday. She pulled on her Nikes and put her hair into a ponytail. In the kitchen, she grabbed several plastic grocery sacks and a small hand-held gardening shovel so she could take care of the goat poop. Finally, she took off in the direction of her office at a fast jog, only to slow down after one block when she became winded.

If only she would follow the advice she gave others and begin an exercise program of her own.

Reaching her office, Maggie dropped the poop-filled bag into the trash can in back, dug her keys from her pocket, and jumped into her white Toyota. She started the engine and pulled a travel packet of hand wipes from the glove compartment. She mopped her face, cleaned her hands, and put the car in reverse. A horn blasted from behind, scaring the wits out of her.

Maggie glanced in the rearview mirror. Queenie and a very large man sat in

Queenie's vintage cherry-red 1969 Chevrolet Impala. Maggie put her car into park and got out.

"I can tell by the look on your face that you've heard the news," Queenie said.

Maggie nodded. Again, she checked the time. "I have to pick up Mel. I'm late."

"I'll take you. You shouldn't be driving right now. You're a danger to yourself and others. You're an accident waiting to happen. You're —"

"I think I get the picture," Maggie said. She cut the engine in her car and locked the door before turning back for Queenie's car. The man inside seemed to be struggling to open the door. Finally, he pushed hard and climbed out. "Sorry," he said. "These doors get stuck once in a while." He leaned close. "You don't look that dangerous to me," he whispered.

Maggie nodded. He wore a black T-shirt that read MAD DOG.

"I'm Everest," he said, offering his hand, which was the size of a small ham.

Maggie hesitated before taking it, praying he wouldn't crush every bone in her hand, but his touch was surprisingly gentle. "Wow, you're big," she said, getting into the Impala.

"Six foot seven, two hundred seventy-five

pounds," he said proudly.

"This is my neighbor's grandson," Queenie said, backing from the drive and heading for Mel's school. "His mother named him Everest 'cause he weighed fifteen pounds when he was born, and she said it felt like she was giving birth to Mount Everest. I figured he might come in handy right now, know what I mean?"

"Then you've heard that the police think Carl Lee is on his way here," Maggie said.

"Everest will protect you and Mel. Carl Lee doesn't stand a chance."

Maggie knew Queenie was trying to make her feel better, but even as big as Everest was, he was no match for Carl Lee and his friends who were, no doubt, heavily armed. "Thank you for coming, Everest," she said, at the same time wondering why he would put himself in harm's way for a complete stranger. "I'm sure you have better things to do."

"The only thing I have to do is be at church on Sunday morning," he said. "I'm the choir director. I don't make much money. That's why I have to moonlight as a thug. I get twenty-five dollars per job. 'Course, I don't charge Granny Queenie."

Queenie smiled and glanced back at Maggie. "Isn't that sweet? He calls me Granny

Queenie. Everest has a wonderful voice. He sounds like Aaron Neville. I get chill bumps when he sings 'Amazing Grace.' Everest, sing it for Maggie."

The big black man broke out in song. Maggie had to admit he was very good, but his talent was difficult to appreciate at the moment.

"Did you get chill bumps?" Queenie asked once he'd finished and Maggie clapped.

"I sure did."

"I told him he should go to that Elvis convention. He would put the others to shame."

"Elvis was a white man, Granny Queenie."

"Nobody is going to care about that," the woman said. "Besides, Elvis sang like a black man."

"I'd rather sing for the Lord," Everest said, then looked at Maggie. "I don't want to give you the wrong impression. I've never actually had to beat up anyone. Mostly, I just have a little talk with them, and they straighten up right away. Some have even joined my church."

"That's great," Maggie said, wishing she could sound more enthusiastic. Finally, she turned to Queenie. "What am I going to tell Mel?" She knew she could trust Queenie to help her decide the best way to approach her daughter. Queenie had been at the Charleston hospital with Maggie's parents the day Mel was born, and Queenie, whose twin sons had already finished college and moved out of state, had moved in with Maggie to care for the baby when Maggie started college. Queenie loved Mel as much as any mother could.

"I've been turning it over in my mind since I heard about Carl Lee's escape," the woman said. "I don't think you should just blurt out everything at once."

Maggie closed her eyes briefly. "She is going to hate me for the rest of my life."

Everest gave Maggie a sympathetic look. "If it's bad news it's best to give it in small doses."

"Everest is so sensitive," Queenie said, as she joined the last of the cars waiting in front of Mel's school. The girl sat alone on a bench. Queenie blew her horn several times and called out to her.

Mel gaped; she sank down on the bench and slapped one hand over her eyes.

"Oh, look, our little girl is so happy to see us," Queenie said.

Finally, Mel pulled her hand away and glanced about nervously. Maggie wasn't sure if her daughter was trying to make certain nobody noticed the car waiting to pick her up or if she was looking for an escape route. Finally, she grabbed her book bag and slunk toward Queenie's car.

"Um. What's going on?" she asked, the minute she spied Everest in the back. She ducked to get a better look at Maggie.

"Hop in," Queenie said, struggling to get her door open. She leaned forward; pulling the seat back with her so Mel could squeeze in. "And don't be scared of Everest," Queenie added. "He's not as dangerous as he looks."

Everest smiled and nodded at Mel. "I'm not dangerous *at all*," he said.

Mel nodded but kept her distance. She looked at her mother. "Where's *your* car?"

"At the office. Queenie wanted me to meet her friend Everest so we all rode together."

"We wanted to surprise you," Queenie said.

"You owe me, Mom," the girl said. "I get to color my hair now."

Maggie sighed. She and Mel had discussed the hair thing many times. "Your hair is beautiful," she said for the umpteenth time.

"It's *orange!* I hate it, and since I'm the one who has to wear it I think I should be able to have it the color I want. I'm tired of being teased."

"Who's teasing you?" Everest asked. "Give me a name."

"Stay focused, Everest," Queenie said. "You don't have time to go around scaring schoolkids."

"I want to go blond," Mel said after a moment.

Queenie glanced at Maggie. "I should probably stay out of this. I should probably keep my mouth shut."

Maggie arched one brow. "You think?" Still, Maggie felt bad for her daughter. She remembered how cliquish kids had been when she was growing up, especially the girls. That she had excelled in math, science, and chemistry, subjects usually preferred by boys in those days, had made her an oddity. She had wanted so badly to fit in, to be invited places after school and on weekends by the other kids. And then she'd met Carl Lee Stanton, town hunk and troublemaker, and everything had changed.

"Are you even listening to me?" Mel said.

Maggie turned and looked at her. "I always listen to you, honey, but I'm not backing down on this one." Maggie wondered how much authority she would have left once Mel caught sight of her father's picture on TV, complete with his jailhouse tattoos.

"Blond is definitely not the color for you," Everest said. "You should look into a rinse. It will tone down your color without harsh chemicals."

Maggie and Mel just looked at him.

"My sister is a hairdresser," Everest said. "All she talks about is hair, hair, hair. So I know what I'm talking about. Hair and makeup should be subtle, less is *always* more. At least, that's what my sister says."

"Yeah?" Mel sounded interested.

"Hey, I have a great idea," Queenie said. "We should stop by the Full Scoop ice-cream parlor."

"That'll work," Mel said.

Maggie noted her daughter's eager expression. She had a secret crush on Abby Bradley's fifteen-year-old son Travis.

"My friends have been carrying on about this new flavor of chocolate ice cream," Queenie said. "They say it's better than sex, and at my age that's as close as I'm going to get to the real thing."

"Don't listen to her, Mel," Maggie said teasingly, having learned long ago that Queenie did not censor her words.

Queenie glanced at Maggie. "I think we could all use a little chocolate about now, don't you? We could buy a whole gallon and take it with us."

Maggie almost hated herself for salivating over the thought of chocolate when she was facing serious problems. Queenie parked in front of the ice-cream parlor and cut her engine.

"I'll wait in the car," Everest said. "It might blow my tough-guy image if people see me going into a place like that."

The three of them barely made it through the door before Abby called out to Maggie. "I hear you have a new goat."

Maggie offered the woman a stiff smile.

"We have a *goat?*" Mel asked incredulously.

"It's only temporary, honey."

Mel gave a huge sigh. "That's what you said about the chickens and the rabbits. I'm the only one in my school who has a petting zoo in her backyard."

Travis Bradley stepped up to the counter wearing a full white apron. "Hey, Miss Queenie," he said. "You're looking mighty fine today."

Mel stared, transfixed.

"Hey, yourself, cutie-pie," Queenie replied. "I'd like a gallon of that new Better than Sex chocolate ice cream. I hear it's good stuff."

Travis grinned. "It must be good because we're selling it faster than I can dip it. I filled some containers in advance for when we get busy." He reached into a freezer behind him and pulled out a gallon-sized carton. "Only problem, you have to be twenty-one to buy it." He looked her over. "I'm afraid I'm going to have to ask for an ID, Miss Queenie."

Queenie preened. "I've always looked younger than my age," she said.

Abby stepped closer and leaned on the freezer case, her gaze fixed on Maggie. "I suppose you've heard about Carl Lee Stanton's escape. It's all over the news. Are you okay?"

Maggie saw Mel's curious look. "I'm fine," she said brightly. "And you?"

Abby went on in a whisper. "They're saying he's probably on his way back here to get that robbery money. I hope he doesn't, um, you know. Try to look you up," she added.

Maggie remembered that Abby had been a big mouth in high school as well. "Honestly, Abby, that's the silliest thing I've ever heard."

Queenie glared at Abby. "When are you going to learn to mind your own business?" she said. "Why, I have half a mind to —"

"Time to go," Maggie sang out and slapped a ten-dollar bill on the counter. She nudged a frowning and grumbling Queenie toward the door.

Everest seemed to pick up on it right away. "Who upset you, Granny Queenie? Give me a name."

"I'll take care of her, Everest, dear. Old Queenie still has a few tricks up her sleeve."

Maggie shot her a dark look. "Don't even *think* it."

"Who is Carl Lee Stanton," Mel asked, "and who did he rob?"

Maggie and Queenie exchanged looks. Maggie turned to Mel. "He and I attended the same high school, although he was a couple of grades higher than me. He made some very bad decisions and went to prison."

"Did he kill anybody?"

"Yes. An FBI agent," Maggie said. She gave her daughter a brief rundown of Carl Lee's crimes.

Mel looked out the window, but Maggie knew the wheels were turning in her head. Her daughter wasn't finished asking questions. Queenie started the car and backed out. Mel turned to Maggie once more.

"Why would he look you up?"

"Um, well." Maggie hedged. "We sort of went out a few times."

Mel was clearly shocked. "You dated a convict?"

"No!" Maggie gave an emphatic head shake. "I had already broken up with him by then."

"You were *going* with him? Like what you call 'going steady'?"

"Goodness gracious," Queenie said. "So many questions. Reminds me of those old *Perry Mason* shows."

"I think I have a right to ask questions," Mel replied. "Everybody in town, except me, knows my mother dated a murderer."

"Melanie Anne Davenport!" Queenie's voice held a note of warning.

Everest shook his head. "I didn't know."

"It was a long time ago," Maggie said. "Those who *did* know have probably forgotten. Except for that bigmouthed Abby Bradley, but most people ignore her."

"Somebody needs to teach Abby a good lesson," Queenie said.

"I can have one of my little talks with her," Everest offered.

Mel looked genuinely concerned. "Are we in danger?"

"Everest is going to look after you and your mama," Queenie cut in, "and tomorrow I'm going to Savannah to stock up on my supplies. And buy a black hen," she added. "Carl Lee Stanton can kiss his sorry bottom good-bye 'cause Queenie Cloud is on the job."

Maggie frowned but said nothing. She didn't know which was scarier, Carl Lee on the loose or Queenie with her black chicken and heaven only knew what else.

Queenie pulled behind Maggie's car a few minutes later and Everest did battle with the door once more. "Granny Queenie, you need to do something about these doors."

"It's the humidity," Queenie said, as though it made perfect sense.

Everest finally managed to get it open. He climbed out and held the front seat forward so Maggie could get out. "Are you coming?" she asked Mel.

Mel shook her head. "I'm riding with Aunt Queenie."

Maggie hesitated.

"We'll follow you," Queenie said. "Don't worry, I'm not going to scold her and remind her how I raised her better than to talk to her mother that way. That's *your* job."

"Thanks." Maggie hurried toward her car. She pulled onto the road a moment later and headed home. She tried to clear her head as she drove. She had accomplished one important step; Mel knew about Carl Lee, and she knew her mother had been

61

involved with him. Maggie figured it was best to let the girl deal with that piece of news before landing the final blow.

She noticed the van in her driveway as soon as she turned onto her street. It was hard *not* to notice. She tried to think who it might be and couldn't. Carl Lee and his cohorts? she wondered and slowed her car. Surely not, she told herself. Like Jamie, she didn't think he would risk getting on an airplane.

She spied a bearded man on her front steps, his long denim-clad legs stretched before him, crossed at the ankles. He wore a red and white floral shirt; a cast was on his right arm and a white bandage on his forehead. She didn't recognize him. Finally, she pulled in, put her car in park, but kept the engine running. She checked the door locks as the man stood and started toward her.

Maggie rolled down her window as the bearded man stepped up to the car. Without warning, and with lightning precision, he reached inside the open window with one hand, hit the master lock and yanked the door open with the other.

"What do you think you're doing!" Maggie demanded in her most menacing tone, at the same time wondering if the man was one of Carl Lee's thug friends. "Get out of here or I'll blow you to kingdom come with my, um, Magnum!" She wasn't even sure what a Magnum looked like, but it sounded pretty scary. She reached beneath her seat, pretending to go for her gun, but all she could find was her compact umbrella. This annoyed the heck out of her since she could never find the damn thing when it rained.

"Amateurs," Zack muttered. "Rule number one, lady," he said. "Don't threaten to shoot somebody unless you have a gun to back it up. Rule number two, keep your windows raised at all times. I can't help you if you're going to do stupid stuff."

Maggie wasn't listening. She put her car in reverse and hit the gas. The tires grabbed the concrete, and the car shot back like a bullet.

The car slammed right into the front of Queenie's car. "Holy hell!" Maggie yanked her head around; she hadn't seen the woman pull in. She cut her engine, grabbed her umbrella, and bolted from the car. She heard a loud yowl and turned, only seconds before Mel jumped the man from behind, wrapped both arms around his neck, and began choking him.

"Run, Mom!" the girl yelled. "He's got a gun tucked in the back of his pants!"

"Mel, no!" Maggie cried. She swung her umbrella, and hit Zack, as hard as she could, in the gut. He grunted. "Let go of my daughter, you scumbag!" she shouted, hitting him again. "Or I'll beat you so hard your mother won't recognize you."

"Hey, wait!" Zack said. "I'm FBI." He reached for his wallet, just as Queenie hurled her cell phone at him. It bounced off the side of his head. Zack blinked several times. "What the hell?"

"Hang on!" Everest said, trying to squeeze through the window on the passenger's side of Queenie's car and getting stuck as a result. He finally pulled free and hit the pavement in a dead run. "I'll save ya'll!"

Zack looked up. "Holy shit!" he said, a split second before impact.

CHAPTER THREE

"I can't tell you how sorry we are, Mr. Madden," Maggie said for the third or fourth time as she and Everest pulled Zack from the ground and insisted on helping him inside the house. Even in her concern she couldn't help notice how solid he was; the muscles in his back and upper arms were hard and defined.

"Look, I'm okay," Zack said. "Really," he added when the tension in her face didn't lessen. She was pretty, despite her distress. "But if you ask me to do jumping jacks I'm going to have to decline." He looked up at Everest. "Have you ever thought of becoming a bulldozer?"

"I feel bad about this," Everest said. "I thought you were Carl Lee Stanton."

"I'm much better looking."

Maggie paid scant attention to the two as she took in the damage. "You're all skinned up and bleeding," she said. "Mel, please hand me my medical bag."

"No big deal," Zack said. "I've hurt myself worse than this going out for my newspaper."

Mel looked awed. "Man, Everest just mowed him down!" she said, grabbing the bag from the top of the refrigerator.

Queenie stared at the badge that Zack had asked Everest to pull from his wallet, even as the big man had held him in a body lock, Zack's face pressed against the concrete driveway. She glanced from the badge to Zack and back to the badge.

"Problem?" Zack asked.

"How do we know this badge is for real?" she asked. "And if it *is* real, how do we know this is you? This man doesn't have a beard. And how come you're driving a hippie van? FBI agents drive black cars with tinted windows."

"Yeah, and they wear black suits and sunglasses," Mel said. "Didn't you see *Men in Black*?"

"And how come somebody from the FBI didn't alert Dr. Davenport to the fact they would be sending an agent to look after the doc and her daughter?" Queenie added.

"I just did," Zack said. "There wasn't a whole lot of time to plan. I was on a plane within minutes of learning about Stanton's escape. You can't get service that quick in a fast-food restaurant. And to tell you the truth, I don't want people knowing. Only reason I blurted it out like I did was because I was losing oxygen, and my aunt Gertrude, rest her soul, was trying to convince me to come to the light."

All four stared back as though they didn't know what to make of him. "I'm kidding about Aunt Gertrude," he said. "I don't even have an Aunt Gertrude."

"So if nobody is supposed to know who you are what are we going to tell people?" Maggie asked.

"I'm a long-lost relative?" He looked at Mel. "I could be your favorite uncle."

"I don't have an uncle. My dad was an orphan."

"We'll pretend."

Everest snapped his fingers. "I get it! He's undercover. But he's smarter than most undercover cops because they like to blend. People like Carl Lee Stanton will be looking for someone who blends. Zack is definitely not blending; you can see that van three blocks away. Not to mention the beard and Hawaiian shirt."

Maggie looked up from her bag. Beard? Hawaiian shirt? She felt the hairs stand on the back of her neck as she recalled Destiny

Moultrie's questions.

"In other words," Everest said. "Zack is so obvious that he's not obvious. Does that make sense?"

"I think I get it," Zack said.

"You need to sit down so I can reach your head," Maggie said, noting how tall he was. The fact that she noticed the width of his shoulders as well stymied her.

"I don't think very many people know my dad was orphaned," Mel said.

"Just call me Uncle Zack," he said, and pulled his pistol from the back of his jeans. Maggie yelped and pushed Mel behind her, Queenie started down the hall.

Everest tried to wrestle the gun from him.

"Hold it!" Zack said. "I'm not going to shoot anybody. I'm just trying to get comfortable."

Everest backed off. "Sorry. Just doing my job."

Zack offered the gun, handle first, to Maggie. "Would you please put this on top of your refrigerator so it'll be out of the way?"

"Huh?" She stared at the weapon. "Do we have to keep it inside?"

Zack shrugged. "I guess I could lock it in the van, but if Stanton and his buddies show up, one of you will have to cover me while I run out for it."

"Okay," Maggie said begrudgingly. She took the gun between two fingers and very slowly crossed the room with it as though it were a hand grenade, and she feared it would explode at any moment. "I hate guns," she added as she placed it on the refrigerator.

Zack gave her a sympathetic nod. "I don't really have a choice. My boss sort of expects me to keep one on me." He glanced about the group. "Listen, if it'll make everybody feel better you can call the bureau and check me out. Thomas Helms, the director, will vouch for me."

"I think we all need to settle down," Maggie said. "Mr. Madden, would you like something to eat or drink? Or should I refer to you as Agent Madden?"

"Just call me Zack. I'm not hungry. I had something called a shrimp burger on the drive from the airport. Now that's something you don't see a lot of in Virginia." He caught Queenie staring, eyes narrowed like slits. "Uh-oh, I'm going to be real embarrassed if you tell me I have a shrimp hull wedged between my teeth."

"I think she's giving you the *eye*," Everest said, almost reverently.

"I'm thinking you don't look so good," Queenie said, pulling a chair from the table and sitting. Everest and Mel sat as well. "You look like you need to be in the hospital."

"You'd think the FBI would have sent someone healthy," Mel said, glancing at the cast on his right arm. "I hope you don't shoot with your right hand."

Zack nodded. "Sorry. But if it'll make you feel better, they actually tried to break my left arm too."

Everest laughed out loud and slapped his hand on his thigh. "You just kill me."

"You don't seem to take your job very seriously," Queenie said. "I would think you'd be plotting and planning and all sorts of FBI stuff, seeing that we might have a cold-blooded killer on the way."

"I need to clean your wounds and make sure you don't have a head injury," Maggie said, feeling a little shy, and a little dopey because of it. But most of the males she was accustomed to treating usually drooled and gnawed teething rings. "Is your vision okay?"

Zack glanced about the room.

"How many fingers am I holding up?" Mel asked.

"Eleven."

"Fun-neee."

Maggie sifted through his coarse dark

hair, her fingers skimming his warm scalp, unleashing the scent of his shampoo. His hair fell well past his collar. "Any tenderness or pressure?" she asked.

"Not yet," he said, knowing there was going to be a whole lot of pressure building if she kept raking her fingers through his hair.

"Excuse me?"

"No," he amended.

"Does anything hurt?"

Zack looked at her. He'd been about to answer, "Only my whole damn body," until he noted the color of her eyes. Sky blue. "I'm good," he said.

"This is going to sting a little," Maggie told him. She put alcohol on a cotton ball and touched the cut at his cheek.

"Ouch!" Zack jumped.

Maggie snatched her hand away. "Sorry about that."

Queenie sighed and shook her head.

"What is that, battery acid?" Zack asked, glaring at the cotton ball. "That hurt worse than having my arm broken."

"You don't want to risk infection," Maggie told him.

"Who says?"

"It won't take me long to clean it if you could just be still for a minute."

"Somebody hand me a bullet from my

gun so I can bite it," Zack said, wincing. "Better yet, just shoot me."

"Are all FBI guys wimps?" Queenie asked.

"Can I ask you a question?" Mel said. When Maggie gave her a questioning look, the girl added defensively, "It's nothing rude." She looked at Zack. "Did you fall off a building or something? Or get hit by a car?"

"I ran into some bad guys on my last case. Things got a little sticky before we arrested them."

"What did they do wrong?"

Maggie dropped the cotton ball on the floor. Zack felt her breasts brush his arm as she bent to pick it up and toss it aside. "Huh? Oh, the usual. Drugs."

"The bandage on your forehead is dirty," Maggie said. "I really need to change it."

Zack looked at her. "Is this some kind of compulsion you have?"

Everest grinned. "If my sister was here she'd insist on doing your hair."

Maggie wished Everest's sister would come over and shave the man's beard. She should have taken a closer look at the picture on his badge. "Stop complaining or I'll take out your tonsils," she said.

Zack gritted his teeth but said nothing as she finished treating him. She stepped away.

"Are we done, I hope?" he asked.

"Yep. You have a nice new bandage."

Queenie suddenly slapped her hand over her mouth. "I forgot to get the ice cream out of my car."

"I'll get it," Mel said, standing.

Queenie suddenly moaned. "Oh, no, I just remembered my car is smashed." She covered her face with her hands. "My baby!"

Everest patted her shoulder. "It's okay, Granny Queenie. I checked while Zack was making Dr. Maggie swear not to let me slam him again if he got up off the driveway. Your car is fine. Dr. Maggie's fender has a dent in it though."

Zack was watching Mel. "Hold on a second," he said as she reached the door. "I'll go with you."

She glanced over her shoulder at him. "Why?"

"I need to get my bags from the van." He shrugged. "Maybe have another look around."

"I'll go too," Everest said. "I want to see how this FBI stuff works."

Zack looked at Maggie. "Before I forget, I'm having a state-of-the-art-alarm system installed first thing in the morning. Sensors on every door and window," he added. "I'll give you and Mel the code and show you how to use it. It's very simple."

"You're staying *here?*" Maggie asked.

"How do you think he's going to protect you and Mel?" Queenie asked.

Maggie nodded. "Oh, yeah."

"You must be pretty sure that Carl Lee Stanton is going to show up," Mel said.

Zack gave her an easy smile as the three of them headed to the door. "*If* he makes it this far," he said, "which is highly unlikely considering everybody in the free world is looking for him."

Maggie watched them go through the door. She was glad Zack was playing down the danger. She tossed the dirty bandage and used cotton balls into the trash and returned her medical bag to the top of the refrigerator.

"You okay?" Queenie asked.

Maggie nodded. "I have a lot on my mind. Surprising as it might seem," she added with a rueful smile.

Mel came through the door with the carton of ice cream, and Queenie put it in the freezer. The phone rang in Mel's room, and the girl started from the kitchen.

"Don't forget what we talked about," Maggie reminded.

"I know, Mom. My favorite Uncle Zack is visiting."

Maggie waited until she heard the door close to her daughter's room. "I should probably go in and have that talk with her," she said to Queenie. "Get it over with," she added.

"Doesn't the poor girl have enough to think about right now without you dishing out more?" Queenie asked.

Maggie no longer knew what was best for Mel. "I'm already frazzled over the waiting," she said. "Waiting and not knowing if or when he'll show up. And we've just begun."

"This is probably a good time for you and Mel to take a little vacation," Queenie said.

"I'm booked solid next week," Maggie said. "I've got new patients coming in. If I cancel they might go someplace else. I need those patients, Queenie." It was all Maggie could do to pay her overhead some months, not to mention living expenses and putting a good chunk of money into Mel's college fund each month. As much as she scrimped, she hadn't made a deposit in her savings account all summer, but she knew it took time to build up a solid practice.

"Is it worth the risk?" Queenie asked after a moment.

They were prevented from discussing it further when Zack and Everest walked through the door carrying Zack's luggage. Maggie noted the serious look on Zack's face. "Everything okay?" she asked.

"I need to replace a couple of light bulbs," he said, setting the small suitcase and a shoulder bag out of the way. Everest placed an olive-colored duffel bag beside them. "The one by the back door is out."

"I keep forgetting to replace it," Maggie said, getting up from the table.

"This is a good time to do it."

Maggie nodded. FBI guys probably changed their light bulbs once a week. "I'll grab a box of bulbs from the laundry room."

"I'm going to check out the inside while you do that."

"You'll have to knock on Mel's door," Maggie told him. "She's on the phone. It could be hours before she gets off."

"That was so cool," Everest said quietly when Maggie reentered the room. "Zack doesn't miss a thing. I can learn a lot from watching him. He says I have what it takes to be FBI. Plus, he promised to put in a good word for me. I'm going to join the gym right away and start working out, and then I'm going to buy a gun and go to the firing range so I can practice, and then I'm going to sign up for the exam. I have to go to the library and see if they have any FBI books I can study." He had to pause to catch his breath.

"But what about your choir job?" Queenie asked. "I thought you were going to sing for the Lord."

He looked thoughtful. "I could maybe start an FBI choir."

Queenie pulled a set of keys from her purse and looked at Everest. "Well, before you strap on your pistol harness, Agent Everest, Granny Queenie needs a favor. Would you please look in the trunk of my car and get my satchel?"

"*The* satchel?" he asked.

"Yes. And there's a box of white candles back there that I'll need."

"Yes, ma'am," he said, heading for the door once again. He tossed her a grin. "I like the sound of *Agent* Everest."

Queenie gave a satisfied sigh. "That young man is so polite. Impeccable manners too," she added. "If I didn't know better I would think I had raised Everest. But I'm not sure about this FBI business. If he leaves I won't have anybody to scare people for me."

Maggie had other things on her mind. "Why do you need your satchel?"

"Oh, I thought I'd make up a protective floor wash. It can be used for a personal protection wash as well, but you already know all that." She got up. "Better put on some water to boil."

"Please tell me you're not going to boil a bunch of basil and smell up this whole house," Maggie said. "Please tell me you don't expect Mel and me to bathe with it because it's not going to happen."

"And I'll leave a jar of basil with you to sweep up with as well," Queenie said, obviously choosing to ignore the question.

Maggie didn't put up an argument as Queenie went about her business. Not that she could say or do anything to stop the woman once she made up her mind. Queenie had tried more than once to convince Maggie that many of her remedies were as good as or better than modern medicine, but Maggie did not use them, and she strongly opposed root work or other practices for harmful purposes.

"I have to make a grocery list," Maggie said after a moment. She needed to occupy her mind and stop her obsessive worrying or she would drive herself nuts. She grabbed a tablet and pen from a drawer in the small built-in desk.

Zack entered the room as Everest came through the back door with the candles and satchel. "Here's your hoodoo-voodoo mojo mumbo-jumbo stuff, Granny Queenie," he said, grinning. "I hope you don't have any cat's eyeballs or lizard's tails in this big old satchel," he added as he placed it on her chair. "Because I'll get a bad case of the heebie-jeebies." He winked at Zack. "Just kidding. Nothing scares me."

"You know I don't use eyeballs and all that nasty stuff," Queenie told Everest.

Maggie gave Zack a questioning look. "Everything okay?"

"I found three unlocked windows, including the one in your daughter's bedroom," he said.

"It cooled off for a change last night so we opened them."

"We need to keep them locked from here on out. Also, I want all the blinds and curtains closed, and I want you and Mel to avoid standing in front of them. Beginning now, the two of you don't leave the house without me. Not even to grab the morning paper." He smiled. "Deal?"

Maggie and Queenie exchanged glances. "Do you think he's already here?"

Zack shook his head. "I seriously doubt it. The airports, bus stations, and even the marinas were crawling with cops and security within an hour of Stanton's escape. My guess is they dumped the car the minute they left the hospital. I suspect they had another one waiting nearby. It's hard to imagine that they would have been dumb enough to steal a vehicle because somebody would report it right away.

"I think the three of them are traveling together by car. Unless, as a witness to the crime suspects, one of the shooters was hit. If that's the case we might be looking for two bad guys instead of three."

"Maybe Carl Lee was shot," Queenie said, her voice hopeful.

Zack smiled at her. "That would help. Unfortunately, we don't have anything to go on, but I want to be prepared." He paused and looked around. "What's that smell?"

"Queenie is boiling basil to protect the house from evil," Maggie said as though it were an everyday occurrence. "She practices folk medicine."

Zack looked intrigued.

"This is powerful stuff," Queenie said. "Carl Lee Stanton will not set foot in this house after I'm done."

Maggie sat quietly for a moment, rolling her pencil back and forth on the table. "Um, Zack?" she said. "I need to discuss something with you."

He joined her at the table. "I'm all ears."

"I didn't want to say anything in front of

Mel, but I think it's too dangerous for her to stay here. I have an old college friend in Charleston. I could take Mel there." Maggie heard a sound from the doorway and looked up.

"No way am I leaving," Mel said. "I don't even like your friend Cheryl. All she does is complain because she can't find a boyfriend."

"I could help her with that," Queenie said.

"Excuse me," Maggie told her daughter, "but I'm having a conversation with Zack."

"I'm not leaving, Mom. You can't make me go."

Queenie stood at the stove stirring. "I should probably stay out of this. I should probably keep my big mouth shut."

Mel crossed her arms. "If you make me go I'll force myself to throw up in your car. Then, as soon as you leave Cheryl's house I'll run away. I'll hitchhike back."

Mel turned, strode across the kitchen floor and into the hall. A second later her bedroom door slammed.

Queenie made a tsking sound with her tongue. "The girl is scared something is going to happen to you," she said to Maggie. "As much as I dislike hearing back talk from a child, I'm going to have to cut her some slack this time." Queenie turned to the stove. "Once this is all past us though, I think you should ground her until she's thirty. Everest, look in my satchel and grab more basil. Get the big jar. I have a feeling we're going to need it."

"Would she actually run away from your friend's house?" Zack asked.

"Oh, yes," Maggie assured him. "She is willful and stubborn and spoiled. Tell him, Queenie."

Queenie looked at Zack. "That girl is willful and stubborn and spoiled."

"You'll have to keep Mel out of school for a couple of days," Zack said. "I want her at your office where I'll be able to keep tabs on both of you."

"I'm really trying hard not to get freaked out over this," Maggie said, her eyes bright with tears.

Zack nodded. "It's tough with kids."

Maggie looked at him, noted that his eyes had softened. She did not want Zack Madden feeling sorry for her. She did not want him looking at her like that because it made her feel even more vulnerable, and if she let down her guard she might start crying and never stop. She cleared her throat and tried to sound casual. "Do you have children?"

"Nope." Zack grasped his hands behind his head. "I discovered early on that my line of work doesn't make for a good family life." His cell phone rang, and he pulled it from the pocket of his jeans and checked the readout on his screen. "I'll take this out-side," he said.

"Man, oh man," Everest whispered once Zack left the room. "I'll bet that call is from FBI headquarters. This is like watching a movie. Zack is one slick dude."

"Yeah," Queenie said. "But I'm thinking it might be tough for him to keep an eye out for Carl Lee Stanton when he can't keep his eyes off Maggie."

Everest nodded. "I noticed it too, Dr. Maggie."

"Know what I think?" Queenie said, mop-ping her face with a paper towel. "I think under that beard is one fine man. And he's got the nicest behind I've seen in a long time. If his front side is as good as his back side —"

"Queenie!" Maggie glanced toward the kitchen door. "Mel might hear."

"Oh, good grief, the girl is thirteen years old," Queenie said. "What? You don't think she knows a man has a front side?"

Maggie almost groaned out loud. She did *not* want to start thinking about Zack's front and back parts. "I thought we were going to have an ice-cream party," she said.

Queenie gave a grunt. "No way am I going to eat Better than Sex chocolate ice cream with a good-looking man around," Queenie said. She pretended to fan herself. "I might have an orgasm."

"Granny Queenie!" Everest said, clearly shocked.

Maggie burst into laughter. It felt good to laugh after the day she'd had, with all the fears and worries swirling around in her mind. "I can't believe you said that!"

Everest grinned at the older woman. "Hey, you could pretend it was gas."

"I don't *think* so," Queenie said, tipping her white head to one side and giving a wicked smile. "Gas doesn't make you go 'ooh-ooh-ahh-ahh-ahhhhhhh' and move like this." Queenie began a hootchy-kootchy dance, swinging the dish towel seductively, then pretending to towel off her behind with it as she began swiveling.

"I may be old, but I'm still hot," Queenie said, touching herself with one finger and blowing hard on it as though she'd just given herself a bad burn. Maggie and Everest laughed so loud it brought Mel into the room, but Queenie paid the girl no mind and began moonwalking across the kitchen.

Maggie shrieked with laughter.

Everest doubled over and held his belly,

then grasped the back of Maggie's chair to keep from falling on the floor.

"What in the world is she doing?" Mel asked.

Maggie couldn't stop laughing, even when she noticed Zack peering through the screen door, an odd look on his face. He stepped inside, tucking his small cell phone into the pocket of his jeans. "Are you okay?" he asked Queenie.

She came to a dead stop, and her mouth formed an O of surprise. Everest snapped upright and threw his shoulders back as though standing at attention, and Maggie tried to swallow her laughter.

Queenie blinked. "Um, I, um. It's just gas," she said.

Zack looked amused. "You might want to have that checked out." He turned to Maggie. "Could we chat for a minute? Alone," he added.

Zack followed Maggie through the living room to the front door. He thought she looked a little stiff; she was probably trying to prepare for bad news, and it pissed him off that he couldn't make things okay for her and Mel.

They stepped outside and Zack decided he liked the front porch, with its large rocking chairs with fat cushions, and ferns and potted plants. He'd noticed it first thing when he'd arrived earlier. Maggie Davenport was all about providing and making a good home for her daughter, and it grated on him that some mean son of a bitch would think nothing of destroying it.

He waited for Maggie to sit in one of the rockers before dragging the one next to it closer to her. She turned to him, her eyes troubled and expectant. "Okay, Madden, lay it on me," she said, and he knew she was trying to sound brave. The faint tremble of her bottom lip told him she was having trouble pulling it off.

"I just got some news," he said. "A security guard spotted the red Jeep Cherokee used in Stanton's escape."

"Where'd they find it?"

"Sitting in a Wal-Mart parking lot, not far from the hospital," he said. "I'm pretty certain Stanton wasn't interested in shopping."

"Not unless there was a sale on handguns," she said.

"As I mentioned earlier, I think they had another car lined up. It would be too risky to steal one, although police are checking stolen-vehicle reports as they come in. Until now, all they've had to go on is the Cherokee." He saw the disappointment in her eyes.

"Which means Carl Lee and his groupies have probably been on the road since ten-thirty this morning," she said.

"Unless they had to look for a place to dump a body," he said. "Our witness was right; the guy who pulled Stanton inside got hit. There was blood on the backseat of the car."

"How do they know it wasn't Carl Lee's?" she asked. "It happened so fast. I understand there was a lot of confusion."

He noted the hopeful look on her face. "It's possible. The crime lab in Houston is going over the vehicle now." She raked her hands through her hair, and Zack wondered if it was just a habit or if she was trying to compose herself. He watched the thick dark strands slide through her fingers and fall to her shoulders.

"What do we do in the meantime?" she asked.

"We wait."

Max Holt walked into his wife's office where she was eyeballing her computer monitor. "Hello, gorgeous."

She looked up. "Oh, *now* you show up." She crossed her arms and tried to look miffed, but miffed wasn't easy with Max standing there grinning. She pulled her thermometer from her desk drawer where she kept it hidden from Vera. She waved it about. "Where were you when my temperature went up?"

He chuckled, rounded her desk, and sat on the edge. "Sorry about that. I was going through the plant, and I accidentally left my cell phone on my desk. I'm not usually so forgetful, but my wife is wearing me down with this sex-on-demand business."

Jamie uncrossed her arms. She knew how anxious Max was to start production at the polymer plant. "We're never going to get pregnant," she said on a sigh. "I'm going to end up on fertility drugs. Women on fertility drugs usually have about eighteen babies."

"Maybe we should stop trying so hard."

Jamie shook her head sadly. "Poor Fleas is going to be an only child."

They both looked at the snoring hound, sprawled on his back in front of the window. Max cocked his head to the side. "Is it me or is he getting better looking by the day?"

"Trust me, it's you." Jamie turned back to Max, her expression suddenly serious. "We have to talk. My friend Maggie is in trouble."

"I know."

She was surprised. "*How* do you know?"

"Helms called me. You can stop worrying now because there's an agent already in place. Zack Madden will be staying with Maggie and her daughter until this thing with Carl Lee Stanton is over."

"Why did Helms call you?"

"They needed more information on Stanton."

"And they know you don't have a problem breaking the law getting it," she said.

"Only if it's for a good cause," Max said with a grin.

"Uh-huh. So what do you know about this Madden guy?"

"His father was the agent Stanton gunned down."

"Holy crap!"

"Yeah. All of this is strictly confidential," Max said. "Helms pulled a few strings so Madden could have the case. To sort of make up for the fact the bureau screwed up. Evidence was mishandled and lost. Which is why Stanton escaped the death penalty," he added.

"I have a vague recollection of the case," Jamie said, "but we were busy trying to get Maggie out of town and do the whole cover-up thing." She paused. "Does Maggie know it's personal for Madden?"

"No, and it is best that she doesn't. Zack Madden has revenge on his mind. He's going to take Stanton out."

Chapter Four

Maggie went about the house pulling shades and closing drapes once she and Zack had finished their conversation. She knocked on the door to Mel's room and found the girl sprawled on her bed sketching. Mel looked up but turned her sketch pad facedown. She was, at times, self-conscious about people seeing her work.

"We need to talk about the new house rules that Zack has put into place," Maggie said, trying to sound casual as she listed them and went about the room pulling the curtains closed. Zack had taken down the café curtains over the kitchen sink and covered the window with aluminum foil, even as Queenie had shaken her head and told him how tacky it looked.

"He's just taking extra precautions," Maggie said, "and it's only temporary." She turned. "This is going to break your heart, but you'll have to miss a couple of days of school."

"What about my friends?" Mel asked. "Will I be allowed to visit them?"

"We'll have to discuss it with Zack." Mel didn't look happy. "It's not forever," Maggie reminded. "The police are doing everything they can to find Carl Lee." Maggie clasped her hands together in front of her. "We should talk."

Mel gave a pained expression. "Mom, I don't want to talk any more right now, okay? If you want to talk to somebody why don't you talk to Aunt Queenie about how she's stinking up the whole house?"

"She's boiling basil to, um, protect the house."

"Can't you make her stop?"

"What do you think?"

Mel made a sound of exasperation. "None of my friends have all this voodoo crap in their houses. It's dumb. Everything that's going on here is dumb. My whole life is dumb." Mel turned on her back and stared at the ceiling.

Maggie prayed her daughter would get through puberty quickly. "Yeah, life can be like that sometimes," she said, heading for the door. "Just one dumb thing after another."

Maggie finished her grocery list and pulled a large container of spaghetti sauce from the freezer to thaw in the microwave. She had decided if the house was going to smell Italian she should cook something Italian for dinner to go with it. Mel had left her room in search of a snack and was in the process of spreading peanut butter, cream cheese, and strawberry jam on a warm bagel as Everest watched. The girl cut the bagel down the center and handed him half. "Try it."

Everest took a bite. "Hey, that's good."

"Told you." Mel took a big bite.

Maggie listened in amusement as Mel went through the list of ingredients carefully so Everest could commit it to memory. "Don't tell him how fattening it is, Mel," she said.

"Oh, right, Mom," Mel said with a grunt of a laugh. "This coming from a woman who eats her weight in chocolate."

"Okay, so I have one teeny-tiny vice," Maggie said.

Mel looked at Everest. "The only reason my mom isn't fat is because she has good genes. My grandmother is thin and so was my great-grandmother."

"Did they eat a lot of chocolate too?" Everest asked.

Mel nodded. "Tons of it."

Maggie opened the pantry and searched through it for spaghetti. All she could find was a box of macaroni and cheese. "If I don't buy groceries soon we're going to be in trouble."

"I want pizza," Mel said. "We always order pizza delivery on the weekend."

"When you're home," Maggie answered, "which you seldom are."

"You could go out on weekends too if you wanted," Mel said, "instead of sitting home reading your dumb medical journals. You're long-suffering."

"Excuse me?" Maggie arched one brow.

"You haven't come to terms with Dad's death. You compare every man you meet to him, and they always fall short. You need closure, Mom."

"That's deep," Everest said.

"She probably heard that on *Oprah*," Queenie said, reading the newspaper at the table. "They're always saying stuff like that on *Oprah*."

"Nope," Mel said. "Caitlin told me. She heard it from her mom who heard it from —"

"Abby Bradley," Maggie and Queenie said in unison.

"Uh-huh." Mel finished her bagel and licked her fingers.

"I'll bet Abby heard it on *Oprah*," Queenie said. "Abby isn't smart enough to come up with something like that on her own. She's not even smart enough to know when to keep her mouth shut. I've said it before, and I'll say it again, somebody needs to teach that woman a good lesson."

"That somebody better not be you," Maggie told her.

"Bottom line, Mom," Mel continued. "You need to start dating. People are going to think you're weird. I *know* you can find *somebody* in this town you're attracted to."

"I could help you with that," Queenie said, giving Maggie a big smile.

"Yes, you've told me. A trillion times," Maggie added. "And the answer is still *N-O*."

"All you would have to do is pick out a man you like," Queenie went on as though she hadn't heard a word Maggie said. "And leave the rest up to me. Mel is right. There has to be *one* man in this town you find attractive. All it takes is one."

The back door opened and Zack stepped through. Four sets of eyes stared at him.

"Why is everybody staring at me?" he asked. "If you tell me I have ketchup on my face it's going to be hard to explain because I haven't been near the stuff."

"Um, we were just trying to decide what kind of pizza to order," Maggie said, "and wondering what you like."

He shrugged. "I'm easy to please."

"Me too," Everest said.

"I'll call Crusty's," Mel said, going for the phone. "I'll order one large pepperoni and one with everything."

Zack looked at Maggie. "I forgot to ask you earlier," he said. "What's the deal with the goat?"

Maggie's hand flew to her mouth. "Oh, no! Poor Butterbean!"

Mel stopped in her tracks and slapped her palm against her forehead. "I forgot we had a dumb goat. It's hard to think with Aunt Queenie doing her smelly voodoo thing."

"Be careful what you say about my practices," Queenie said sternly. "I'd hate to have to put the root on you."

Mel rolled her eyes back so far in her head that Maggie was certain she'd caught a glimpse of her brain.

"And don't you roll those eyes at me, young lady," Queenie said. "You know I don't tolerate eye-rolling. You keep rolling those eyes, and you might just find them stuck like that for a while."

"Okay, I'll do this instead." Mel stepped closer; raised her fingers to her eyes and turned the lids inside out.

"Oh, Lord!" Queenie cried, backing away and giving a huge shudder. "Stop that!"

Zack grinned and looked at Maggie who simply shook her head. "Ignore it," she whispered.

"Wow!" Everest said. "That's the ugliest thing I've ever seen. How long can she do that?"

Mel stuck her head forward, giving Queenie a better view. "I can't find my eyeballs," the girl wailed.

"Get away from me," Queenie cried, grimacing, "or I'm going to smack your backside so hard with this wooden spoon that you won't be able to sit for a week."

"Cut it out, Mel," Maggie said, trying to concentrate on what to do with the goat.

Mel turned toward her mother's voice, arms flailing. "Is that you, Mom?" she said, putting her hand on Maggie's face and exploring it with her fingertips.

Zack and Everest laughed.

Maggie's expression was deadpan, even though it was hard to remain straight-faced over her daughter's antics, no matter how juvenile. "Please fix your eyes," she said calmly.

"They're gone. Aunt Queenie stole them for her witch's brew."

Maggie shrugged. "Guess that means you can't order pizza. Too bad."

Finally, the girl rubbed her eyes and blinked several times until the lids were back in place. She headed for the phone.

Queenie looked relieved.

"I forgot about Butterbean too," Maggie told Zack, feeling sorry for the little pygmy with the kooky-looking eyes that nobody seemed to want. "I don't have any goat food. I don't even have a place to keep her. Except for maybe the garage. She'll need hay."

"I can get it," Everest said. "Carter's Hardware and Feed is ten minutes from here."

"Take the van," Zack said, tossing him the keys.

Maggie was relieved. "I really appreciate it," she said. She reached for her purse and pulled out a twenty-dollar bill. "Go ahead and grab two bales of hay if you have enough money."

"Oh, wait," Zack said and pulled out his wallet. "How about picking up half a dozen good-quality night-lights from the hardware department."

"Wow, you must really be afraid of the dark," Mel said as the others gave him a questioning look.

Zack shrugged. "You never know when they might come in handy."

"I'm on it," Everest said. He opened the back door and jumped at the sight of a young man with tousled brown hair and a wrinkled coat. A camera hung from his neck. "You half scared me to death!" Everest said. "Who are you?"

"Mike Henderson from the *Gazette*." He had to look straight up to see Everest. "Wow, you're big."

Everest nodded. "I was born big. That's why I was named after a mountain."

"Is your name Matterhorn?"

Zack joined Everest at the door. "What can I do for you, Mr. Henderson?" he asked.

The reporter pried his eyes off Everest. "I was hoping to have a word with Dr. Davenport."

"Why?"

Mike looked surprised. "Well, um, I'd like to talk to her about an old friend of hers by the name of Carl Lee Stanton."

"Why?" Zack repeated.

"I'm writing an article about his escape

this morning, and I wanted Dr. Davenport's response."

"Did he say his name was Henderson?" Queenie suddenly shouted. "That's the smart-aleck reporter who wrote the nasty article about my family." She stepped up to the door, hands on hips.

Everest frowned. "Do you want me to have a little talk with him before I go to the feed store, Granny Queenie?"

Mike instantly paled. "I don't know what she's talking about."

"You called my grandfather a witch doctor," Queenie said.

Everest grabbed the lapels of Mike's jacket and lifted him off the floor. "You don't talk about Granny Queenie's family like that."

"Wait! There has been a mistake," Mike said. He looked at Queenie. "Who was your grandfather?"

"Dr. Cloud."

"The Root Doctor? Oh, crap."

"If I hadn't been nursing my sick neighbor I would have marched right up to that newspaper office and given you what for. I let her talk me out of it. But now I'm mad again just seeing your face."

Maggie and Mel exchanged sighs.

"Okay," Zack said. "Let's just settle down. Nobody is going to hurt anybody."

Everest lowered Mike to the floor. "I'll be on my way, then," he said. "Excuse me, Mike, I need to get by."

Mike quickly moved out of his way. He straightened his jacket, but it did little good. "Look, lady," he said to Queenie, "I barely remember writing that article, but I would never have called your grandfather a witch doctor. I may have quoted someone. Most people don't believe in that stuff anyway."

Queenie started for him, but Zack blocked her. "Dr. Davenport can't see you right now," he said. "She's in surgery."

Maggie crossed the room. Enough was enough. "Excuse me," she said, squeezing between Zack and Queenie. "I'm Dr. Davenport. You needed to speak with me, Mr. Henderson?"

Mike looked relieved. "I just wanted to get your reaction to the news about Carl Lee Stanton's escape."

"My *reaction?*" she repeated.

"You know, on account of the two of you were kind of tight at one time."

"You need to leave before I do something you'll regret," Queenie said.

Maggie shot the woman one of her "don't even think about it" looks. "Does Jamie know you're here?" she asked Mike.

"No."

"I didn't think so. My reaction to Carl Lee Stanton's escape is no different from anyone else's," she said, an edge to her voice. "I want him caught before he hurts or kills someone else."

"Are you afraid, Dr. Davenport?"

"What kind of question is that?" Queenie blurted.

Maggie looked at Zack, and their gazes met and held. "Absolutely not."

"Wow!" Mike pulled a small notepad from his pocket. "You know he's dangerous, right? And everybody says he has a score to settle with you. I'll bet you regret ever laying eyes on the guy, huh?"

Maggie opened her mouth to answer, but nothing came out. How could she regret having known Carl Lee Stanton when the result had been a daughter she adored? She could feel everyone's eyes on her. "I'm finished answering your questions."

"Could I get a quick picture?"

Queenie pushed past Maggie. "Take a picture of this door," she said, and slammed it in his face so hard the house shook.

"Holy shit!" Cook shrieked the words.

Carl Lee Stanton jumped, and the car swerved to the center lane, almost sideswiping the pickup truck that barreled past them. He yanked the steering wheel to the right, and they rode the shoulder for a few seconds before he managed to get control. In the passenger seat, Cook twisted around, covered his eyes and gave an enormous shudder.

"What the hell is wrong with you?" Carl Lee yelled. "Are you trying to get us killed?"

"It's Loopy," Cook said. "He's deader'n hell."

"Are you sure?" Carl Lee glanced around, trying to get a look. "Did you check his pulse?"

"I don't have to, man. He's stiff as a board." Cook's voice was muffled behind his hands. "His eyes are open, Carl Lee. He's staring right at me."

"Just what I need," Carl Lee muttered. "A dead clown in the backseat."

"I can't ride in a car with a body. No way can I —"

"Shut up!" Carl Lee shouted. "I don't need you freaking out on me on top of everything else."

"You don't understand. I have a serious *phobia!* Some people fear heights, elevators, and snakes, but I fear dead people."

"So don't look at him."

Cook babbled on. "I was raised way up in the mountains," he said. "When somebody in my family died the undertaker put them in a casket and delivered it to the house. It would sit there for three whole days! Somebody had to sit up with the dead person all night; I was five years old my first time."

"We'll just have to make an appointment for you to see a shrink once we get to Beaumont." Carl Lee turned on the radio. He searched for a country-western station and paused when he found a news station. He turned up the volume. "Be quiet, I want to see if they mention us."

"And when my grandma died the ground was frozen so she couldn't be buried until it thawed. My old man put her in a junk car at the back of our property and covered her with a blanket. I still have nightmares." He wiped his hands down his face. "You gotta let me out of this car, man."

Without warning, Carl Lee backhanded him.

Cook reared back. "Why'd you do that!" he demanded. "Look, my nose is bleeding! I've got blood all over my good western shirt." He reached for a dirty handkerchief on the floor, shook it out and pressed it to his nose. "I don't want to be part of this anymore if I have to ride with a dead man in the backseat staring at me. Stop the car and let me out."

Carl Lee reached beneath his seat, pulled out a pistol, and, darting a quick look at Cook, put it to his head. The man froze. Carl Lee listened to the newsman who was in the process of recounting Carl Lee's crimes and giving a description of him. In the distance ahead, a police car sat on the side of the road. Carl Lee checked his speed and lowered his gun, pressing it below Cook's rib cage. He passed the patrol car and glanced in the rearview mirror several times until they were well past it.

"Now, you listen to me carefully," he told Cook. "I'm not going to dump a body in clear daylight, you got that? It'll be good and dark by the time we get to the other side of Shreveport; then we'll get rid of it."

Cook swallowed so hard his Adam's apple bobbed several times. "Whatever you say, Carl Lee," he said, eyes fastened on the barrel of the gun. "I can wait until it gets dark."

"And just so you know —" Carl Lee looked at him. "I can dump two bodies as easily as one."

They found Butterbean eating a cardboard cereal box from the recycling bin. "Uh-oh," Maggie said. "I didn't think to move the bin, but I feel better knowing she's had a snack." The animal didn't let their sudden presence interfere with her dinner. She chewed right on.

"She's so small," Mel said.

"I don't think pygmies get much larger than that," Zack said. "I read an article about them in *National Geographic.*"

"I don't know why Joe Higgins names all of his animals after food," Mel said, and looked at Zack. "He gave us a cat named Okra."

"Joe's little girl is a patient of mine," Maggie told Zack. "He pays her medical bills with animals."

"Ah, the old barter system," he said.

Mel was keeping a respectful distance. "Does she bite?"

"Nope." To prove it Maggie stroked Butterbean's forehead. Mel did the same.

"She's kinda cute," the girl said. "I was expecting some ugly, disgusting-looking goat."

"I'd better have a look at the garage." Maggie turned, and they followed. The wooden structure was as old as the house but she hadn't had the time or inclination to scrape, repaint, and repair, after she, her parents, and a handyman named Yap had spent so much time working on the house. Her grandfather had let things go after her grandmother's death. Decades-old wallpaper had been stripped, carpeting pulled up, the wood floors beneath sanded and varnished, and the list went on and on.

The garage doors swung out on hinges that squawked like a nettled blue jay. Inside it was dark and cool and musty. Maggie caught only a hint of the paint thinner she'd used restoring several of her grandparents' antiques in the garage. Still, it was orderly, Maggie noted thankfully, having devoted an entire Saturday to cleaning it back in the spring. She had hauled off years of forgotten junk, organized and stowed items in the built-in cabinets along the back. Yap had cleaned decades of dirt and mildew, inside and out, with a power washer.

"It's gloomy in here," Mel said.

"I think we should open those two windows and take off the screens so Butterbean can stick her head out," Maggie said. "She'll be able to get fresh air and won't feel so closed in." She shrugged. "It'll just have to do for tonight until I figure out another solution. I've put an ad in the newspaper. Hopefully somebody will call."

"I'll take care of the windows," Zack said, "if you and Mel have something else you need to do."

"We can start carrying all these yard tools to the back storage shed," Maggie told her daughter, "then I'll sweep up some of this dust."

Zack walked to a window, unlocked it, and tried to raise it. "It's stuck," he said. "Is there a screwdriver nearby?"

Maggie already had her arms full. She pointed to the built-in cabinet. "First drawer on the left," she said. She and Mel began carrying rakes, shovels, garden hoses, and ladders from the garage to the shed where a rusted tiller sat, reminding Maggie how much her grandfather had enjoyed keeping a garden at one time. Mel pushed her bicycle from the garage and leaned it against a wall in the shed.

Zack had managed to pry one of the windows loose and pull the screen off by the time they returned. He had moved on to the next window. He was already sweating, and dust and grime covered his face and hair. He blinked several times when some of the dust landed in his eyes. "How long since these windows were opened?" he asked with a grin. He pulled off his shirt and mopped his eyes and face.

The first thing Maggie noticed was the gun, tucked into the back of his jeans. She and Mel exchanged looks. The girl shrugged, lifted a five-gallon gas can by its handle and carried it out as Maggie grabbed the broom and began sweeping. She had no choice but to leave her riding lawn mower parked in the corner, but Butterbean would still have plenty of room to move around.

Her gaze drifted back to Zack. The muscles in his upper arms and back rippled beneath dark olive skin as he struggled with the window.

Maggie swallowed. As a physician who'd served time in the ER, she was well acquainted with the male anatomy, both young and old, in all shapes and sizes. But there was little time to appreciate a fit male body when it was in dire need of medical attention; and sterile exam rooms with glaring lights and beeping machines pretty much stole the ambience.

There was little time to appreciate a man's wide shoulders or the way his backside looked in jeans that rode low on his hips and —

"Something wrong?" Zack asked.

"Huh?" Maggie met his gaze. Hell's bells, he'd caught her looking! "I just, um, didn't mean to stick you with all this work. Especially with your injured arm," she added. "Let me help you." She stepped beside him and together they pushed. She could smell the sweat on his body, feel his heat along her arms and down her thighs. She wished the FBI had sent an ugly agent. Finally, the window gave, and Zack shoved it all the way up.

Everest pulled the van into the driveway and parked near the garage. He immediately began unloading the hay. Zack cut the twine, and he and Maggie spread the hay, forming a soft mound beside one of the windows where a light breeze sifted through. By the time Mel led Butterbean into the garage, Zack had tucked the screens inside the outbuilding and Maggie had put out food and water.

Butterbean stood there for a moment as if uncertain what to do. Finally, she walked over to the hay and nudged it about with her nose, then turned to her bowl of oats and ate with gusto.

"She should be comfortable here," Zack said, putting on his shirt without bothering to button it.

Mel didn't look convinced. "What if she gets lonely?"

Maggie wondered if her daughter's heart was beginning to soften toward the little pygmy. "She'll probably go to sleep after she eats."

"I'm going to bring my portable radio out here," Mel said, already hurrying from the garage.

Everest looked surprised. "I thought she didn't like goats."

Maggie shrugged. "I've yet to figure out how a thirteen-year-old thinks, but I'm working on it."

Mel returned with her radio. "I put new batteries in it a couple of days ago so it should last a while." She placed it on the lawn mower seat and selected a station with soft music. "That should keep her calm, don't you think?" She looked at Maggie who nodded.

Queenie was packing her satchel when they entered the house. Her black eyes immediately took in Zack's gaping shirt before turning to Maggie.

"Mind if I grab a quick shower?" Zack asked.

Queenie made a sound in her throat and began fanning herself with a notepad.

Maggie tried not to think of Zack naked in the shower. "I'll show you to the guest room," she said. He grabbed his duffel bag, and the odd-shaped suitcase, and Maggie reached for his shoulder bag. She led him up a flight of stairs just off the hall. A step creaked beneath her feet. Maggie knew and loved every creak, crack, and cranny in the old house. She took comfort in the sharp pings of raindrops hitting the tin roof, the window at the end of the hall that shuddered in its casing during a strong wind, and the feel of the pine floors beneath her bare feet. Some nights, as she lay in bed reading, she could hear the house settling on its foundation before growing quiet, as if it were telling her good night and giving a final sigh before calling it a day.

"I like your place," Zack said, as though reading her mind.

"Thanks. It belonged to my grandparents. The house was built in the 1930s, but my grandmother had it updated a couple of times and put new furniture in it. Said she was sick of being around old stuff. She passed it on to my parents who didn't care for antiques either. You wouldn't believe how much of this furniture was stored in my parents' barn. It was piled as high as the ceiling in one of the stables and covered in plastic." She shook her head sadly. "There should be a law against that sort of thing."

They entered the guest room, where a magnolia comforter covered an iron bed. "Just so you know," Zack said, "I'll be hanging out on the couch at night. I want us all on the same floor."

"Thanks. I'll rest easier having you down there," Maggie said. Zack set down his bag and looked around, nodding at what he saw.

He looked at her and smiled, and Maggie wondered how he could possibly appear so at ease. "I can't believe this is happening," she said. "It feels so —" She shook her head. "Unreal and weird," she added. It felt kind of weird standing in a bedroom with a stranger too, she thought.

Zack took the small suitcase and shoulder bag from her. "It's going to be okay, Maggie."

He seemed to project some sort of energy and confidence that Maggie wished she had. "How can you not be afraid, Zack?" she asked. "I mean, I know you've had all this training, but aren't you worried? Or is this just 'another day at the office' sort of thing?" She hated that her voice shook.

"I would probably be afraid if I didn't know what I was doing, but Stanton isn't the first badass I've had to deal with." He reached up and touched her shoulder. "I've been at this a while, Maggie. As long as Stanton doesn't break my other arm we'll be fine."

Maggie didn't know which surprised her more; the fact he was touching her or that he was making jokes. She was glad when he moved his hand. "What's in this odd-looking suitcase?" she asked, nodding at the oblong case on the bed.

Zack glanced over at it. "That? Oh, it's my makeup case." He smiled.

"Gee, why don't I believe that?"

"If you really want to know I'll tell you."

"I really want to know. I think," she added under her breath.

"There's a sniper rifle inside."

Maggie covered her eyes with one hand. "I wish I hadn't asked. I wish you hadn't told me. I wish none of this was happening. I don't like guns. I *hate* guns. I hate having guns in my house." She knew she was babbling. She paused and sucked in air.

He shrugged. "I'm fresh out of straws and spitballs."

"I hate exposing my daughter to this sort of thing," she said. She closed her eyes and pressed the ball of her hand against her forehead. "Queenie is right. I'm overprotective. I should have let Mel watch more violence on TV so she would be better prepared for this sort of thing."

"I'm sorry," he said, "but this isn't just about you and your daughter. Other people are in danger as well."

CHAPTER FIVE

"I'm going to be sick, Carl Lee," Cook said.

Carl Lee glared at him through the lenses of the fake glasses. "Sick, hell," he said. "You throw up in this car you're going to be dead."

Cook removed his cowboy hat and fanned himself. "I sometimes have a problem with motion sickness, and —" He paused and swallowed. "I think Loopy is beginning to smell."

"Go back to sleep," Carl Lee said.

"It's after midnight, man, and you promised to dump Loopy as soon as it got dark."

"Well, there was a change of plan on account of half the eighteen-wheelers in the country decided to drive the back roads tonight."

"They aren't supposed to do that," Cook said.

"You're absolutely right, Cook, but not everybody is a stickler for following rules like we are."

There was a noise from the backseat. Cook jumped so high he hit his head on the roof of the car. "Holy shit, what was *that?*" He reached for the door handle.

"Take your damn hands off of that door right now," Carl Lee all but shouted, reaching for his gun.

"Is it Loopy?" Cook managed to ask, as he tried to gulp in air. "What's he doing?"

Carl Lee sighed. "He's not doing a damn thing. He's dead. Dead bodies sometimes make sounds."

"I can't take it!" Cook cried. He wiped his hand down his face. He had already begun to sweat. "I can't breathe! I'm hyperventilating. Stop the car, I'm really getting sick!"

Carl Lee muttered a string of four-letter words as he braked and pulled off the road. Not a moment too soon either. Cook barely made it out of the car before he lost the stale sandwich he'd eaten earlier.

Carl Lee watched the rearview mirror for oncoming headlights. "I ought to leave your cowardly ass right here in the middle of nowhere," he told Cook as the man continued to heave. "What I want to know is how you had the guts to shoot those prison guards today."

"I didn't shoot anybody." Cook choked the words out. "That was all Loopy's doing. I fired over their heads. I'm a thief, Carl Lee, not a killer."

Carl Lee just looked at him. "You're pathetic. Get in the car and close the door."

"You're on your own," Cook shouted. "I'm out of here."

Carl Lee slammed the gear into park, opened his door and climbed out. He walked around the car and yanked open the back door. "Get over here and help me pull him out," he ordered.

"I can't touch a dead person," Cook said, sweat pouring from his brow. "Honest to God, man."

Carl Lee pointed the gun at Cook's head. "You've got two seconds."

Cook took a deep breath and stepped up to the door. Carl Lee tucked the gun in the waistband of his slacks and together they pulled Loopy from the backseat and lowered him to the ground. Cook began heaving again as Carl Lee flung four-letter words at him and wrestled to get the clown suit off Loopy.

"What are you doing?" Cook asked, barely able to lift his head.

"I thought it would be nice if the police didn't recognize him immediately." He cussed and tugged until he pulled the suit free. Finally, he grabbed Loopy's wallet, looked inside, and pulled out what cash was in it. He checked his other pockets.

"You just robbed a dead man," Cook said.

Carl Lee ignored him and tossed the wallet into the backseat. "We have to drag him across that ditch to those pine trees," he said. He straightened and wiped his brow; saw the headlights in the distance. "Hold it."

They waited. The car, an old sedan, slowed and pulled off in front of them. "Shit!" Carl Lee's eyes darted to the body as the sedan backed toward them. He grabbed a worn baseball cap from the back floor, slapped it on his head, and reached into his shirt pocket for his glasses and fake teeth.

The driver's door opened, and a teenage boy climbed out. He walked toward them, trying to shield his eyes from the glare of their headlights. "Ya'll having car trouble?" the kid said.

"Let me do all the talking," Carl Lee told Cook.

Cook was doubled over, trying to gulp air. "Don't kill him, Carl Lee," he said with difficulty.

Carl Lee quickly walked toward the kid.

He chuckled. "My friend is carsick," he said.

The boy nodded. "That's too bad. My sister has problems with that. I think my old man keeps motion-sickness pills in the glove compartment. You think your friend could hold one down?" He tried to see past Carl Lee.

Carl Lee stepped in front of him. "He'll be okay."

"Well, if you're sure. Sorry I couldn't be of help." He turned.

Suddenly, Cook gave a loud heave and fell against the car, making a loud thud.

The teenager whipped around. "Oh, man, he sounds bad. I should probably help you get him into the car."

"No." Carl Lee's tone was cold as he tugged the bill of his cap low on his eyes. "You need to move on, kid."

The young man looked up quickly. "Hey, I didn't mean to make you mad, mister."

Carl Lee sounded more relaxed when he spoke again. "My friend is embarrassed," he said. "You understand."

"Yeah, sure." The teenager turned and walked away but glanced over his shoulder a couple of times as he went.

Carl Lee waited until the car pulled away before he joined Cook. He yanked him up straight. "Get in the car before I shoot you in the kneecaps and leave you on the side of the road."

"I'm sorry, man." Cook did as he was told.

Carl Lee dragged the body across the ditch, glancing up from time to time to check for headlights, pausing once to catch his breath before pulling Loopy up the incline leading to a stand of pines. His glasses fell off, and he had to stop and look for them. Once he pulled the dead man into the copse, he let go of his feet and they hit the ground with a thud. "Sar-ro-nar-o, asshole," he said.

"Ladies, thank you for all your hard work," Zack told the hens shortly after six A.M. the next morning. They didn't seem interested in what he had to say as they plucked the feed he'd tossed on the ground inside the henhouse. He held out the basket of eggs he had just collected and bowed. "You can take the rest of the day off." He carried the eggs inside the house, left them on the kitchen counter, and went back out to feed the goat and rabbits.

Zack led Butterbean from the garage and staked her beneath the big oak tree in the backyard. She watched him curiously as he filled her bowls with food and water. His cell phone rang, and he pulled it from the pocket of his jeans. Max spoke from the other end.

"The fingerprints lifted from the Jeep Cherokee were put through AFIS and hit pay dirt on Carl Lee Stanton's buddies."

"How'd you get into AFIS?" Zack asked.

Max chuckled. "I could tell you, but then you'd have to arrest me."

"Forget I asked."

"Both men spent time in Texas Federal Prison. Raymond Boyd, aka Sam Griffin, Peter Hardy, nickname Cook, was skimming money from an S and L."

"I recognize the name Sam Griffin from Carl Lee's visitor's log," Zack said. "Griffin was there several times over the past six months. Or should I say Raymond Boyd."

"We have photos of Boyd, using the name Sam Griffin, from prison security cameras. Obviously in disguise," Max added. "The other guy, Luis Perez — his friends call him Loopy — was a postal worker with a bad habit of stealing checks that came through the mail. He had quite a racket going until he got busted and became Boyd's room-mate."

"How about the blood in the backseat?" Zack asked.

"Type O. Both Stanton and Perez have O. But the hair on the backseat was black like

Perez's. Stanton's hair is dark red; several strands were lifted from both headrests in the front. There was quite a bit of blood, by the way, and its location on the seat suggests an abdominal injury. For all we know he could be dead."

"So we could have a possible body," Zack said.

"Could be. As soon as your new office is up and running, give me a call, and I'll fax or e-mail you everything I've got."

"Great. Anything on stolen vehicles?"

"We found the owner of the Jeep Cherokee. He's out of town and had no idea the car was gone. I'm sure Boyd or Perez planned it that way. We don't have a make or model on what they're driving at the moment," Max added. "In other words —"

"We don't have a clue in hell," Zack finished for him.

Maggie's hair was still wet from her shower when she entered the kitchen wearing white shorts and a navy pullover. She saw the basket of eggs and a folded newspaper on the table. She couldn't help but smile at the thought of Zack collecting eggs from a flock of fussy hens. She peeked into the living room where a bed pillow rested against the arm of the sofa, and she wondered how much sleep he'd managed to get.

She poured a cup of coffee, sat down at the kitchen table, and opened the newspaper.

Carl Lee Stanton's face stared back at her. Her mouth went dry.

It was an older version of Carl Lee, but she recognized in him the young man she had known so many years before. He was still attractive, despite the deep lines at his mouth and brow, and the flat, emotionless eyes that painted a picture of a man who'd grown hard sitting in prison. Maggie scanned the article quickly. Two guards still listed in critical condition, several others wounded but expected to recover. Witnesses were unable to give a description of the shooters; one was dressed in a clown suit, and the driver wore a bright orange wig and oversized cartoonlike sunglasses.

The last paragraph generated a sigh from Maggie.

Local pediatrician Dr. Maggie Davenport, who had close ties with Carl Lee Stanton before his crime spree fourteen years ago, refused to talk to the press.

Maggie folded the newspaper and stuffed it in the trash beneath the sink so Mel wouldn't see it.

Now what?

She would close her practice and move, that's what. She wondered if Mel would like Portland or Seattle or maybe Canada.

The telephone rang. Maggie hurried to answer it before it woke Mel.

"Dr. Margaret Davenport?" a man asked.

"Yes?"

"Dr. Davenport, you don't know me. I'm Dr. James McKelvey. I'm the psychiatrist at Texas Federal Prison, and I'm calling in regard to Carl Lee Stanton."

Maggie felt as though all the oxygen had been sucked out of the room. She sat down. Took in air. "I'm listening," she said, wishing she didn't sound like she'd just finished a 5K run.

"I'm sure you've heard he has escaped. I just want to make sure you have adequate protection."

She wouldn't mention Zack. "I'm having an alarm system installed today," she said instead. "Do you have reason to believe Carl Lee will come here? You obviously know him." It would be unprofessional for her to come right out and ask if he was treating Carl Lee, and it would be unethical for him to say.

"I wish I knew," McKelvey said. "I

shouldn't be getting involved in this, but —" He paused. "I feel I know you."

He had just answered her question; deliberately, but in a roundabout way. Carl Lee had talked to McKelvey about her. "I don't know what I'm up against," Maggie said, trying to toss another line to the man on the other end. "I worry that he might be, um, *unstable*," she said, instead of coming right out and asking if Carl Lee was psycho.

Silence. Finally, "He's been sitting in a jail cell for fourteen years, Dr. Davenport." McKelvey sighed. "I've said too much. We never had this conversation, okay?"

Maggie had more questions, but the next thing she heard was a click. "Damn!"

The dead bolt turned in the door. Zack stepped inside. "The people installing the alarm system just pulled into the driveway." He frowned. "Why does your face have a greenish tint to it?"

Maggie stared at the caller ID. No number listed. She could call McKelvey at the prison, but she suspected he wouldn't like it, and he'd be less inclined to talk to her.

Zack crossed the room, took the phone from her and put it to his ear, then checked the ID. "Who called?" he asked. "Was it Stanton?"

She looked up, did a double take. He'd

shaved his beard! Queenie was right. The man was about as good-looking as they came.

"Maggie?"

"Dr. James McKelvey," she said.

"The prison psychiatrist? What did he want?"

Zack had done his homework. "He called to warn me about Carl Lee and make sure I had enough protection. I didn't mention you, of course."

He smiled. "Good girl. Are you okay?"

Hell, no, she wasn't okay, she wanted to shout to the rafters, but she was determined to keep her cool. She saw that Zack was looking at her legs. Oh, great, she had obviously nicked herself shaving. She glanced down quickly, half expecting to see blood trickling down from one knee, and was relieved to see that it wasn't. Finally, he looked up.

Maggie gave herself a mental shake. "I got the feeling Dr. McKelvey knows Carl Lee very well," she said. "He's probably treating him for some terrible and dangerous psychiatric disorder. What do you know about it?"

"Same as you," Zack said. "Carl Lee Stanton doesn't give a damn who he hurts as long as he gets what he wants."

The doorbell rang. Zack started to turn,

but Maggie touched his arm and looked into his eyes. He had somehow managed to get his hands on Carl Lee's psychiatric records. She didn't know how he had accomplished such a feat, but she knew instinctively that he had. "Is there any mention of Mel?"

"He knows you have a daughter, Maggie, but it's all about you. Stanton has kept tabs on you over the years. He has newspaper clippings, which were obviously sent by a family member or friend."

The doorbell rang again. "I need to get that." He surprised her with a grin. "You might want to change out of those shorts. These guys I hired are good, but they won't be able to concentrate once they get a look at those legs." He suddenly smacked his head. "Uh-oh, the FBI manual clearly states that I'm not supposed to notice things like that. Forget I said anything."

Maggie watched him go. She was supposed to forget that Zack Madden liked her legs? Oh, yeah, *right*.

Destiny Moultrie sailed through the double glass doors leading into the *Beaumont Gazette* shortly after nine A.M. Oversized breasts were barely contained in a stretchy leopard print tank top, and a thigh-high denim skirt exposed shapely legs. Her long dark hair had been pinned up, no doubt due to the heat.

Vera gave the outfit a disapproving look. "I hope an animal didn't have to die for that blouse," she said, even though it was obviously not the case.

Vera and Destiny's relationship consisted mainly of squabbling, although it had never been mean-spirited. *Gazette* employees had grown to expect it, and they found it amusing. This was why Jamie had given Destiny the desk closest to Vera.

Destiny ignored the barb and gave Vera a pleasant smile. "Wow, it's hot out there! I am wet and sticky in places I didn't even know I had."

"Please don't share," Vera said. "I don't want to have to think about it." She gave an exaggerated shudder.

"You know, Vera," Destiny said, "a good roll in the hay would go a long way toward improving your disposition. Even old people have needs."

"Who are you calling old? Even if I was old, which I'm not, I'd rather be old than crazy, which you are. Miss Love Goddess," she muttered.

"My advice column has brought in tons of new readers."

"Goes to show you how many nutso cases there are in this town."

Destiny looked thoughtful. "You'd better be nice to me or I'll send my new friend Earl G. Potts to haunt your house. Before he met his untimely demise in a bad fall during his famous trapeze act, his hobby was cross-dressing. He paints his toenails."

Vera just looked at her. She made no secret that she thought Destiny strange, and Destiny did all she could to live up to it.

Jamie opened the door and stalked from her office, her expression furious. "I don't know why the two of you come in on Saturday. You should be enjoying your weekends."

"So should you," Destiny said.

"I have no place else to go. My house is filled with contactors, remember?" She looked at Vera. "Has Mike called?"

"No. Did he do something wrong?" Vera asked. "Again?" she added.

"He decided to tack on a few lines to the article he wrote about Carl Lee Stanton. Which he did not run by me for approval before it went to press," she added.

Vera held out her hand. "Let me see."

Jamie handed her the newspaper and crossed her arms. "Read the last paragraph."

Vera read quickly and pressed her lips in annoyance. "What was he thinking? Like

129

Maggie Davenport doesn't have enough problems."

"I'm just worried she'll think I gave him the okay," she said. "I need to talk to her."

Destiny read the paragraph next. "Jerk," she said. "I'm glad I didn't sleep with him."

Jamie took a deep calming breath. "I'm going to handle this like a professional businesswoman," she said. "I'm going to have a meeting with him, discuss those areas I find problematic, put him on a probationary period, and follow up with a letter to him, a copy of which will go in a folder for future reference," she added.

"That's an excellent plan," Vera said.

"And then, once it gets dark, I'm going to slash his tires," Jamie added.

Vera looked impressed. "An even better plan! But slashing tires is hard and dirty work when I can just as easily shoot holes in them with my thirty-eight."

Destiny handed Jamie a purple folder with gold moons and stars adorning the front. "I just stopped by to drop off what mail I've answered." Jamie took it.

Vera stood. "I need to run this to the back real quick," she told Jamie. "How about catching the calls for a minute?"

"Sure."

"Sooo, how's it going?" Destiny asked,

once she and Jamie were alone. "Any luck in the you-know-what department?"

"Huh?"

"I know you're trying to get pregnant," Destiny whispered. "I'm psychic, remember? Plus, I've seen the way you look at Frankie Jr."

"I didn't know I had any maternal instincts until he came along," Jamie said quietly. "I wonder if anyone else suspects."

"I doubt it. And I'm not going to say anything."

"Well, to answer your question, so far nothing has happened. I finally tossed my home pregnancy kits in the trash like Maggie suggested. She thinks I'm trying too hard." She paused and looked at Destiny. "Do you ever think about having children?"

"No way. I don't even want a dog." Vera returned and went to her desk. "I can't handle pets after what happened to my goldfish," Destiny added.

"What happened?" Jamie asked.

"He committed suicide."

Vera sighed but didn't look up.

"How awful," Jamie said.

"Yep. I came home one day and there he was lying on the coffee table. Jumped right out of his bowl. He'd been depressed."

Vera just looked at her.

"How do you know it wasn't an accident?" Jamie asked.

"Do you have any idea how hard it is for a goldfish to jump out of his bowl? That little bugger had to practice. He hated me. We never bonded."

"That's so sad." Jamie shook her head.

"He was obviously desperate to get out of our relationship. I know what it's like because that's exactly how I felt with my third husband. I think we all feel stuck in our fishbowls from time to time, just like poor little Petey."

"Oh, good grief!" Vera said loudly, looking at Destiny. "That is the dumbest thing that has ever come out of your mouth. You made that up."

Destiny looked indignant. "I did *not.* I still have the little box containing his remains. I had him cremated."

"I can't listen to this," Vera said, "or I will go crazy."

Destiny reached for the phone messages on her desk. "Oh, no, Freddy Baylor called! Three times!" She waved the messages at Jamie. "See, I told you trouble was on the way. First, that convict escapes, and now *bait store owner* Freddy Baylor, who keeps his hands in disgusting *stuff*' — she paused

132

and gave a huge shudder — "is hot on my trail!"

"Maybe he wears latex gloves," Jamie said.

Destiny ignored her. "It's worse. I heard his friends had him chewing tobacco!" She grimaced. "It seems I've always got some strange man following me," she said. "I don't know what to do."

Vera gazed at her computer screen. "You could maybe stop dressing like a tramp."

"Uh-oh," Jamie said.

Destiny looked Vera's way. "And do what? Shop for my clothes at the Bargain Barn? Haven't you already cleaned them out of polyester?"

"Be nice," Jamie said, although it was all she could do to keep a straight face.

Vera opened her mouth to respond, but the phone rang.

"Remember, if it's Mike I want to talk to him," Jamie said.

Vera nodded and answered the phone in a pleasant voice. No one would have suspected she had offered to put bullet holes through someone's tires only minutes before.

Jamie stepped close to Destiny. "You were just kidding about having your goldfish cremated, right?"

Destiny winked. "I've never even had a

goldfish, but don't tell Vera."

Vera finished with the caller and hung up. "No, it wasn't Mike," she said to Jamie's questioning look. "And if you're going to spend the afternoon fretting over what Maggie might think, you need to drive over and set the record straight."

Jamie climbed from her car and opened the back door so Fleas could get out. She had wanted to leave him at the office, but the hound had caught her sneaking out and had given her the same look he did when they ran out of his favorite butter pecan ice cream.

A man stepped out the back door and smiled. "You must be Jamie. I recognize you by your dog. Mel described him to me."

Maggie hadn't mentioned Zack Madden was good-looking. She grinned. "You must be Zack. I recognize you by your injuries." Jamie offered her hand, and they shook. "It's a relief knowing my friend and her daughter are being looked after by a professional. How *is* Maggie, by the way?"

"She's worried, of course. Mainly about her daughter," he added.

Jamie hated to think the newspaper article may have added to Maggie's worries. She had not been able to reach Mike Henderson on his cell phone during her drive over. "I think some girl talk might be in order," Jamie said.

"She's in her bedroom. I saw her haul two laundry baskets in there."

"Thanks." Jamie headed toward the house; Fleas didn't follow. Instead, he moseyed toward the backyard. Jamie found Mel sitting at the kitchen table in oversized pajamas eating pizza. She was reading a magazine and tapping one hand to the beat of the music spilling from her room. "Hi, kiddo," Jamie said.

Mel looked up and smiled, showing a mouth full of braces. "Hey. You want some cold pizza?"

"No, thanks. I just dropped by to say hello to your mom. By the way, how's the new goat?"

"She's cute. Except her eyes are weird," Mel added.

Jamie tapped on Maggie's bedroom door a moment later and peeked in. She found Maggie sitting on her bed surrounded by a mountain of laundry, a phone tucked between her jaw and shoulder.

She motioned Jamie inside. "Okay, listen up, Queenie," she said into the phone, "You know how I feel about harmful root work, even if it's aimed at Carl Lee Stanton. Just remember, if you get into trouble, I am *not* going to bail you out of jail or smuggle a hacksaw to your cell, baked in a Lady Baltimore cake. Oh, and tell Everest I said to drive safely." Maggie hung up and shook her head. "That woman is a danger to herself and others. She won't rest easy until she gets a black hen, despite having to drive all the way to Savannah to get it."

"What does she plan to do with it?"

"She uses the eggs in various ways, depending on what kind of magic she's trying to work. We're better off not knowing."

Jamie nodded toward the bed. "I hear you're on a laundry-folding marathon. You doctors really do lead glamorous lives."

"Yeah, ain't it grand?"

Jamie hesitated. "Um, just so you know; I had nothing to do with what was written about you in the article. As owner of the paper, I take all responsibility, and I —"

"Let's just forget about it," Maggie said. "Besides, it's old news. Abby Bradley has already told everybody. *But* if you're really feeling guilty you can match these socks for me." She nodded toward the stack.

"I hate matching socks." Jamie kicked off her shoes, climbed onto the bed, and pulled the mound toward her. "Yuk."

Maggie grinned and produced a pillowcase from beneath a pile of sheets. She reached deep inside and pulled out two Tootsie Rolls. "Chocolate?" she offered.

"That's a pretty unique hiding place," Jamie said, taking the candy. She and Maggie wasted no time unwrapping their goodies. "Now, fill me in on the good-looking FBI guy."

Maggie shrugged. "I don't know much about him other than he seems good at his job, and I feel safer having him here." She bit into her Tootsie Roll.

"Wife? Children?" Jamie asked.

"He said his job isn't conducive to family life. I know I wouldn't want to be married to a man who spent most of his time away from home. Plus, I'm sure undercover work is dangerous." She paused. "Speaking of family, how is the baby-making business?"

Jamie shrugged. "Nothing to report."

Maggie could hear the disappointment in her voice. "You know, Queenie claims she has a surefire fertility recipe," she said.

"Really?" Jamie looked up.

"It's so simple anyone can do it. All you need is a rosebush," she added. "You can only use red roses though. They signify desire." She knew Max and Jamie had rosebushes at their new house.

Jamie looked eager.

"You dig up the rosebush at dawn while the petals are still dewy. Before you cover the hole, you drop a shiny new penny inside. Then, you pluck all the petals from the roses. You don't have to measure them out or anything, but you drop half the petals in your bathwater with your favorite bath salts, and you sprinkle the other half on your sheets at bedtime."

"And it's supposed to make people fertile?" Jamie asked.

"That's what I hear."

"Gee, I hope I don't have quintuplets."

"That's fairly rare." Maggie folded one of Mel's T-shirts and smoothed her hand across it like an iron, to get the wrinkles out. "Which is a good thing because you don't want to have five thirteen-year-olds," she said.

Jamie was quiet for a moment, committing the recipe to memory. She looked up, noted the worry lines on Maggie's brow. "I hate seeing you like this."

"Yeah, it's a little tense around here these days." She tried to smile but failed.

Jamie studied her. "What is it you're not telling me?" When Maggie looked surprised, Jamie arched one brow. "You think I don't know you by now? I can tell when you're hiding something. Give it to me, Davenport.

Don't make me wait to hear it from Abby Bradley."

"I got a call this morning from the psychiatrist at Texas Federal Prison." She told Jamie about her conversation with McKelvey. "The fact that he would put ethics aside in order to warn me is pretty scary. Carl Lee has newspaper clippings. Mel's picture has been in the paper twice since I returned. The picture you took of the two of us sitting on the trunk and —"

"The art show last year," Jamie said, remembering the close-up she had taken of Mel holding the blue ribbon for the sketches she had been so hesitant to share.

"I'm afraid Carl Lee might have figured out the truth. If he hasn't, his mother probably has. Mel and I ran into her at Wal-Mart six or eight months ago so I know the woman got a good look at her. What if she sent the clippings?"

"Did the psychiatrist mention anything?"

"No. But Zack has seen the file. Carl Lee knows I have a daughter. What if —"

"Okay, time out," Jamie said. "I would think if Carl Lee knows, it would be in the file and Zack would have said something. Don't go borrowing trouble, as Vera would say."

Maggie stood and walked to the closet

where she pulled a large hardbound book from the top shelf. "This was in my grandmother's old trunk, along with a ton of other stuff, including incriminating material like love letters and notes from my friends, teen magazines and sexy paperbacks that my parents would never have approved of," she added. "The trunk was in the barn crammed inside a stall with my grandparents' other antiques so it was a good place to hide things." She held up the book. "Remember this?"

Jamie groaned. "Why would you keep our middle school yearbook? Do you remember how crummy our hairstyles were back then?"

Maggie didn't answer. She flipped through the pages until she found what she was looking for. "I'll bet you forgot Carl Lee has a younger sister. She was two grades behind us."

"I don't remember her," Jamie said.

"Well, here she is." Maggie handed Jamie the book and pointed to one of the school photos, a thin girl with bright red-orange hair, freckles, and braces. "Meet Kathleen Francis Stanton," she announced, "who could easily be my daughter's twin."

Chapter Six

Police Chief Lamar Tevis pulled the old pickup truck into Maggie Davenport's driveway and parked. He wore a cap adorned with several fish hooks; the words BITE ME were written just above the bill. A blue tick hound sat in the back of the truck, scratching as though his life depended on it.

Zack climbed inside the truck a few minutes later and found Tevis on his cell phone. The chief held up one finger, indicating to Zack the call would only take a minute.

"Now, listen here, Clancy," Tevis said, "I put you on alert the minute I caught wind of Carl Lee Stanton's escape, and you've been jerking me around ever since. If this is your way of getting back at me for winning the last poker game then you need to start spending your Wednesday nights at the senior citizen's bingo parlor."

Zack grinned and leaned back in the seat.

"You're not listening to me," Lamar went on. "I am spread real thin on manpower, Buddyroe, on account of this whole dang town has gone completely nuts on me, and these Elvis impersonators aren't making things any easier. I've got four of them locked in a cell right now for public drunkenness, and if I have to listen to 'Jailhouse Rock' or that hound dog song one more time I'm going to turn my dang gun on myself." He paused for air. "Now, then, I need every fireman and volunteer fireman you got, you hear?" He paused. "What do you mean, they're sitting in the lobby at the station? Since when?"

Tevis looked at Zack who shrugged.

"Well, dang, Clancy," Lamar said, taking on a sheepish tone, "you could have told me you were sending them over and saved me this phone call. Hello? Clancy, are you there?" Lamar hung up. "Well, I guess I can kiss off my free ticket to the next fireman's ball." He gave Zack a thoughtful frown. "Did you or Max have anything to do with this?"

"You underestimate your powers of persuasion," Zack said.

"Yeah, could be." He held out his hand. "Zack, it's good to finally meet you. Sorry it took me so long for a face-to-face; as you can guess, I've been preoccupied." They shook hands. Lamar gave him the once-over. "Who broke your arm and knocked you upside the head? Was it a woman? No, don't tell me, it's none of my business. And speaking of business, let's get to it because these waders are hot."

"Have you been fishing?"

"Oh, no, this is my disguise so Carl Lee Stanton won't know the police are hanging around," Lamar said. "I borrowed this truck from my cousin, and that old blue tick in the back belongs to my neighbor. This cap is mine though."

"It's a great disguise," Zack said.

"While we're on the topic of disguises, I should mention to you that only a couple of my key men know you're FBI. We're following the brother-in-law thing."

"That's good. Do you think you're going to have enough people?"

"We're working as fast as we can, Zack, what with all this craziness going on in town right now. I've had more domestic disputes, vandalisms, car accidents, you name it, in the last twenty-four hours than I usually have in six months. And now I've got half the force working roadblocks."

"Where do we stand as of now?" Zack asked.

"The sheriff has deputies coming in from several other counties, the highway patrol will have more cars on the road, and Clancy is providing backup. Dang, I've got to get back and deputize some people."

"I'll be brief," Zack said. "I just want to make sure we see eye to eye on how to best handle this."

"Firm things up, so to speak," Lamar added.

"As we discussed, no patrol cars on this street," he said. "I don't even want them in the neighborhood."

Lamar nodded. "I read you loud and clear, Buddyroe. I've put unmarked cars and plainclothes officers in the vicinity, but you'll be hard-pressed to find a cruiser." He pulled a lime-green tackle box from behind his seat. "There's a radio inside. Bottom line, nobody makes a move without your say-so."

Zack gave him a curious look. "Are you always this agreeable?"

"We're just two guys trying to do our jobs, right?" Lamar turned slightly in his seat. "You know, I thought about signing on with the FBI."

"Yeah?"

Lamar nodded. "I'd been on the force a good five years, and things were pretty dull around here so I entertained the idea. Sent off for information. Matter of fact, it was the same year Carl Lee committed his crimes. I put in a lot of hours on the ATM robbery. They caught him a couple of days later in Virginia, of course. After he shot and killed that agent."

Zack nodded and reached for the tackle box. "Well, I'd better get back —"

"I even took a week's vacation and drove up to Virginia so I could watch some of the trial," Lamar added.

Zack looked at him.

"I will never forget the look on the step-son's face when Stanton got off with a life sentence. I have no sympathy for cop killers, know what I mean? Not one iota." Lamar held out his hand. "Zack, it was nice meeting you."

"Same here." They shook hands once more. Zack climbed from the truck and watched Lamar drive away.

Maggie had finished putting away laundry, and Mel was reluctantly showing Jamie some of her latest artwork when the doorbell rang. Maggie and Zack met up in the living room.

"Check the peephole first," he said as he looked through a slit in the living room drapes.

"It's okay," Maggie said. "Just my neighbors from across the street." She opened the door. Ben and Lydia Green stood on the other side. Maggie smiled, unlocked the door, and opened it wide. "Come in," she said, stepping aside so they could enter.

"We brought goodies," Lydia announced. "My homemade chocolate chip cookies and a Coca-Cola cake," she added. "I don't dare keep them in the house on account of Ben's diabetes."

"Thank you!" Maggie said, her mouth watering at the sight of chocolate.

Mel suddenly appeared. "Uh-oh," the girl said. "I'd better eat some quick before Mom adds it to her stash." Lydia handed both containers to Mel, and she carried them into the kitchen.

"Didn't you bake that for your granddaughter?" Maggie asked, remembering the six-year-old was due to fly in from Ohio the following day.

Lydia gave a sigh of disappointment. "Emmy is sick, bless her heart. It's her tonsils again. But my daughter promised she could come at Thanksgiving so she'll be able to see her new room after all." Lydia looked at Zack. "My granddaughter loves Barbie. Maggie and Mel helped me decorate one of the guest rooms just for Emmy. Barbie stuff everywhere," she added.

Maggie noticed Ben and Lydia darting looks at Zack and his injuries. "Oh, I'm sorry," she said and made the introductions, remembering to tell them Zack was her brother-in-law. "Zack is staying for a few days," she added. She saw relief in Lydia's eyes and knew she'd heard the news about Carl Lee.

Zack and Ben shook hands. "We're the old fogies from across the street," Ben said. He regarded Maggie. "So where did you get the goat?" he asked her.

"You remember Joe Higgins who dumped all the hens on me," Maggie said, "and we spent the weekend building a chicken coop?"

"Oh, yeah. He must owe you money."

"I don't plan to keep her, of course," Maggie told him. "For one thing, I don't have a place for her. I hate keeping her tied to a tree, and I don't like sticking her in a dark garage every night. I put an ad in the newspaper. Maybe I'll hear something soon."

"Tell you what," Ben said. "If Zack is up to it, I've got a few posts we can stick in the ground and enough chicken wire to make a temporary pen. Won't take but a couple of hours since I have a post-hole-digger," he added. "I've also got an old tarp I can throw over one corner to keep her dry in case it rains."

"Oh, that's too much trouble," Maggie said.

Lydia waved off the remark. "Let him do it, hon. You know how Ben loves having projects, and it keeps him out of my hair."

Ben looked at Zack. "If you're willing and able we can get on it right away. You'll have to help me carry things over."

"Sure." Zack turned to Maggie. "Just shout if you need me."

"That's one handsome brother-in-law you've got there," Lydia said as the men hurried across the street. She smiled, but her eyes were troubled. "I'm very anxious for you and Mel after reading the newspaper this morning," she said softly. "I would think you'd have police protection. Why aren't they here?"

"I can't go into details, Lydia, but Mel and I *are* being looked after. The police and FBI are doing everything possible to find Carl Lee Stanton."

The woman still looked worried as she stepped outside. "If you need anything —"

"I know." Maggie took her hand and squeezed it.

A moment later, Maggie found Jamie and Mel eating cake and cookies at the kitchen table. "You started without me?" She tried to sound hurt.

"Hey, I matched all the socks for you," Jamie said. "I have to build up my strength."

Maggie pulled a plate from a kitchen cabinet and grabbed a fork. Jamie and Mel watched her cut an enormous piece of cake. She looked up. "What?"

"Carl Lee, are you still mad?" Cook's voice shook.

He'd barely dared to breathe during the five hours since one of the tires had blown on the car and sent them walking. He'd simply followed Carl Lee, no questions asked, through the wooded area that, to their advantage, had replaced cow pastures and would make detection by the police more difficult. Not to mention the fog that had rolled in shortly after and still hugged the road.

"Mad doesn't come close to what I'm feeling," Carl Lee finally said. "In fact, I'm about two seconds from putting a bullet between your eyes, and the longer I walk the more I think about it. Does that answer your question?"

Cook maintained a safe distance. "How was I supposed to know there wasn't a spare in the trunk?"

Carl Lee let out a mouthful of cuss words. "I'm not listening to any more of your pissy excuses, you got that?" He checked his watch, and the scowl on his face turned menacing. "I can't believe how much driving time we've lost because of your stupidity. How you managed to get an accounting degree *and* a job with a federal savings and loan is beyond me."

"Maybe I'm smarter than you think," Cook said. He suddenly stopped and gazed through the trees on the other side of the road. "Is that a water tower?" he asked.

"How the hell would I know? I can't see my hand in front of my face."

Cook hurried toward the edge of the trees. "Hell, yeah, that's the Columbiana's water tower," he said in obvious delight. "I know right where we are. My friend Jonesy, or Reverend Jonesy, as they call him," he added with a laugh, "lives a stone's throw from it."

"Great. You can stop in and ask him to save your soul before I put you out of your misery."

Cook looked worried for a moment. "He's not a *real* preacher, and he's as crooked as my mama's arthritic finger. He'd *sell* his mama if he could make five bucks. Trust me, he has spent a time or two behind bars. He's a traveling preacher. If he's not on the road he'll give us something to eat."

Carl Lee looked doubtful. "There's probably a reward out for our capture," he said. "I'm not taking any chances."

"That's where you're wrong, Carl Lee. Jonesy wouldn't turn in a con. It wouldn't be ethical. Besides, he's rich. Made a butt-load of money scamming truck drivers, leading them to Jesus," he added. "And guess who showed him how to hide all that money? Yours truly, that's who. And Jonesy has connections coming out the ying-yang. He might be able to find us a ride to Beaumont."

Carl Lee seemed to ponder it. "Okay," he said. "We'll go by and see your friend, but if he even looks like he's going to blow the whistle on us I'll bury a bullet so deep they'll never find it."

They crossed the highway and picked their way through the woods. On the other side, they found a brand-new double-wide mobile home. Beside it sat an eighteen-wheeler, the words PRAYER MOBILE painted on the side.

"What's *that?*" Carl Lee asked.

"That's Jonesy's traveling church," Cook

said. "He holds religious services at truck stops and roadside parks. Goes all over the country spreading the Good Word," he added. "Truckers are very generous."

A man's voice called out to them from the mobile home. A shotgun poked from a window, trained on the men. Cook identified himself. A moment later a gray-haired man in black slacks, black shirt, and priest's collar appeared at the door. He still held the rifle, even as he and Cook pumped hands enthusiastically. Cook introduced him to Carl Lee.

"CNN has been flashing pictures of you boys all day," Jonesy said. "A motorist decided to take a leak in the woods along the side of the highway and almost tripped over your pal's body. They found him several hours ago; ID'd him at the scene from a couple of tattoos."

"We didn't kill him," Cook said. "He got hit by a guard during the escape."

"Anyway, some kid heard about it and called the cops. Claims he ran into you guys last night." Jonesy had to pause to catch his breath. He looked at Carl Lee. "Gave the make and model of the car and said you looked like Jerry Lewis in that professor movie," he added.

"Uh-oh, there goes your disguise," Cook said.

Carl Lee muttered a couple of four-letter words.

"Hold it right there, son," Jonesy said. "This is the Lord's house. We don't use that kind of language."

Carl Lee looked at Cook. "Is he for real?"

Cook nodded soberly before looking at Jonesy. "We don't have the car anymore. The tire blew out. We were able to ride the rim to a dirt road and push it into a ravine. Hopefully nobody will see it for a while."

Jonesy looked at Carl Lee. "I know what you did," he said, "but God loves you anyway, and so do I. I'll invite you in to break bread, but you'll have to leave your gun outside. I don't allow weapons in my home."

Carl Lee looked pointedly at the rifle.

"This doesn't count because it's for protection," Jonesy said. "A man has a right to protect his home."

Cook pulled his gun from his waistband and put it on the front step. Finally, Carl Lee did the same.

"You boys hungry?" Jonesy asked when they stepped inside. "I've got a pot of red beans and rice on the stove."

"I hear you've got a lot of money," Carl

Lee said once Jonesy served up three bowls of beans and rice and thick slices of buttered bread. "How come you're not living in some fancy mansion?"

"I'm storing my treasures in heaven," Jonesy said. "There are mansions galore up there, all sitting on streets of gold. Also, I don't want the IRS asking questions."

They ate in silence. Jonesy refilled their bowls. "Where are my manners?" he said. "I'll bet you boys are thirsty."

"A cold beer would be nice," Carl Lee said, only to receive a look of warning from Cook.

"Then you've come to the wrong place," Jonesy said. "I don't allow alcohol, drugs, cussing, or poker playing." He pulled several soft drinks from the refrigerator and passed them around.

"So how are you fellows planning to make the rest of the trip without getting caught?"

Carl Lee looked up. "Cook said you might be able to hook us up with a ride."

"Depends on how much you're willing to pay," Jonesy said. "I understand you got a quarter of a mil waiting for you in Beaumont. I might be willing to help for a fair cut. First thing I'd do is get you two out of those clothes."

"What do you consider a fair cut?" Carl

Lee asked after a moment.

Jonesy considered it. "Takes a lot of gas to fill up an eighteen-wheeler," he said. "I reckon twenty-five will do it."

Carl Lee's eyebrows shot up. "Twenty-five *thousand!* Are you crazy?"

"I'll take you right down I-20 to Atlanta, go through Augusta, turn south in Columbia, South Carolina, then on to Beaumont. All in all, I'll have you there in about seven hours."

Carl Lee shook his head. "Forget it. I can charter a damn jet for less than that."

Jonesy reached for his gun.

Carl Lee sighed and looked at the ceiling. "I meant to say 'darn.' "

Cook stared at Carl Lee in disbelief. "Take the deal, man! We don't have wheels, and now the cops have a description of you."

"I'll give you ten," Carl Lee told Jonesy.

"Fifteen."

"No."

"Okay, make it twelve," Jonesy said, "and I'll let you take a well-needed shower, put you both in a priest's outfit, rub a little black shoe dye in your hair, and ask the Lord to speak to your hearts."

"I'm out of here," Destiny told Vera, grabbing her purse and pushing her chair from her desk. She gave a sudden squeal that startled Vera so bad the woman dropped a file folder, scattering papers across the floor.

"It's Freddy Baylor!" Destiny said, dropping to her knees and scrambling beneath her desk. "Don't tell him I'm here," she hissed.

"Oh, I'm going to enjoy this," Vera said.

A man with longish blond hair and a scruffy reddish-blond beard walked through the front door wearing ragged jeans and a torn T-shirt with the words BORN TO BREED on the front. He walked up to Vera's desk. "How are you today?" he said politely.

"Why, I'm just fine, thank you." Vera gave him her best smile.

"I'm Freddy Baylor. Is Destiny —"

"Freddy Baylor!" Vera bolted from her chair and held out her hand. "It's *so* nice to finally meet Destiny's new beau! Why, she can't say enough wonderful things about you. I'm Vera, by the way."

He arched both brows, but took her hand and shook it. "Destiny has mentioned me? I'm glad to hear it."

"She's wondering why you haven't invited her to go fishing."

"I had no idea she enjoyed that sort of thing. But then, I haven't had much of a chance to talk to her since she's always in a hurry."

"Oh, she's just playing hard to get," Vera said, giving him a wink.

He grinned. "Is she around, by any chance?"

"As a matter of fact, she is," Vera said. "She's hiding under that desk." She pointed. From where Vera stood, she could see Destiny clearly, but Freddy, on the other side, could not.

He chuckled. "Destiny never mentioned she worked with somebody so personable and funny," he said.

"Destiny, come out from under that desk right this minute!" Vera said, only to receive a menacing look from the woman scrunched beneath it.

Freddy laughed again. "You ever thought about doing stand-up comedy?" he asked, as Vera continued to talk to the desk. "How about telling Destiny I stopped by?"

"I've got a better idea," Vera said. "Why don't you wait for her? You just make yourself comfortable on the sofa over there and help yourself to a magazine. I have a feeling she's going to pop up any moment."

"Thanks." Freddy turned for the sofa, just as Mike Henderson pushed through the front door.

"Look at me!" Mike all but shouted to Vera, motioning wildly at his face. "I've got this rash all over my body."

"You've got chicken pox," Vera said.

Mike shook his head. "No way! That voodoo woman, Queenie Cloud, did this to me. I'm going to report her to the police."

Freddy Baylor suddenly looked anxious and backed away from the other man. "I have to get back to the bait shop," he said. "Would you tell Destiny I came by?" He was gone.

"Who was *that?*" Mike asked Vera.

"Destiny's new boyfriend."

"What!"

"Stop shouting," Vera said. "If you think you look bad now, just wait until Jamie gets her hands on you."

"Uh-oh. I shouldn't have added that part about Dr. Davenport in my article."

Vera arched one brow. "You think?"

A relieved Destiny crawled from beneath her desk, startling Mike so bad he jumped. "What is going on here?" he asked.

Destiny shot Vera a dark look. "You're going to pay."

"Was that man your lover?" Mike demanded. "Are you actually having *sex* with a bait store owner? After turning me down *three* times! Do you know what that does to a man's ego?"

Destiny ignored him.

The phone rang and Vera grabbed it. "You called in the nick of time," she told Jamie. "Mike just walked in. I would slap him for you, but he's under the weather. Has the chicken pox," she added.

"I do *not* have the chicken pox. I'm telling you, I'm hexed!"

"He claims Queenie Cloud is responsible for it. Says he's going to call the police. He's gone wacko. Flipped out. Lost it. Gone off the deep end. You need to get back here fast."

Jamie hung up the phone and looked at Maggie. "I have to get back to the office." She relayed the message and Maggie closed her eyes and shook her head. "I have no idea why he thinks Queenie did something to him," Jamie added, "but the police aren't going to take him seriously."

"Queenie made threats against him last night," Maggie said and told Jamie about Mike's visit. "He could report threats. I'd better ride over and take a look at him. Maybe calm him down." She turned to Mel. "Would you please go outside and see how much longer Zack and Ben will be working on the pen for Butterbean? Tell Zack I need a lift to the newspaper office as soon as they're done."

Mel nodded and hurried out.

Jamie reached for her purse. "You don't really think Queenie, um —" She paused. "Never mind. I don't want to know. I'll see you at the office." Jamie stepped out the back door and called Fleas several times.

"He's back here with Butterbean," Mel shouted from behind the house.

Jamie hurried to the backyard. An amused Zack and Ben were using a heavy-duty staple gun to fasten the chicken wire in place on the wooden poles. Mel grinned at Jamie and pointed. Standing on opposite sides of the makeshift fence, Fleas and Butterbean were trying to rub noses through the octagon-shaped holes in the wire. "I think they're in love," Mel said.

Jamie shook her head sadly. "Just when I think my life is as strange as it can get, my dog gets the hots for a goat. Okay, Romeo, time to go." Jamie grasped his collar and tugged gently, but Fleas wouldn't budge. He was too busy making goo-goo eyes at Butterbean.

"Oh, great," Jamie said, as Mel continued to laugh and the men's amusement grew. She reached into her purse and pulled out the leash she kept on hand. She hooked it to Fleas's collar and tugged.

He gave a huge hound-dog sigh, gave Butterbean a lingering look, and followed Jamie toward the car.

"We're going in *that?*" Mel asked a half hour later as they were getting ready to go to the newspaper office. "Your hippie van?"

Zack grinned. "Yeah. I wish I had thought to put on my tie-dyed T-shirt." He unlocked and opened the doors for them. "Ladies?"

"I'll die if anyone I know sees me," Mel said once they were on their way.

"Hey, look," Zack said, reaching for several cassette tapes on the dashboard. "We've got Janis Joplin, Joe Cocker, and Jimmy Hendrix. Hey, Mel, I'll bet you fifty cents you don't know the words to 'Bobby Mc-Gee.' " He put the tape into the cassette player and sang along.

"Oh, brother," Mel mumbled and scooted down in the backseat.

Maggie chuckled as Zack sang to the music, obviously unaware that he couldn't hold a tune. She liked that he had a sense of humor; it would go a long way toward easing the tension over the next hours or days as they waited for Carl Lee's appearance.

They arrived at the *Gazette,* and Maggie

161

hurried inside, with Zack and Mel right behind. Maggie followed the sound of voices and found Jamie and her staff trying to calm Mike. "Okay, I'm here," she called out.

"Finally!" Mike said. "I'm going crazy with all this itching. It's *everywhere!*"

"Men are such babies," Vera said.

Maggie noted the rash on Mike's face and arms as she opened her bag and pulled on her latex gloves. "Have you ever had the chicken pox, Mike?" she asked.

"When I was about three years old," he said. "This isn't the chicken pox."

"Sure looks like it. Have you been exposed to anyone within the past couple of weeks who had chicken pox?"

"No."

"When did your symptoms begin?"

"My head started itching like crazy last night. I thought it was my new shampoo. I woke up this morning to *this,*" he added, pointing to himself.

Maggie doubted it had come on quite *that* fast. The rash had probably started on his back where he couldn't see it. She followed up with more questions, slipped a thermometer beneath his tongue, and reached for a vial containing an antihistamine. "I'm going to give you something to stop the itching," she said, drawing the medication into a syringe and giving him an injection. The thermometer beeped. One-oh-one. "And something for your fever," she added.

"You don't have a cure for what I have," he said, sounding hopeless. "Queenie Cloud is the only one who can stop it."

"She's in Savannah for the day. Sorry."

"I could be dead before she gets back. Is there something you can do to break the hex?"

Maggie looked at him. He was genuinely afraid. "I promise you'll feel better in a few minutes, Mike." She tore open another package and shook two tablets into his palm. His hand trembled so badly he almost dropped them. Jamie went for water.

"You're being silly," Vera told him. She looked at Maggie. "He's the worst hypochondriac I've ever seen. If he gets a headache he swears it's a brain tumor and won't shut up until the doctor does an MRI."

"May I speak with you for a moment, Maggie?" Jamie said.

Mike's eyes widened. "Uh-oh, it must be bad if they have to talk in private."

"Try to relax, Mike. I'll be right back." Maggie followed Jamie out of the office. Zack and Mel sat on the sofa in the reception area reading a magazine.

"You have to do something," Jamie said, once she and Maggie reached the small kitchen at the end of the hall. "Mike will end up making his condition much worse if he doesn't get a grip."

"He'll feel better once his fever goes down."

"Not if he continues to think Queenie put a hex on him. I'll have to take him to the ER and sit with him day and night like when he had the flu and was sure it was acute leukemia."

Maggie had no time to think about hexes and poxes and root work, what with the threat of Carl Lee looming. "I've tried to convince him otherwise. What do you want me to do?"

"You'll have to remove the hex."

"What hex?"

"The hex he swears Queenie put on him."

"Even if it was a hex, which it isn't, I don't know how to remove them," Maggie said. "Queenie uses some kind of Uncrossing Oil, whatever that is, and a bunch of other weird stuff."

"You're not *really* going to remove a hex; you're just going to make Mike *think* you removed one. Do like Queenie. Use weird stuff."

"I don't *have* any weird stuff on me at the

moment, and I don't have time for Mike's weirdness."

Mel came to the door. "Mom, Miss Vera says you'd better check on Mike. His face is red. Miss Vera says he's burning up."

"See?" Jamie said. "In an hour he'll be dead."

Maggie tried not to show her annoyance as she rechecked Mike's temperature. She was stunned to find that it had gone up two points.

"I feel so weak," Mike said, falling sideways on the sofa. His voice was barely audible. "Where is that pretty music coming from?"

"Oh, brother," Maggie said under her breath.

"You have to do something!" Jamie said.

"What he needs is a good kick in the behind," Vera told her. "He's nothing but a big baby."

Maggie could not remember feeling more frustrated. "Okay, you want to help me uncross this hex?" she asked Jamie. "Fine."

Vera gave Maggie a funny look.

"What do you want me to do to *break* the hex?" Jamie asked loudly.

"Hmm, let's see," Maggie said thoughtfully. "First, I'll need a frog."

Jamie looked surprised. "Frog? Did you say *frog?*"

"Not just *any* frog. I need a young male frog."

Jamie opened her mouth to speak, saw the smug look on her friend's face, and smiled pleasantly. "Okayee, one young male frog coming up," she said, grabbing her purse.

"I'll go with you," Destiny said, following Jamie to the door.

"Hold it!" Maggie said. They turned. "I absolutely positively must have grave dust in order to undo this particular hex."

"Grave dust!" Vera said.

Maggie shrugged. "Dirt from a grave."

"Can't you make a substitution or something?" Jamie asked.

"Oh, my goodness, nooo!" Maggie gasped and covered her chest with both hands as though fearing her heart would stop beating at the mere thought. "The results could prove disastrous."

Jamie crossed her arms and gave Maggie a peeved look. "Anything else while we're at it?" she asked sweetly. "Eye of an owl? Hair of a dog?"

Maggie spoke softly. "The grave must have been dug within the past forty-eight hours and sit within twenty-five feet of an oak tree."

Jamie's eyes crossed.

"It must be empty. It looses its purity once a body has been placed in it."

Mike raised his head slightly. "Hank Judd is being buried at one o'clock this afternoon at Oaklawn Cemetery," he said, as though it might be the last words that slipped from his lips. "There are oak trees all over the place. That's why they call it Oaklawn." His eyes rolled about, and his head fell back on the sofa with a flump.

Destiny checked her watch. "We have thirty-five minutes. You drive, and I'll jump out and grab the grave dirt. I tossed an empty Midol bottle in my trash. I'll get it on the way out and put the dirt in it."

Vera looked at her. "Somewhere out there is a straitjacket with your name on it."

Destiny looked amused as she turned to Jamie. "After we get the dirt we can go by my place for the male frog. I have dozens. I keep them in Mason jars under my bed just in case one decides to turn into a prince."

"How do you tell the difference between a male and female frog?" Jamie asked.

"By the color bow around its neck," Destiny said.

Vera pressed her lips into a thin line and looked at Jamie. "I'll be at my desk writing my letter of resignation."

Jamie and Destiny hurried from the building. They climbed into Jamie's Mustang, and she put her key into the ignition and started it. "You know this whole thing is a hoax."

"Of course," Destiny said.

"So where are we *really* going to get the frog?"

"There's a pond near my place. I've seen bunches hopping around. We can grab some dirt from there as well."

Max stepped inside the kitchen and found Maggie and Zack carrying cups of coffee to the small table. "Vera said I could find the two of you in here," he said. He offered his hand to Zack and introduced himself. "It's nice to finally meet the voice on the other end of my cell phone," he said.

Zack nodded. "Same here. You've been a great help."

"You two know each other?" Maggie asked.

"Max is my info man," Zack said. "The coffee is fresh," he told Max.

"Great." Max poured a cup, and the three of them sat down. He looked at Maggie. "So, if I understood Vera correctly, my wife is out gathering frogs and grave dust so you can remove a hex."

"Why else would I have spent all those years in medical school?" Maggie asked.

"Now I understand." He turned to Zack. "Have you heard anything?"

Zack leaned back in his chair. "Not since they found Luis Perez, the guy they call Loopy. The police are scouring the highways and byways, but they can't put a chopper in the air because of the fog."

Maggie took a sip of her coffee. "Do they have any idea how long it will take for the fog to lift?" she asked.

"A couple of hours at least," Zack said. "They're ready to move the minute it does."

"What's it been, twenty-seven or twenty-eight hours since Stanton took off?" Max asked.

Zack nodded. "They're smarter than I thought. I'm trying to think which way Stanton and Boyd are traveling. Remember, Boyd drove a beer truck for a southeastern distributor while taking correspondence courses to become a shyster accountant. He knows his way around. If they've listened to the radio they know we have a description of the car. In that case, they'd be smart to avoid heading east to Atlanta and go straight south, maybe as far as Albany, Georgia, then grab 82 East to Brunswick. From there, I-95 North is a straight shot to Beaumont."

"It would still be risky," Max said.

Zack nodded. "I think they ditched the car. They've either stolen another one or caught a ride with somebody."

"I can't imagine anyone would be willing to pick up a couple of strangers," Maggie said.

"Unless they had a gun to their head," Max offered.

Maggie could tell the men were deep in thought and could probably use some time alone for brainstorming. "I'd better check on Mike." She left the room.

"These guys are going to give the police a run for their money," Max said. "They could be zigzagging all over the place in a dune buggy for all we know."

"Yep." Zack clasped his hands behind his head. "So the smart thing is to wait," he said, "and let them come to us."

CHAPTER SEVEN

"I don't know which is worse," Jonesy said, trying to make himself heard over a gospel song blaring from the radio and the slapping windshield wipers. "This dang rain or the fog," he added. "Cook, hit that defroster; the windows are steaming up on me again."

Cook flipped a switch and hot air fanned the windshield. Outside, the wind whipped about and from time to time the semi shuddered.

Carl Lee sat quietly, arms folded across his chest, a frown marring his face as passing motorists openly gawked at the Prayer Mobile and the three priests in the front cab. He checked his wristwatch, sighed, and leaned his head back against the cracked leather seat. He tugged the collar at his neck.

"Your friend doesn't say much," Jonesy told Cook.

Cook nodded. "He's got a lot on his mind."

Jonesy chuckled. "Hope he's not trying to remember where he hid the money."

Carl Lee ignored him. Instead, he reached into his back pocket and carefully pulled a sandwich bag containing a folded newspaper clipping. He unfolded the clipping; it was worn despite his attempts to protect it, the ink smudged in places from overhandling. Dr. Maggie Davenport and her daughter smiled back at him from a black-and-white photo as they leaned against an antique trunk that Maggie claimed she had lovingly restored, just as she had a number of other antiques belonging to her grandparents. It was her hobby, she said.

"She's a beauty," Cook said, shooting a quick look at the clipping. "Too bad she messed you over, huh?"

Carl Lee regarded Cook with a look of contempt. "Keep your fat mouth shut or I'll shut it for you."

Cook shrank away. "Hey, I didn't mean anything by it."

"Okay, boys," Jonesy said. "I'm not going to have none of that. I've got enough to tend to with this crazy traffic. Couldn't pay me enough to live in Atlanta, no siree."

The traffic began to thin as they passed over the city toward Covington, Georgia. Jonesy was able to pick up speed, despite

the still whirling wind and rain and sometimes heavy patches of fog. The speedometer
rose steadily.

"There's something up ahead," Carl Lee
said. "Lights flashing," he added. "A wreck
maybe. You need to slow this thing down,
man."

Jonesy pumped the brakes several times
but was not prepared when suddenly the
cars in front of him braked and stopped
dead on the interstate. "Oh, Lord!" he said,
unable to slow the big rig quickly enough.
He slammed his foot on the brake, and the
trailer began to fishtail, even as the smell of
burning rubber filled the cab.

"Oh, hell," Cook said, crossing himself.

Carl Lee shouted a foul litany.

Jonesy lost control of the vehicle, and the
Prayer Mobile skidded. Ahead, passengers
threw open car doors and raced from the
road, only seconds before impact. The
eighteen-wheeler slammed into an SUV,
creating a domino effect. From behind, a
large pickup truck hit the driver's side.
Jonesy cried out a split second before his
head hit the steering wheel in a bone-
crunching blow, only to be tossed back
against the seat. He fell across Cook's lap.

"Sheee-ittt!" Cook cried as he stared in
horror at the gash in Jonesy's forehead. "Do

you think he's dead?" He struggled to get out from under the man.

"I'm not going to hang around long enough to find out," Carl Lee said, yanking hard on the door handle. He shoved the door of the cab open with his shoulder and started to climb out. He reached for the canvas bag that held their belongings, including their guns that Jonesy had refused to let them carry inside their pants while dressed as priests.

"Don't leave me," Cook cried, and grabbed the straps to keep Carl Lee from taking the bag.

"Let go!" Carl Lee shouted.

"You *need* me," Cook yelled back as he tried once more to free himself from Jonesy. "Her neighborhood will be crawling with cops. I know how to get you in."

Carl Lee gritted his teeth. "Grab his wallet and cell phone," he said.

"You mean *rob* Jonesy?"

Carl Lee grabbed Cook by the shirt. "Can't you smell, you dumb shit? There is fuel all over the road. You want to burn to death?"

Cook gaped in horror but wasted no time. He worked Jonesy's wallet from his pocket and grabbed his cell, then shoved him hard and pulled his legs from beneath the man.

Carl Lee dragged him from the cab. They hurried toward the exit sign, passing dazed motorists and crying babies. Several men and women had already begun helping people from their vehicles; one man was trying to open a smashed car door with a crowbar.

"Father!" A middle-aged woman came out of nowhere and grasped Carl Lee's arm. "My husband is badly hurt," she said, pointing to a nearby car.

Carl Lee gave her an odd look as though he'd forgotten he was dressed as a priest. He shook his head as if to clear it. "I'm going for help, ma'am," he finally said and pulled free. He turned and walked quickly as Cook followed.

Sirens whined in the distance.

"I've got blood on my hands," Cook said, "and you've got black shoe dye leaking from your sideburns." He reached into his pocket and brought out a wad of tissue.

"This sucks about as much as prison," Carl Lee muttered as he mopped each side of his face. They made their way down the exit ramp and crossed the street to a convenience store where a number of people stood outside and stared at the commotion on the interstate. Carl Lee opened the door leading into the store. "Go wash your hands," he told Cook and shoved him inside. "You got two seconds." He barely got the words out of his mouth before a sudden explosion shook the ground and rattled the windows in the store. People outside screamed. The clerk raced outside.

Cook threw open the door of the bathroom. "What was *that?*" He looked out a window. "Man, would you take a look at that fireball!" The cash register rang out, and he turned and frowned at Carl Lee who stood behind it. "What are you doing?"

"Don't ask stupid questions." Carl Lee grabbed the bills and stuffed them into his pocket. "This way," he said.

They left through the opposite door and started across the parking lot as fire trucks raced down the road toward the interstate.

Maggie was only too happy to escape the newspaper office by the time Zack led Mel and her to the van. "I hope I never have to go through something like that again," she said, climbing inside and closing her door.

"At least you didn't have to chase a stupid frog all over Jamie's office," Mel grumbled from the backseat. "Do you think Jamie is going to be mad at you for long?" she asked.

Maggie gave a small shrug. "I probably shouldn't have laughed over her falling into a frog pond. I'll make it up to her by taking her someplace nice for lunch next week."

"If we live to see next week," Mel reminded.

Zack frowned.

"Please don't say things like that," Maggie said, even as her own worries came rushing back.

"Who's hungry?" Zack asked as though trying to change the subject.

"I'm starving," Mel said.

"Where do you want to go?" he asked. "You choose the place, *any* place, and remember, money is no object because I'm loaded."

Maggie wondered how Zack could be so upbeat with the possibility of what lurked ahead. Of course he was used to dealing with mean and dangerous people. The only mean person she knew was Henry Filbert. Maybe Zack was merely pretending to be cheerful and buoyant so she and Mel wouldn't be so anxious. Even so, she noted how alert he was, how *aware* he was of everything going on around them. She knew he watched the rearview mirror, that he kept an eye on the side mirrors and back door when they stopped at a red light or pulled up to a stop sign. Those dark eyes didn't miss much.

"If you're loaded, how come you're driving this dumb-looking van?" Mel asked. "How come you're not driving a cool car?"

That was her daughter, Maggie thought. No tact.

"There weren't any cool rental cars left when I arrived in Beaumont," Zack said. "They were all rented to Elvis impersonators."

"Gross," Mel said, then suddenly brightened. "Let's stop at Harry's Burgers. They have awesome foot-long hot dogs."

"You up for that?" Zack asked Maggie, slowing.

"Sure," she said. "Who cares about high cholesterol?"

"Would you park in the back?" Mel asked, ducking low in the seat.

"No problem." Zack turned in and drove to the farthermost parking space. "How's this?"

Mel wasn't listening. She was peeking out the window, obviously checking the vicinity for someone she might know. Finally, she threw open the door, jumped out, and took off.

Zack looked amazed. "Wow, did you know she could run like that? Faster than a locomotive, faster than a speeding bullet, faster than the speed of light?" he added.

Maggie laughed. "She learned to run like that when she turned thirteen. To avoid embarrassing situations." Once again, she saw him staring out the side window, his eyes fixed on Mel, obviously wanting to make certain she was safely inside the building.

"Are you embarrassed easily?" he asked as they walked toward the restaurant, his gaze scanning the parking lot.

"Are you kidding? You're talking to a woman who led a goat right through town in broad daylight. Nothing embarrasses me."

"How about when toilet paper sticks to your shoe and you drag it from the bathroom?"

"Nope." Maggie liked the sound of his voice, liked having him nearby and knowing he genuinely cared about their safety. It allowed her to take a breather from time to time. She could enjoy the feel of the afternoon sun on her face and the smells coming from Harry's. She could almost pretend there wasn't a deranged killer headed her way holding a score card with her name scrawled in big bold letters. Almost.

"How about when spinach gets stuck between your teeth?" Zack asked. "Or diving into a pool and losing the bottom of your swimsuit? Or being kissed by me right here in this parking lot?"

"I wouldn't flinch. Uh?" She looked up just as Zack slid his arm around her waist and pulled her against him. She barely had time to get out a small "eek" of surprise before he planted his lips squarely on hers.

Maggie was stunned. She hadn't seen it coming. Had she missed some cue? Was she so out of touch with the opposite sex that she was just plain *clueless?* She didn't have time to answer her own questions because his mouth was hot and wonderful, and his tongue slipping past her lips was just so good. Good like chocolate.

Okay, better than chocolate. Chocolate didn't make her tingly and shivery. Chocolate didn't make her X chromosomes dance and leap and twirl like ballerinas on a caffeine buzz.

Maggie slipped her arms around Zack's neck and kissed him right back. Right in Harry's parking lot! Amid horns, whistles, and catcalls.

What was she *doing?*

She broke the kiss and stepped back so fast she almost lost her balance. "Why did you do that?" she asked, her brain still spinning crazily like some wild carnival ride.

"Damned if I know," Zack said, looking

dazed. "I just had this wild impulse to kiss you. I wasn't thinking. I lost my head." He frowned. "Hey, wait, you lost your head too, because you did a pretty good job of kissing me back."

Maggie could not believe it. She *had* lost her head. They had *both* lost their heads! She almost gasped as the thought hit her. Queenie! The woman had put some kind of spell on them. That was the only possible reason she could think of for necking with a man in Harry's parking lot.

"We need to get inside," Zack said. "Mel is probably wondering what happened to us."

Mel was already in line and waving frantically. "I need money," she mouthed. Maggie gave Zack her order and searched for a table in a sea of teenagers. Harry's was a happening place, she decided.

Zack and Mel joined her a few minutes later. "Now which of you ladies wants to share her seat with me?" Zack asked.

Mel scooted to the center of her seat.

Zack smiled at Maggie and slid in beside her, and the booth seemed to shrink to the size of the kiddy table used at Thanksgiving. This sorta, kinda, explained why his thigh kept brushing against hers, Maggie thought, even though the other side of her was practically smushed against the wall.

"Where *were* you guys?" Mel asked her.

Maggie tried to think of a good answer.

"We were kissing in the parking lot," Zack told the girl, earning a surprised look from Maggie and an eye roll from Mel.

"Next time would you try not to take so long?" Mel said, obviously not taking him seriously.

"Okay, the grilled chicken sandwich, no mayo, no onions, with extra lettuce and tomato goes to the boring person at our table." Zack passed it to Maggie. "The same person who ordered bottled water," he added, handing it over as well. "You know, Mel, this is probably going to gross you out, but when I was a kid we drank water right out of the spigot on the side of the house. My mother wasn't worried, though, because she caught me eating dirt when I was two years old, and that didn't kill me."

Mel regarded him as she grabbed her foot-long hot dog, fries, and milk shake. "You are strange," she said. "Mom, don't you think Zack is strange?"

"Very strange."

"Whoa, that's pretty scary coming from a woman who chants over frogs and scatters grave dirt on sick guys," Zack said. He unwrapped his double burger with all the fixings. "Nothing like a home-cooked meal," he said, biting into his sandwich.

"Zack, my man!" a male voice called out from across the room, drawing a questioning look, not only from Zack, but Maggie and Mel and the entire restaurant as well. He was dressed in a sparkly Elvis outfit. He waved and hurried over, followed by a group of Elvis clones, their capes flowing, rhinestones flashing.

Mel looked at Zack. "Please tell me they aren't coming to our table."

"I could, but that would make me a liar," Zack said as the men approached.

"You remember me, right?" the man said to Zack. "Lonnie Renfro. You gave me a ride." He offered his hand.

"How could I forget?" Zack said as they shook hands. "Good to see you again, Lonnie."

"You didn't tell me you had a family, Zack." Lonnie introduced himself to Maggie and then Mel, who had already slid so far down in the booth her chin almost touched the table. "Meet my new friends," he said, calling out the names of the other Elvis impersonators.

Maggie nodded politely. She saw the expression on Mel's face change and followed the girl's look as Travis Bradley and several friends stepped inside Harry's. They paused and stared at the many Elvises.

"Are you an Elvis fan?" Lonnie asked Maggie.

"Absolutely."

Lonnie grinned at his friends. "Boys, what d'ya say we give Zack and his lovely family a little song? How about 'Heartbreak Hotel'?"

Maggie saw the panic in her daughter's eyes, but there was no escaping the men, who'd formed a solid Elvis wall around the booth.

Lonnie grabbed the salt shaker off their table and put it to his lips. "Well, since my ba-buh left . . ." he began loudly and the other men followed. People stopped talking. Heads turned.

Maggie noted the grin on Zack's face as she forced herself to nod and smile as well. The men were obviously encouraged by their reaction and began swiveling their hips.

"You *so* owe me," Mel said out of the side of her mouth.

The customers at Harry's Burgers applauded once the Elvis ensemble finished their song and moved to the counter to place their food order. Travis came over and gave them a big silver grin. "Guess where I've been?" he asked Mel, pointing to his new braces.

Her eyes widened in surprise. "The orthodontist?"

"Uh-huh. Everybody calls me 'Metal Mouth' now."

"That happened to me too," Mel said sympathetically. "They'll stop after a while."

"Was your mouth sore in the beginning?" he asked.

She nodded. "It'll get better."

He grinned at Maggie and Zack.

"They look great," Maggie said, and introduced him to Zack.

"I'm Mel's favorite uncle," Zack said. "I'll bet she has told you all about me."

"I heard you were visiting," Travis said. "My mom knows everything that goes on in this town."

"She talks a lot, huh?" Mel said.

"She isn't talking right now," Travis said. "She woke up this morning with laryngitis."

"Laryngitis?" Maggie said. "Oh, no."

"Actually, my dad says it's a day for celebration. He even upped my allowance." Travis glanced back at his table. "Well, I'll see you around." He gave Mel a small wave.

Mel gazed at him dreamily as he walked away.

"Nice kid," Zack said.

Mel turned to Maggie. "I'll bet Aunt

Queenie gave Mrs. Bradley laryngitis. Right after she put a hex on Mike Henderson."

"It's just a coincidence," Maggie said.

"Too bad she didn't lose her voice before she blabbed stuff about you and Carl Lee Stanton all over town. Caitlin said everybody is talking about it. People don't think the cops will catch him before he gets here. They think he's more interested in hurting you than getting his money."

"I seriously doubt it," Maggie said.

"He looks mean. I saw his picture on CNN last night. Paula Zahn was interviewing the warden from the prison in Texas."

"What was Paula wearing?" Zack asked.

Maggie and Mel just looked at him.

"You can tell me later," he said.

"Since when do you watch CNN?" Maggie asked, annoyed with herself for not remembering her daughter had a TV in her room and access to the news. No wonder she had spouted off in the van.

"I think I should know what he looks like," the girl said. "They showed a picture of the ATM driver he shot, and that FBI agent he killed. And he just dumped his friend's body in the woods on the side of the road. That is so sick. Now I'm glad Grandpa bought me that softball stuff last year. I'm going to keep the bat by my bed just in case."

"You play softball?" Zack asked as though trying to change the subject.

"In gym class," Mel said. "I wasn't very good at it and nobody wanted me on their team. My grandpa bought all this equipment so we could practice, but he is so impatient. I quit when he got annoyed and said I swung the bat like a girl."

Maggie was only vaguely aware of the conversation between the two. She was fuming mad at Carl Lee Stanton for making her daughter afraid. She was surprised that she could hate someone so intensely, that she could despise another human being. But Carl Lee wasn't much of a human being as far as she was concerned.

"I don't want you watching any more news shows," she told Mel. "I don't want you to get all caught up in that crap because it will only make you worry more."

"Nobody has to worry about anything," Zack said, "because I am here to serve, protect, and take care of the farm. I gotcha covered, ladies. Stanton doesn't stand a chance."

Mel looked at Zack. "What kind of gun do you have?"

Zack and Maggie exchanged looks. She gave a slight nod. She trusted Zack to say the right thing.

"It's a Glock," he said. "It's powerful, and I know how to use it if I have to. You and your mom are safe."

"Are you going to kill him?" Mel asked.

Maggie looked away. She felt frozen and hard. It didn't matter that Mel's question was tactless.

Zack put his elbows on the table and leaned closer to the girl. "Okay, here's the deal," he said. "I'm going to be honest with you, but you have to promise to trust me. Bottom line, I am going to do what I have to in order to protect the two of you. Whatever it takes."

Carl Lee and Cook hadn't walked far when an older-model baby-blue Cadillac convertible pulled off the road. The top was down; the driver sat low in the seat.

"Would you get a load of that car?" Cook said, giving a low whistle. "That sucker's an antique. It's in perfect condition. No telling what it's worth. He keeps looking at us. You think he plans on giving us a ride?"

"We're priests," Carl Lee said. "Of course he wants to give us a ride."

The driver backed toward them, swerving from side to side. "Uh-oh, he drives like he's drunk," Cook said. "I'm not riding with a drunk driver. I am totally against driving and drinking. Plus, drunk drivers have too many wrecks. I can't take being in another wreck today."

"Hell, look at him," Carl Lee said. "He's not drunk; he's old. Let me do the talking." Carl Lee walked toward the car, a big smile fixed on his face.

The man at the wheel smiled and waved. His face was a web of wrinkles, his bald head speckled with liver spots. White hair sprouted from his ears, one sharing space with a flesh-colored hearing aid.

"Good afternoon, Fathers," he said, peering at Carl Lee and Cook over a pair of bifocals that rested low on his nose. He wore an old terry-cloth bathrobe that bore grape juice stains. "Going my way?" he asked.

"Well, hello there, old-timer," Carl Lee said as he and Cook stood next to the car.

"Old?" the man said, drawing bushy white eyebrows together in a frown. "Who are you calling old? I'm only ninety-nine. I'm still as spry as a young rooster."

"My mistake," Carl Lee said. "Where are you headed?"

"Say what?" The man cupped his ear as he looked from Carl Lee to Cook. "I'm hard of hearing, and I was in such a hurry to get on the road that I forgot my hearing aid."

"It's in your ear," Cook said loudly.

"Really?" The man touched it. "Hey, you're right. I forgot to turn it on." He fiddled with it. "That's better," he said.

"I asked where you were going," Carl Lee repeated.

"Can you fellows keep a secret?"

Carl Lee nodded. "We're in the business of keeping secrets."

"I'm running away to Canada because my daughter is sending me to a nursing home in a couple of days. She says I'm not in my right mind. She's seventy-five years old; her mind isn't as sharp as she thinks it is."

"You sound okay to me," Cook told him, "but I'm still in shock because we were just in a terrible —"

Carl Lee stepped on his foot. Cook winced but shut up quickly.

"If you boys need a ride, I could use some help driving 'cause I've been at this wheel a while and I missed my nap," the old man said.

"How long have you been on the road?" Cook asked, stepping back, obviously trying to avoid Carl Lee stepping on his foot again.

"About an hour now," he said.

"Sure, we'll help you out," Carl Lee said. "That's what we do." He opened the driver's door. "Why don't you relax in the backseat and let me take the wheel?"

"I'd be much obliged," he said as Carl Lee helped him out. "My name is Ed White, by the way."

"I'm Father Tom, and this is Father Jerry," Carl Lee said, motioning to Cook. "But you can call us Tom and Jerry. You're safe in our hands, Ed."

"Does anybody need me to make a stop before we head to the farm?" Zack asked.

"I need —" Maggie sighed. "I need groceries, but I left my list at home."

"Do you want me to drive you to the house to pick it up?"

"No, I can probably remember." Maggie tried to sound confident, but her mind was racing in too many directions. Ultimately, though, every thought led straight to Carl Lee. Except one, she reminded herself. She hadn't stopped thinking about Zack's mouth on hers.

Inside, the store was crowded with Saturday shoppers. Maggie grabbed a cart and was surprised when Zack did the same. He and Mel took off in one direction while Maggie tried to decide where to start. Her mind drew a huge blank, and she pushed her cart aimlessly for a few minutes before deciding to concentrate on buying the essentials. Milk and bread, she thought. She was always running out of milk and bread.

Zack and Mel came up behind her a few minutes later. Mel wore a huge grin. "Look what Uncle Zack bought me." She pointed to the cart.

Maggie looked at their cart. Potato chips, dips, cocktail wieners, cookies, a twenty-four-pack of Pepsi, several teen magazines, a sketch pad, glitter nail polish, and *poker chips?* "Wow," she said.

Zack wore a sheepish smile. "I know it's a little over the top, but how many times do I get to spoil my favorite niece?"

Mel nodded. "Plus, I think we should be able to eat junk food on weekends. All my friends eat junk food, and they haven't come up with any incurable diseases. And look —" She paused and dug through the cart. "We got you some bath spritzers. You just drop one into your bath water, soak for about an hour, and all your tension goes away. The frown lines between your eyebrows will magically disappear."

"I have frown lines?" Maggie asked, touching the area between her eyes and finding the skin puckered. "Gee, I guess I do."

Zack pulled into Maggie's driveway a half hour later with only a few bags since Maggie hadn't been able to remember all that she'd needed. Zack gave them the code, showed them how to punch it in so they'd know how to arm and disarm it. Maggie and Mel took turns trying it out.

Mel helped Maggie put the grocery items away before heading toward her room with a handful of cookies. Maggie checked her telephone messages and was relieved to find the lab from Beaumont Memorial had called. She quickly dialed the number, spoke to one of the techs, and learned that the tests she'd ordered on eight-year-old Jimmy Sanders had indeed pointed to lead poisoning. She found the doctor, also a personal friend, who was taking her calls that weekend, and they discussed an aggressive treatment plan.

Zack came through the door just as she hung up and gave a smile of relief.

"Good news?" he asked.

"Yes." She told him about Jimmy Sanders.

Zack looked pleased for her. He crossed his arms and leaned against the kitchen counter. "Your grandfather was a doctor," he said. "Is that why you decided to practice medicine?"

"Hey, I've been practicing medicine since I was five years old," Maggie said with a chuckle. "Right at this very table," she added. "My grandfather discussed all of his cases with me. My mother claims my first word as a baby was 'diverticulitis.' "

Zack grinned. "Was your grandfather disappointed when your father didn't become a doctor?"

"You know a lot about my family," she said, only to get a shrug in return. "He was at first. But my dad had no desire to be stuck inside an office all day, which is why he became a cattle farmer." She crossed her arms as well. "Since you know about my family tell me something about yours."

"I grew up in Richmond where I still live when I'm not out of town on a case. My mom is still there and works in real estate. Each time she finds a house she can't live without she buys it and sells the old one."

"What about your father?"

"He hasn't been around for a while."

"Oh." Maggie didn't pry.

"I'm an only child like you."

"Was it lonely for you?"

He shook his head, and his smile was nostalgic. "I had a best friend. He's the reason I went to work for the bureau."

Maggie opened the refrigerator and pulled out two decaffeinated sugar-free soft drinks. She offered one to Zack who arched a brow.

"They're not that great," Maggie said, "but I like to think they cancel out my morning coffee and chocolate."

"I think I'll pass," he said.

Maggie put the second one back and closed the refrigerator. "What does your mom think about your working a dangerous job?" she asked, turning in time to see the surprised but troubled look in his eyes.

He shrugged. "You know how moms are. But my job isn't as dangerous as it sounds."

"Uh-huh." She clearly didn't believe him. She opened her soft drink and sat at the table.

"You just have to know what you're doing, Maggie. There's a lot of up-front work, a lot of planning. I don't just walk in blindly."

"Have you ever been scared?"

"Never."

"Liar." She laughed.

"Okay, I was a little nervous when the guy broke my arm. I just do my best to act the part and not flub up my lines."

"Like performing in a play," she said.

He looked thoughtful. "I guess."

Zack was still thinking about the conversation with Maggie an hour later as he cleaned his rifle in the upstairs guest room. When she had likened his work to being in a play, he should have mentioned that he didn't usually kiss the other characters. Or notice their legs and the way their hips swayed when they walked. Okay, that was a lie. He noticed. He'd fantasized. But he hadn't touched.

CHAPTER EIGHT

Maggie folded back a small section of the aluminum foil from the kitchen window and gazed out at the backyard. She knew Zack would insist she re-cover the window once he came downstairs, but she did not like having the world and the light blocked from view so that it felt as if she were living in a tightly sealed box.

The shadows, cast by the tall oaks and pines, had lengthened. It would be dark in an hour, making it easier for Carl Lee to slip unnoticed past police who had embedded themselves in the neighborhood woodwork and would go unnoticed by most people. But Carl Lee Stanton was not like most people. He was dangerous and cunning. And he might already be in Beaumont. He could be watching the house this very minute. She was comforted by the sound of Zack's footsteps overhead.

She was not comforted by their earlier

conversation.

I just do my best to act the part and not flub up my lines.

He hadn't been referring to people like Mel and her, Maggie reminded herself. He was talking about the bad guys who did things like break his arm. She and Mel posed no threat. He did not have to hide behind another character. He was free to be himself, and the real Zack Madden genuinely liked her daughter. He genuinely cared about their safety. Of that she was certain. What she didn't understand was why he had checked them out beforehand. And where the hell did that kiss fit in? And when it was all over, then what? Would he just fill out his paperwork, stick them all into a file, and stamp it CASE CLOSED?

Queenie and Everest arrived at Maggie's shortly afterward. Maggie disarmed the alarm system, and the two stepped inside the kitchen, Everest grasping the handle on a pet carrier that contained a squawking black hen. Mel came into the room and peered inside the carrier.

"She looks strange," the girl said.

"She's not your average hen," Queenie told her. "This is a *special* hen. She cost me seventy-five dollars."

"You paid seventy-five dollars for a *chicken?*" Maggie said in disbelief.

"She's *not* a chicken," Queenie said, clearly insulted. "This hen comes from championship stock. She has breeding. She's a blue blood."

Everest held up the carrier and talked to the bird inside. "Her name is Flo."

Queenie gave a sigh. "I guess we have no choice but to keep her out in that chicken coop with the *others.*"

"You want me to take her out there, Granny Queenie?" he asked.

"Yes, Everest. Be very gentle with her," Queenie said. "And watch where you're walking. You don't want to drop her and shake up anything inside of her that might interfere with her egg production."

"All the floodlights are on," Maggie said, but handed Everest a flashlight to help. Once again, she disarmed the security, waited for him to step outside, and then turned it back on. "This security business is driving me crazy," she said irritably. "I feel like I'm guarding a bank vault." She went back to preparing a cold-cuts platter of turkey, fat-free ham, fat-free cheese, and carrot sticks.

"Not in a cooking mood tonight, huh?" Queenie said, looking over Maggie's shoulder at the simple fare.

"Nope."

"You sound tired."

"Yep."

"Uh-oh, somebody is in a bad mood tonight," Queenie said, and turned for the table.

Mel sat in one of the chairs, an annoyed look on her face. "Ask Mom *why* she's in a bad mood."

"Okay, why?"

"Because she had to undo one of your hexes," Mel said before Maggie could speak.

Queenie gave Maggie a questioning look. "What's she talking about?"

"Mike Henderson is covered with a rash and he was practically clawing himself because he was itching so badly. He already had blisters popping up. If his fever had gotten any higher I would have had to get him to the ER."

"Sounds like chicken pox."

"Exactly." Maggie turned to Queenie. "The problem is, you threatened to do something to him last night so he swears you put a hex on him. The fact that he's a hypochondriac and planned to report you to the police made it even more fun."

"I didn't do anything to that smart-aleck boy."

"You didn't *have* to," Maggie said, raising her voice slightly. "With some people just *saying* it is enough, but you already know that. So I spent two hours trying to make him think I was undoing a hex."

"And Abby Bradley has laryngitis," Mel said.

Queenie smiled. "Now that's some good news."

"Like you didn't already know," Mel said.

Queenie crossed her arms and gave the girl her most formidable look. "Are you smart-mouthing your aunt Queenie, young lady? You know I don't put up with that nonsense."

Mel flounced from the room.

"Somebody needs to yank the attitude right out of that girl," Queenie said.

"And another thing," Maggie said, this time her voice little more than a whisper. "Did you go against my wishes and put some kind of spell on Zack and me?"

"What kind of spell?"

Maggie blushed. "Something to make us, um, *attracted* to each other?"

Queenie grinned. "I knew it! I knew you two were hot for each other. It's well past time you got hot for a man, and that's one hot man."

"If you did something I want it undone,"

Maggie said. "And don't expect me to try to protect you the next time somebody threatens to report you to the police. I'm a medical doctor. I can't go around removing hexes. I don't even know *how* to remove hexes, for Pete's sake!"

"First thing, you need some uncrossing oil," Queenie began.

"I don't *want* to know how to remove hexes," Maggie said. "I have enough to worry about. And while we're on the subject, no more boiling basil or anything else in this house," she said. "And no more making people hot for each other!" she added emphatically.

"How am I supposed to protect you and Mel from that madman if I'm not allowed to use my special talents?"

"That's why Zack is here."

"A gun may not be enough."

A tap on the back door forced Maggie to deal with the alarm system again. Everest stepped inside carrying a lime-green bag with decorative handles. "I don't think Flo likes it out there," he said.

"She's probably used to living in a four-star chicken coop," Queenie told him.

Zack came downstairs. "I heard you down here talking about your new hen," he said. "Where is she?"

Queenie opened her mouth to answer, but the words didn't come out.

"I put her out back," Everest said.

"You shaved," Queenie said. She looked at Maggie. "You didn't tell me he shaved. You are so lucky. I wish I had a crazy killer after me so the FBI would send a good-looking man to my house."

Maggie had no idea how to respond so she kept quiet. Everest handed Maggie the bag. "I forgot to bring it in earlier. I hope you won't get mad at me, but I asked my sister about a rinse for Mel's hair. She gave me the stuff she uses. It has no harsh chemicals, and it washes out after a couple of weeks. It will tone down the orange, that's all. Oh, and my sister put some makeup in there for Mel too."

"Makeup!" Maggie cried. "She's only thirteen years old, for Pete's sake."

"Well, it's not like *real* makeup. It's a tinted moisturizer, and it's good for the skin." When Maggie looked doubtful, he went on. "I'm telling you, I know all about women's products and how to use them. Who do you think my sister practiced on?" He looked at Zack. "I hope this won't get in the way of me being a big-time FBI agent."

"No problem," Zack said. "Diversity is good."

Mel walked into the kitchen. "Is there any chocolate cake left," she asked Maggie, "or have you already hidden it?" She saw the bag and stepped closer to her mother. "What's that?"

"Hair color," Everest said.

"For me?" He smiled and she squealed in delight. "Yes!"

"I'll color it for you if your mom agrees to let me," he said. "I'm really good at it."

"Please, Mom," Mel said.

"You're sure it will wash out?" Maggie asked Everest.

"It'll take two or three weeks of shampooing, but yes. It won't take me long to put it on her hair."

Maggie saw the eager look on Mel's face. "Okay."

Mel threw her arms around Maggie and hugged her, then exchanged a high five with Everest. "We can use the front bathroom," she told him. "It's plenty big enough."

Maggie shook her head as she opened the refrigerator and began pulling out the condiments. "I hope Everest knows what he's doing," she said.

"He's the one who gave me my perm," Queenie said.

"He'll make a fine agent," Zack said.

Maggie half listened to Queenie sing Everest's praises as she tried to unclog the tip of a squeeze bottle of mustard with a toothpick. When that didn't work, she pulled a case knife from a drawer and struggled to pry off the top.

"Do you need any help over there?" Zack asked. "Looks like that mustard container is kicking your behind."

"I can get it." Maggie gripped the plastic bottle tightly to keep it from slipping from her hands, and she tried once more to free the top. It popped, the lid flew off, and mustard spewed from the bottle and plastered her blouse. "Damn!"

Queenie looked up. "I have a remedy that will get that stain out."

Maggie rinsed the mustard off her hands and wiped her blouse with a paper towel and watched the stain spread. "Excuse me," she said, "while I slip into something less messy."

The phone rang as soon as Maggie stepped inside her bedroom. She closed her door and headed for it, pulling off her blouse as she went.

Dr. James McKelvey spoke from the other end. "Dr. Davenport, I thought I should call you," he said quickly. "Carl Lee Stanton has been in touch with me. Within the last hour," he added.

Maggie felt her stomach give a sudden lurch. "Where is he? What did he want?"

"The call came in on my home phone," McKelvey said. "It wasn't a lengthy conversation, and nothing on my caller ID. But the fact he called is a good sign, although I'll have to admit I never would have expected it."

"Did he say anything that might help police find him?"

"He said if I *notified* the police he would not call me back," McKelvey stated flatly. "I have to call them, but —" He paused and sighed. "You know it'll leak out. Hell, it'll probably be on the front page of the newspaper within a matter of hours. Carl Lee will find out, and he'll go into one of his rages, probably kill the first person who steps within firing range."

Maggie sank onto her bed. "What are you going to do?"

He gave a rueful laugh. "I *need* to get out of the prison system and go back to my ritzy practice and listen to rich people bitch about how much they hate their lives. As for Carl Lee, I don't know."

"Why do you think he called you?" Maggie asked.

"Hypothetically?" he asked.

"Of course."

"A man on the run? Police closing in? Feeling trapped and desperate? All of the above? And maybe searching for a voice of reason?" McKelvey added. "Having said that, I really don't have a clue," he added.

"Do you think he'll call you back? Do you think he would listen to you?"

"If he listened to anyone it would be me. I *think* he'll call back, but I'm not putting any money on it."

"What would you tell him?"

"I'd try to negotiate his surrender," McKelvey said, "and see that he was taken in without incident. I'd promise to be there for him. That's about all I can offer him. That doesn't mean he would agree to it and certainly not in one or two phone calls. I'm just thinking fewer people would get hurt."

"I don't know what to say," Maggie told him. "I can't tell you not to call the police."

"I need to think. I'll let you know. Oh, and we never had this conversation."

"Ladies and gentlemen, may I have your attention, please?" Everest said from the kitchen doorway. "I would like for you to meet the new and improved Miss Melanie Davenport." He stepped aside and Mel swept into the room.

"Ta-da!" The girl struck a pose.

"Oh my God!" Queenie gaped.

Maggie, in the process of carrying the platter of food to the table, almost dropped it. Her daughter had been transformed.

Zack leaned back in his chair. "Wow."

"Well?" Mel asked, grinning wide at her mother. Behind her, Everest grinned as well. "What do you think?"

"Um." Maggie tried to find the right words.

"No more orange hair!" Mel said. "And Everest cut it; look, it's all layered. And he showed me how to apply makeup." At the look Maggie shot her, she hurried on. "Just a teeny-tiny bit to tone down my freckles and bring out my eyes."

"It's very subtle," Everest said. "It's called the 'Barely There' look."

"Mom!" Mel planted her hands on her hips. "Say something!"

"Um." Maggie stepped closer. Her daughter's hair was now a lovely shade of red, cut and styled into a flattering look. Her freckles *had* been toned down as well, and there was a hint of mascara, but Maggie had to admit it all looked very natural. "Honey, you are beautiful," she said.

"Stunning," Zack said. "If you were twenty years older and knew how to cook, I'd marry you."

"Everest's sister knows all about fashion," Mel went on excitedly. "He's going to ask her to help me go through my clothes and —" She paused and looked at her mother. "What?"

Maggie realized she had tears in her eyes. She was still reeling from her phone call less than an hour ago, and she was unprepared for Mel's new grown-up look. She smiled and swiped at her tears. "I'm just so happy that —" She laughed self-consciously. "I can't believe I'm getting teary-eyed over my beautiful daughter. I think I need to blow my nose. Excuse me." She hurried from the room.

Queenie folded her arms in front of her as she studied Mel. "You look so good I'm going to have to put together a little something to protect you from the boys."

"They already have something like that, Granny Queenie," Everest said. "It's called a chastity belt." He slapped his hand over his mouth, and cut his eyes at Mel. "I shouldn't have said that," he whispered.

"I need to check on Mom," Mel said, obviously more concerned about her mother than what was being said around her. She disappeared down the hall.

Maggie was dabbing her eyes with a tissue

when Mel tapped on her bedroom door and came in. "Are you okay?" she asked.

"Yes, honey, I'm fine." Maggie forced a smile. "I just —" She shrugged and sat on the edge of her bed. "I've been selfish, Mel. I should have taken you to that new hair salon in town that everyone is raving about. I should have taken you to the mall in Savannah or Charleston, to a store geared toward young people."

Mel patted her shoulder. "It's okay, Mom. We can still go to the mall together. I don't want to hurt Everest's feelings, but I'd rather you help me pick out clothes instead of his sister."

"Really?"

"Uh-huh. I still have my birthday money. I could even take you to lunch as long as you don't mind eating a burger."

Maggie smiled and touched her daughter's hair. It was thick and silky and healthy looking, not how she imagined it would look after putting a color on it. "You look very pretty, sweetheart. I'm so proud of you. But you need to know, I've always felt that way about you."

"I'm proud of you, too, Mom."

Maggie gazed into her daughter's green eyes and wondered how proud Mel would be when she learned the truth about her father. "Honey, we need to talk."

"Okay, but I'm really hungry. I didn't eat much of my hot dog after the Elvis guys showed up at our table."

"How about we chat after you eat something?"

Mel started for the door and turned. "Do you think Travis Bradley will notice me now?"

"What do you mean, *now?*" Maggie said. "Did you not see the way he was looking at you at Harry's?"

"Yeah?"

"Uh-*yeah,*" Maggie said, answering like Mel sometimes did.

Maggie followed Mel into the kitchen and discovered Queenie and Everest had left. She suspected Queenie was annoyed with her. Zack sat at the kitchen table playing solitaire. "FBI guys do a lot of this while on stakeout," he told Mel, as she prepared her sandwich and a side order of chips and dip.

They had just finished eating when the phone rang. Mel snatched it up. "Who else is going?" she asked after a moment. "Hold on." She turned to Maggie. "Caitlin and Emily are going to see the new Johnny Depp movie. It's PG. Can I go?" When Maggie hesitated, Mel added, "I sorta have to know right now because the movie starts at seven-fifteen."

"It's five till seven now," Maggie said.

"This is the soonest they could call. They don't officially get off restriction until seven on account of they missed the school bus twice last week, and their mom had to take them."

"Honey, I don't know if that's a good idea," Maggie said and looked at Zack.

"Mom, I need to get out of this house! I can't go outside and I can't look out my window."

"We could go too," Zack told Maggie, "and sit in the back row."

Mel gave an enormous sigh. "Never mind."

"Or park out front and wait for her," he added.

"I can go!" Mel said and hung up. She started from the room and turned. "Could we please not take the van?"

Maggie made the drive in her car in record time while Zack laid out the rules.

"Stay with your friends and sit in the first row. If somebody you don't know approaches you, use this." He handed her a whistle that hung from a sturdy chain. "See this button on the side? Press it, and I'll be there in two minutes. Then, blow the hell out of the whistle to attract attention. It's a good way to scare people off. Hang it around your neck."

Mel frowned. "I'll look like a dork."

"Tuck it inside your blouse," Maggie said, thankful that Zack had such a gadget.

"We will be parked out front the whole time," Zack said. "Once the movie ends we'll pull right up to the steps, and I'll come in and get you."

Mel gave him a pained look. "I want to walk by myself. It's like twenty feet from the door to the car."

He nodded. "Okay, but don't come out until you see the car."

Mel climbed out and hurried to the glass entrance where Caitlin and Emily waited. Zack watched them buy their tickets and disappear through a doorway. "I'll be right back." He opened the door.

Maggie shot him a questioning look. "But where —"

"I want to know what time the movie ends, and I want to see which theater they're in." He climbed out, hit the master lock, and shot her a quick look. "Keep the engine running just in case —"

Maggie sighed. "I hate this," she mumbled. She folded her arms across the top of the steering wheel and buried her face in it. Someone knocked on her window. She jumped and snapped her head up and around. A policeman stood outside her door. She lowered it a few inches.

"Ma'am, you'll have to move your car. You're in the fire lane."

"Oh." Maggie glanced at the doors leading inside the theater. "Is it okay if I wait for my friend? He'll be right out."

"As long as you don't mind me writing you a ticket for illegal parking," he answered.

"I'll move," she said. She pulled forward and turned down the first aisle, searching for a parking place. She was at the far end of the parking lot when she saw Zack come out. He planted his hands on his hips and looked around. She headed his way.

When he saw her he shook his head and held his hands out in question. He climbed into the car. "I ask you to do one simple thing —" he began.

"You big-shot FBI agents probably don't worry about illegal parking, right?" Maggie said. "If a cop walks up and tells you to move your car out of the *fire lane,* you just flash your big shiny badge, and say 'beat it, pal.' Am I right?"

Zack nodded. "Yep. That's what we do."

Maggie spied a car pulling from a parking

slot near the front and gunned her engine. She backed in so they had a clear view of the front doors.

Maggie cut the engine. "So, how much longer till the movie is over?" she asked with a half smile.

"One hour thirty-nine minutes."

"I can't believe I agreed to sit in a parking lot for two hours so my kid could go to a movie with her friends."

"Look at the bright side," Zack said. "You get to spend all this time with me. Play your cards right, and I'll let you sign my babe cast. You can have Paula Zahn's coveted spot."

"I think *not*."

He grinned. "So, now, what should we do to pass the time?" He stretched his arms out wide, then lowered them so that his left arm fell on the back of Maggie's seat and finally her shoulder.

She shook her head sadly, but it was all she could do to keep from laughing. "That is so seventh grade."

He looked wounded. "It always served me well in the past."

"You must date some really dumb women. Like, uh, *Bambi?*" she added, pointing to a name on his cast.

"She was the ER doctor who took care of

me after I got beat up," Zack said.

"You're yanking my chain, Madden," Maggie said.

"I was a perfect patient. Never complained. Thanked the nurses profusely for each morphine shot. The only time things got ugly was when the nurses fought over who was going to sign my cast first."

Maggie studied his smile. "Do you ever have a serious moment?"

"Oh, yeah, plenty of times." He touched her hair, rubbed a thick strand between his thumb and forefinger. "I've been seriously fighting the urge to touch your hair since we met," he said. He slipped his hand beneath her hair and brushed the back of her neck with his fingers.

The shiver started at her tailbone and worked its way up her spine, leaving each vertebra tingling. Maggie tried to keep her breathing steady. She shifted in the seat, leaned away slightly. "Hey, aren't you on the clock? You're supposed to be doing your FBI thing."

"I got it covered, babe. I can stoke your fires of passion, *and* protect your daughter. I can encourage the rabbits to consider planned parenthood, keep the hens on a tight production schedule, *and* offer emotional support to a disabled goat on the verge of womanhood. My specialty is multi-tasking."

He had a sexy, mischievous smile. Infectious too; Maggie couldn't help but smile back at him. "I've got your number, Madden," she said. "You're a flirt and a sweet-talker."

"You could be right." He leaned over and pressed his lips to the side of her neck. Her lips parted in surprise, and he raised his finger and tilted her jaw so that he could kiss her. Just like before, Maggie felt completely disarmed beneath his warm mouth. All her defenses seemed to melt like warm chocolate, and she couldn't resist responding eagerly.

Zack raised his head and winced. "I think your stick shift just punctured my spleen. We should get in the backseat."

"Hmm. The last time a guy suggested that to me I got pregnant."

"So, does Mel know she was conceived in the backseat of a car or is this something I can hold over your head?" He didn't give her a chance to answer. He kissed her again. He pressed his lips against the hollow of her throat, kissed her chin, her nose, and closed eyelids. He slid his fingers through her hair, covered her breast with one palm. Maggie sucked in a short breath. Everything inside felt as if it were jingling and jangling, like pots and pans swinging from a rack. She was almost certain her heart missed three full beats.

She opened her eyes and blinked several times, bringing the world back into focus. He reached for her again, and she pressed her hands flat against his chest. "We have to stop!" she said, a little too loudly.

"I'm moving too fast?"

"We have an audience." She scooted down in the seat as a security car slowly passed, both officers staring. "Oh, great," she said. "I think the driver is the father of one of my patients."

"They're gone now." Zack reached for her.

Maggie resisted. "You and I shouldn't be doing all this kissing, Zack." She tried to sound firm. "It's too, um, confusing. And I'm not thinking straight as it is. My brain is numb. I didn't sleep well last night." It was the truth. Each time she'd closed her eyes she had seen Carl Lee's face as it had appeared in the newspaper. And then there was McKelvey's call, and her silent promise not to say anything, and wondering if Mc-Kelvey was going to inform the police as they both knew he should, or if he planned to try and deal with Carl Lee on his own. It was too much.

But the main reason she didn't want to keep kissing Zack Madden was because she knew she was getting too wrapped up in him, and that would have consequences that she didn't have time to consider at the moment.

"Okay, Maggie." He gave her cheek a final caress. "Why don't you close your eyes and relax? I'll be here with you, and I won't take my eyes off that door."

Maggie leaned back in her seat and closed her eyes. She was surprised how weary she suddenly felt. Stress and worry did that to people. How many times had she said those words to friends and family, and they didn't even have a psycho-wacko on their trail? She wished she could lean her head against Zack's chest, but there was a lot of comfort just knowing he was close. She dozed.

Maggie was only vaguely aware of the door opening, and the overhead light flashing on for a few seconds. Obviously, the movie had ended and Zack was going for Mel. She would wake up when they returned, maybe ask Zack to drive them home. Voices hummed in the parking lot. Car doors slammed and engines cranked. Then everything grew still.

Maggie heard the car door open again and knew she had to wake up, but the short nap had left her heavy with fatigue.

"Maggie?"

She thought she heard something different in Zack's tone. "Huh?"

"Maggie, you need to wake up."

She opened her eyes, saw his expression in the faint yellow light above his head. Something was wrong. She twisted around and found herself looking into an empty backseat. "Where —"

"Babe, we can't find Mel."

CHAPTER NINE

Fear sent an adrenaline rush through her body and sucked the air from her lungs. "What the *hell* do you mean, you can't *find* her?" she yelled as she struggled to take a breath. She yanked the door handle and slammed from the car. She started to run and stumbled; Zack caught her before she hit the pavement. She tried to pull free, but he wouldn't release her.

"Maggie, you need to calm down," he said. "The police are on their way."

"Calm down?" she said loudly, drawing stares from those lingering in the parking lot. "My daughter is missing, and I'm supposed to *calm down!*" She pulled free. "Find my damn daughter!"

She ran toward the theater, Zack beside her. She opened the door, and one of the employees looked as though he might stop her, but he stepped back instead. The expression on her face obviously convinced him she was somebody he didn't want to tangle with.

Maggie scanned the lobby where people stood in line for the nine o'clock shows. "Where are Caitlin and Emily?"

"This way." Zack took her hand and led her to the hall. He opened the first door they came to, and Maggie hurried into the auditorium. The lights had been turned up; a teenage boy sweeping up a popcorn spill moved from her path.

A heavyset man in dark slacks and a white dress shirt was talking to Caitlin and Emily, as their mother Roberta stood beside them looking anxious. They paused and looked up as Maggie approached.

"Where is Mel?" she demanded, eyes darting from one girl to the other.

"She told us she was going to go to the bathroom," Caitlin said.

"How long ago?"

"Right after the movie started," Caitlin answered.

"Two hours ago?" Maggie was incredulous, even though her heart felt as though it were being squeezed and twisted like modeling clay.

"I'm going to look around," Zack said, then glanced at Maggie. "Do *not* leave this theater, got it?"

She nodded. "Why didn't you tell somebody when Mel didn't return?" she demanded of Caitlin because she was the older of the two sisters. "Didn't you think it odd?"

"Maggie, the girls feel bad enough," Roberta said. "Shouting at them is not going to help matters."

"You would be yelling too if it was your daughter," Maggie said sharply. "Isn't that why we insist the girls go in a group?" The woman looked away.

The man in the white shirt stepped forward. "Ma'am, I'm Len Besser, the manager. I have a security guard searching the premises now. The police will be here any second. Do you think your daughter would have left the theater?"

"Absolutely not! Someone took her."

The manager looked surprised. "Do you actually have reason to believe that?"

"I wouldn't have said it otherwise." Maggie noted the kid had stopped sweeping and was listening. He glanced away quickly when he realized she was looking at him. "Did you ask that young man if he saw my daughter?" she asked Besser.

"I've questioned everyone," he said. "Nobody saw anything, but this is our busiest night of the week so I'm not surprised."

The boy started up the aisle toward the door. "Hold it right there!" Maggie said.

"I don't know where your daughter is, lady," he said defensively.

"Did you or anyone else let someone in through the exit doors? A man?" she added.

"I didn't," he said. "I don't know about the others."

Maggie's mind flew in a hundred different directions. Had Carl Lee seen them leave the house? Had he followed them to the theater and watched Mel go inside? He would have tried to get in through an exit door if he knew they were parked out front watching the entrance.

"My employees know that's against the rules," Besser said. "They can get fired for it."

Two police officers stepped inside the auditorium, and the manager quickly introduced himself and explained the situation. "I have a security guard searching the premises now," he added.

Maggie reached inside her purse for her wallet. "I'm her mother, Maggie Davenport," she said. "Here is a school picture of my daughter taken last year." Her voice trembled, and her hands shook as she handed it to one of the officers. "I have every reason to believe she was abducted, and I demand that you call for backup immediately."

Both men looked surprised.

"Don't just stand there!" Maggie said loudly.

"Mrs. Davenport, we need a little more information," one of them said.

"Carl Lee Stanton," she said. "Tall, dark red hair, killer," she added. "Is that enough information for you?"

Maggie heard Roberta gasp.

The look on the officers' faces turned to disbelief. "Why would Stanton —"

"This is *not* the time to ask questions," Maggie interrupted. "You need to be out there searching. You need to call —"

"Mom?"

Maggie snapped her head around at the sound of Mel's voice. "Oh, thank God!" she cried. Seeing that her daughter was alive and in one piece left Maggie weak-kneed. She hurried toward the girl and pulled her into her arms. Tears stung her eyes as she stepped back to get a closer look. "Are you okay? Are you hurt? What happened?"

Mel looked embarrassed. "I'm fine. I went to the bathroom."

"For two hours! Are you sick?" Maggie touched her forehead to see if she was feverish.

"I had one of my girls check the bathroom," Besser said. "Several times."

"Did you leave the theater, young lady?" the officer asked kindly.

Mel looked at her mother, then back to him. "Yes."

"What?" Maggie almost shrieked the word. She released the girl.

"Is it okay if I take my daughters home now?" Roberta asked.

The officer held up his hand. "One minute," he said.

Maggie looked stricken. "What is going on, Mel?" she demanded, resisting the urge to shake the words from the girl. "Where *were* you?"

"I just stepped outside for a little while, Mom. I was planning to come right back in, but the door was locked." Her eyes darted toward Caitlin and Emily for a split second.

"She left with Travis Bradley," Emily blurted. "She asked us to let her back in before the movie ended, but we were afraid we'd get into trouble." She looked at Mel, whose face was now a bright red. "Why should *we* get in trouble when we told you not to do it?"

Mel looked down at her shoes.

Maggie felt a flash of hot anger. "Where is

Travis now?" she asked.

"His parents picked him up." Mel's voice was little more than a whisper.

Zack and the security guard returned. They were clearly relieved to see that Mel had returned and was safe.

"How did you get back inside?" Besser asked, as though he were still concerned that one of his employees was involved.

"One of the shows must've just ended because a bunch of people were leaving through the side exit. I came through it."

Maggie was embarrassed that she had lost her temper with everyone. "I'm very sorry that all of you were dragged into this," she said, glancing at everyone in the group, including Roberta and her daughters. "And that I was so rude." She could see the understanding in their eyes, and she felt her own eyes burn. She looked at Besser. "I'm sure you have people waiting to come in for the nine o'clock show so we'll get out of your way now."

"Don't leave my side," she told Mel, and without another word, Maggie left the auditorium. Zack and Mel followed closely. They exited the building and headed for Maggie's car. She handed Zack her car keys. "Please drive."

"Mom?"

Maggie stopped and looked at her daughter. "You do *not* want to speak to me right now," she said.

"I was just standing outside talking to Travis, for Pete's sake!" Mel said. "It's not like I committed some great sin."

"You left the theater!" Maggie shouted, startling Mel so that she jumped. "You intentionally disobeyed us, knowing damn good and well *why* you were told to stay inside. And you scared the ever-living hell out of me!

"You are grounded," Maggie went on fiercely. "The first thing coming out of your room is your telephone. You have absolutely no privileges, understand? And you can bet that I am going to have a little talk with Travis Bradley's parents about this."

Mel opened her mouth to speak.

"Don't even think of talking back to me, kiddo," Maggie said. "You do *not* want to make me angrier, because if I get any angrier, flames are going to shoot right out of my mouth and smoke will pour from my ears."

Mel winced.

Zack arched one brow as though thinking it might be interesting to watch.

"Just get in the car and don't talk," Maggie said.

They made the ride back in silence. Inside the house, Maggie marched straight to Mel's room and unplugged her phone from the jack. "No TV, no stereo, no computer —"

Mel's expression was pained. "What if I get bored?"

"Read a book."

Carl Lee gripped the steering wheel tight and tried to hold his temper. "How can you possibly have to go to the bathroom again?" he asked Ed. "You just went twenty minutes ago. And twenty minutes before that."

"He has prostate trouble," Cook said.

"Like I told you," Ed said. "I have a problem with my prostrate."

"Pros-*tate*," Cook said, having already reminded him several times.

"And this time I want to pee in a real bathroom and not in some ditch on the side of the interstate."

"There's a rest area less than ten miles from here," Cook said, looking at Carl Lee. "We could be in and out in five minutes."

Ed remained quiet until they pulled in. Cook headed toward the men's room with him. "What's the matter with Father Tom?" Ed asked. "How come he's mad all the time? I thought priests were supposed to be kind and patient."

"He's under a lot of stress," Cook said. "Just try to stay quiet."

"I really need my pills from my suitcase," Ed said. "It's important that I take them first thing in the morning and every night."

"I'll get them for you." They returned to the car. "I need the keys," Cook said, "so I can get Ed's medicine."

Carl Lee sighed and tossed him the keys.

Ed took his pills and lay down on the seat, pulling his blanket with him.

"Is he asleep?" Carl Lee asked Cook some twenty minutes later. "I want to listen to the news."

Cook turned around. "Yeah, he's out."

Carl Lee switched on the radio and punched several buttons. He finally settled on a country-western station. They sat through two songs before a newsman came on.

Escaped prisoner Carl Lee Stanton is still at large and thought to be traveling with Raymond Boyd, one of the two men who aided Stanton's escape from a medical facility Friday morning at 10 A.M. A car fitting the description given by a witness was found early this evening in a ravine.

Carl Lee and Cook exchanged looks.

In other news, an explosion rocked I-20, east of Atlanta, this afternoon as rain and fog made driving hazardous and created a gridlock that surprised motorists and resulted in an accordionlike collision course. An eighteen-wheeler, bearing the name Prayer Mobile, exploded shortly after impact, when sparks ignited a gasoline spill and engulfed the fuel tank. The driver, the Reverend Will Jones, was pulled unconscious from the cab only minutes before the blast. He and several bystanders were rushed by ambulance to the emergency room and are listed in critical but stable condition.

"Oh, thank goodness," Cook said. "Jonesy is still alive."

"I hope he's not stupid enough to think he's going to get any money out of me," Carl Lee muttered.

Witnesses reported seeing two priests jump from the cab and run from the truck before the explosion. Shortly afterward, the priests were caught on camera entering a nearby convenience store, and one of them robbing the store. Police are presently reviewing the tapes and plan to show them to TV viewers.

"Turning to politics —"

"Shit!" Carl Lee hissed between his teeth and cut the radio. "It won't take them long to figure out we're the ones in the video." He yanked off his priest's collar and tossed it out the window.

"I can't believe you did that," Cook said. "You're a litterbug. They put people like you in jail and give them a stiff fine."

Carl Lee ignored him. "Put on your country-western shirt and cowboy hat. See if you can find something I can slip over this stupid shirt. And hand me the teeth and glasses."

Cook reached to the backseat floor for the bag they'd stuffed their belongings into and shook his head sadly at the sight of his ten-gallon hat. "It's smushed," he said.

Zack found Maggie sitting on the sofa in the living room, feet propped on the old trunk, when he returned from checking the property. The house was dark; the only light in each room was provided by the night-lights that Zack had plugged in.

"You okay?" he asked, sitting next to Maggie.

She nodded. It was a lie. Her thoughts were spinning in her head like a child's top.

"You've been crying."

"It helps with stress."

"So does sex."

She heard the smile in his voice, but that didn't stop the small flutter in the pit of her stomach. "So does chocolate, and it doesn't hog the covers or snore." She sniffed.

"That's why I'm such a great bed partner. I'm warm-blooded and don't like sleeping beneath a pile of blankets. And I've been told I don't snore."

Maggie decided it was best to ignore the remark, even as the flutter in her stomach suddenly turned into one gigantic quiver. He sat too close. It should have made her feel safe. Instead, she felt even more anxious.

"You know, I have a friend with a daughter close to Mel's age," Zack said. "From what I understand, it's normal for them to rebel a little now and then."

Maggie looked at him. "She put herself in danger. You and I both know what could have happened."

"But it didn't. She's okay."

"I've been too lenient with her. I should have put my foot down a long time ago, but I didn't want to be like my parents. They were so strict. That's why I preferred being around my grandfather," she said, a hint of a smile on her lips. "He let me get away with murder."

"How old were you when he died?"

"Seventeen. I was a senior in high school. I'd already lost my grandmother by then, and even though I was really sad when that happened, it was nothing compared to losing him." She paused. "He was my best friend."

Zack nodded thoughtfully. "I lost someone close shortly after I signed on with the bureau. It was tough. I got through it by focusing on my job."

"I got through it by focusing on Carl Lee Stanton," she said.

"You left out the part about what happened in your parents' barn," Zack said.

Maggie looked up. "What are you talking about?"

"How he drove to your parents' house and hid his car in the barn. And waited for you to get home from school," he added. "He wanted you to go with him, and when you didn't he punished you."

"It could have been worse. He could have shot me. I think I sort of halfway convinced him that I was afraid to go with him while he was running from the police, but if he could maybe go to Mexico or some other safe place I would agree to join him."

"That would have taken a lot of convincing," Zack said.

"I did this 'Oh, I'm so terrified' thing, backed it up with a lot of tears and trembling. Of course, I actually *was* terrified since he had a gun; but I still like to think I put on an Oscar-winning performance." She paused. "Sort of like you do in your job," she added. "So he grabbed the keys to my dad's old truck and took off.

"Unfortunately, when my parents got home they just assumed I had taken the truck so, of course, nobody looked inside the barn until late that evening. I'm really too tired to go into the rest of it, but I'm sure you already know so why are you asking?"

"Would you believe it's because I need material for the crime novel I'm writing?"

"That's, like, *so* lame, as my daughter would say."

"Okay, let me give you one of the lines I use to impress women." He stroked the back of her hair. "It's because the more I know you, the more I *want* to know you."

Maggie looked at him. "That's *it?* That's your best line? Are there really that many desperate women out there?"

"I wasn't finished."

"It gets *worse?*"

"The other reason I asked you is because files tend to be impersonal, and I'm feeling like I'm sort of *personally* involved with you. Maybe even a lot," he added. "Much more than the FBI manual thinks I should be."

Maggie did not see the teasing light that she often found in his eyes. She saw hope and tenderness and what looked like uncertainty, although it was hard to imagine that Zack had ever doubted himself in his life. He was putting all his cards on the table, and she was holding a full hand.

"Zack, where are we going with all this?"

"I'm hoping it's a good place."

She shook her head in confusion. "Is it me or does this feel like bad timing?"

"Yeah, I'd have to agree the timing could be better."

"I don't know what to say. I have so much unsettled stuff going on in my head, and not all of it is about Carl Lee. I've got to get my kid under control, and then I've got to settle some business with her and it's not going to be pretty."

"Maybe I can help. Mel is crazy about me and with good reason."

"No, you can't help with this one, Zack.

I've done Mel a terrible injustice, and I have to set it right, and there are going to be consequences." Her eyes misted. "I've lied to her about things. I can't even begin to count all the lies. I thought I was protecting her, but I was protecting me, too, and now Mel is going to hate me for the rest of her life. She'll never trust me again. You don't want to get involved with me, Zack. I'm a terrible mother."

"Damn, Maggie, what did you do, shoot her favorite dog?"

"I kept the truth from her, Zack, and the truth is Carl Lee Stanton is Mel's father." Maggie was afraid to look at him and see the disgust on his face. Instead, he put his arm around her and pulled her against him.

"I know, babe."

CHAPTER TEN

Maggie jerked back and stared at him. His expression was relaxed, laid-back. "You *know?*" she said. "*How* do you know?"

"There's no marriage license or certificate of marriage to back up your marriage claims, Maggie. There's no certificate of death on your so-called late husband, and no record anywhere of a man named Tom Davenport dying in a car accident around the time it supposedly happened. Not even for the entire year," he added. "I *did* find records where you had your last name legally changed to Davenport, your great-grandmother's maiden name." He shrugged. "Other than that, all you have are newspaper clippings provided by Jamie and her father. Which I thought was pretty clever, by the way."

"You left no stone unturned, as they say, when you checked me out. Is there *anything* you don't know about me?"

He gave her a lazy smile. "Oh, yeah."

"Don't you think you went overboard, Zack? This isn't about me; this is about Carl Lee Stanton. Unless you were just curious to know what kind of girl would fall for a cold-blooded killer," she added, feeling a little hurt and put off.

"Yes. And I apologize for that."

"But why did that matter? You came here to protect Mel and me. Did you feel I deserved less protection because I was his ex-girlfriend?"

"Of course not! That's a crazy thing to ask." He shrugged. "I guess I wondered why your parents practically moved you out in the dead of night and why Queenie packed up and went with you."

"I was sick a lot during the first few months of my pregnancy, that's why. Queenie's children were grown and had moved away so she decided to help me with the baby while I went to college and med school. But why does that matter?"

"I guess I wondered why Stanton picked this particular time to escape," he said. "Was it a simple case of opportunity? It wasn't that long ago that another prisoner managed to escape using a similar method; only he got caught on the run. Or was it the newspaper clippings that reminded him of how much he hated you? Or the young girl in those clippings who bore a strong resemblance to him?" Zack added.

"But you said there was no mention of that in Carl Lee's psychiatric notes. Carl Lee would have said something."

"I wasn't impressed with McKelvey's file on Stanton if you want to know the truth. He treated Stanton for three years, which is how long McKelvey has been with the prison system. The weekly visits were dated, but there were few entries."

"Then we don't know if Carl Lee suspects Mel is his daughter or not," Maggie said, her body tensing all over. "Why didn't you say something?"

"I wanted to do more checking after McKelvey called here. He has had some problems."

"What kinds of problems?"

Zack hesitated. "He drinks. It cost him his family and his private practice. One or two patients filed complaints. Do you really want to worry about *his* troubles when you have enough of your own?"

They were quiet for a moment. Maggie thought about the call she'd received from McKelvey earlier, and she suspected he had not contacted the police and wouldn't. She hoped he was getting help for his problems because she sensed he was genuinely concerned that Carl Lee might kill someone if he had no one to reach out to. Surely it was a good thing; police trying to catch Carl Lee and McKelvey trying to reel him in.

"Maggie?"

She looked up, startled.

He grinned. "We're going to look back on this one day and laugh."

She laughed just hearing him say it. "Madden, you need help, you know that?"

"You're about thirty-six years too late, pretty lady." He pulled her back into his arms, cupped the back of her head and fit it in the hollow between his shoulder and neck.

"You laugh and joke because it helps you deal with the hard things you see in your job," she said softly.

"It was either that or get drunk a lot." He stroked her hair and pressed his lips to her forehead. He kissed her eyelids. "Maggie," he said, her name slipping between his lips on a sigh.

Maggie liked hearing her name whispered from his lips. Being in his arms wasn't bad either. "Zack?"

"Yeah?"

"Is this, um, part of your job?"

"Uh-huh. How'm I doing?"

She looked up, and their gazes met briefly before he lowered his head. The kiss was slow and lingering. It reached down deep and awakened her tired muscles and weary nerve endings and even her organs; although she would have thought it medically impossible for a kiss to send her liver aquiver.

His tongue explored her mouth, his hand caressed her breast, and she felt the first wave of arousal. She kissed him back. She kissed him with meaning. She kissed him until her lips were numb. Warm stuff flowed through her body and met low in her belly as he stroked her with one hand.

She touched him back, and he moaned and reached beneath her blouse. Found her nipple; rubbed it between his thumb and forefinger.

He began unbuttoning her blouse. "Not here," she whispered no louder than a thought.

"Where then?" he asked.

"Upstairs." They stood, and she linked his hand in hers. "I'll lead the way. I know this house like the back of my hand." She started forward and immediately stubbed her toe on the leg of an armchair. She tripped and fell against it, and the chair scooted several inches, shoving the table beside it. The furniture scraped the wood floor; and the noise sounded as loud as a squawking parrot in the still house. Zack caught the lamp before it hit the floor.

They came to a dead stop; waited and listened. No sound from Mel's room.

Finally, Maggie gave his hand a gentle tug. "Watch out for the chair," she whispered. They moved to the stairs. "The fifth step creaks," she warned.

"Is it the fifth step going up or the fifth step coming down?"

She shushed him, and they climbed the stairs slowly, using the night-light to guide them. In the guest room they undressed each other in the almost nonexistent glow of yet another night-light. Maggie was thankful for Zack's no-lights rule since she hadn't gotten naked in front of a man in longer than she would admit even to her reflection in the mirror.

Zack pulled the covers aside on the bed, and they sank onto it, hands and mouths searching. Fingers roamed intimately, skin touched skin. Bodies ached.

Maggie guided him inside her, and the pleasure was so incredible and intense that she felt her eyes cross. Every touch, every kiss, every movement was beautiful and sensuous and golden.

And then everything changed and became

sexier and pulse-pounding. Kisses turned hot. Anticipation turned to urgency.

Ecstasy in its purest form.

Maggie exhaled a long sigh of contentment as they lay side by side. She had a smile on her face and a song in her heart. She felt sexy and desirable and feminine. She felt like buying a thong.

Propped on one elbow, Zack gazed down at Maggie's seductive body and wanted her all over again. He noted her soft smile and smooth forehead, no longer creased with worry lines. She had one leg draped over his. "Another satisfied customer," he said proudly.

Maggie punched him.

"So what do you think, Dr. D.?"

Maggie stretched and gave his body an appreciative look. "I think all of my five senses like you. And I think I was an idiot to give up sex." She yawned. She felt warm, her arms and legs weighted and relaxed. "Well, I didn't *really* give it up," she corrected. "I just —" She looked thoughtful. "Refused to settle," she said.

"And it's not going to get any easier now that you've met me because I have been told I'm a hard act to follow."

Maggie chuckled. She felt relaxed and playful. "And I discovered the world is not round after all because I think I went right over the edge." She glanced up, noted the dark eyes and sexy mouth. She could feel the pull between them. She trusted him. With her daughter and her heart, she thought.

It had happened in just . . . *two days!*

"Uh-oh." She frowned. "I thought I just had the hots for you."

He frowned. "I thought you had the hots for me too. I could have *sworn* you had the hots for me. Like five minutes ago. Has the newness worn off?"

"I think what we have might be more serious."

"That's just good sex talking, Maggie. Hell, people get engaged over stuff like this. Tomorrow you'll feel differently. I'll just be an annoyance to you like before."

"Are you saying you don't feel anything special for me?"

He gave her an odd look. "You know, I think I *do* feel something more than just lust now that you mention it. Damn. I might be, you know —"

"Falling in love with me?"

"No way. Nobody falls in love in two days, Maggie. Only in movies with Jennifer Lopez does that happen."

"You know what I think?" she whispered.

"I think something very peculiar is going on here." She looked about the room.

He followed her gaze. "Like what?"

"Magic."

He looked at her, touched her cheek. "I agree."

"Not that kind of magic. *Queenie's* kind of magic. Think about it, Zack. What other explanation is there for me just falling into bed with you like I did?"

"Other than the fact I'm witty, intelligent, good-looking, and hung like a stallion?"

"There's a crazed murderer out there," Maggie said, "and we're in bed."

"Which is a good thing," he said, "because that means we're not standing in front of any windows. What does Queenie have to do with this, by the way?"

"She threatened to put some kind of love spell on us."

"And you believe she's capable of that?"

"I just know that I want you, Zack," Maggie said solemnly. She curled her arms around his neck. "I want to be in your arms. I want to taste your lips. I want you inside of me."

"Oh, babe." He slipped his arms around her neck and kissed her deeply.

Maggie kissed him back, exploring his mouth with her tongue, hungry for him. She pulled him down on the bed and covered his body with hers, arching against him intimately. She raised her head. "See that? I can't get enough of you!"

His eyes were closed. "Okay, so be it."

She sat up. "I'm sorry, but I can't fall in love with an undercover agent. What kind of life would that be for Mel and me? We wouldn't see you for months at a time. Plus, your job is dangerous. I mean, look what happened on your last job. You could have been shot or knifed. You could have ended up a floater."

He sighed. "Okay, Maggie, I know what you're saying is important, but here we are, naked, in bed, and your daughter is asleep. Isn't there something better you'd rather be doing than discussing my bleak and dismal future?"

Maggie stood and reached for her clothes. "I'm sorry, Zack, but I just can't take any chances. I'll talk to Queenie tomorrow and once she assures me she hasn't cast some spell on us and we're not going to fall in love, I will gladly have sex with you again."

A few minutes later, Zack stepped outside into the night air. He stood there hoping it would clear his head. It did not. He tried to find logic in Maggie's earlier statement. It eluded him. She did not seem like a woman who wanted sex without strings attached. This was Maggie Davenport, respected pediatrician and loving mom. Stop being a dumbass, he told himself. It was his job. She'd made it plain it was his job. He didn't blame her. She had no business getting involved with a man who spent much of his time living on the fringes of society and crawling through sewers looking for bad guys. And it wasn't like he didn't know. He had already tried a couple of times to have a serious relationship, but both had turned into one big flop.

Bottom line, he had chosen the sheer adrenaline rush of each new assignment over love. It was the reason he'd spent sleepless nights rehearsing in his mind the smallest details and committing them to memory so he wouldn't make a mistake. And get shot. The reason he struggled with paranoia, not always knowing who his friends were, unable to trust anyone in case . . . Well, in case he got shot. Seemed like he was always one breath away from a taking a bullet.

Zack nodded. Yep. Maggie Davenport would do well to stay as far away from him as possible. And Carl Lee needed to show his sorry ass so he could do his job and move on because he knew he was in too deep.

His cell phone rang and he reached for it.

Maggie grabbed the Better than Sex chocolate ice cream and scooped several large servings into a bowl. Several times she had to refrain from turning on a light.

She stepped inside her bedroom a moment later, kicked her shoes off and sprawled across the bed on her stomach. She spooned a mouthful of chocolate into her mouth, closed her eyes, and sighed.

Zack's perfect naked body sprang to life in her mind. Wide shoulders and chest, flat stomach, and —

What was *wrong* with her? Had she gone wacko?

Zack was right. It was the sex talking. Leave it to Maggie Davenport to fall head over heels in love with the first man to climb between the sheets with her in Lord knew how many years.

This was what being a prisoner in your own home did to a person, Maggie thought. She was obviously suffering a breakdown of sorts, thanks to Carl Lee Stanton. That would explain her irrational behavior; why she had acted like the worst kind of slut with a man she barely knew, and then —

She closed her eyes and groaned. *Then,* she had confessed she might be falling in love with him.

Okay, it was *not* her fault that she had made a complete and utter fool of herself in front of Zack. She would simply and calmly explain to him about the breakdown, and he would understand and maybe not run in the opposite direction when he saw her.

Knowing and accepting her problem was half the battle, Maggie reminded herself; then she wondered if that meant she was already half cured. She needed to look at it from a physician's perspective.

People in the throes of emotional problems usually lost interest in food and activities and sex. She spooned more ice cream into her mouth and thought about Zack's body again. A shiver climbed her spine and raised the tiny hairs on the back of her neck.

That had to be a good sign. Maybe she wasn't having a breakdown after all. She was just confused and stressed, and who the hell wouldn't be under the circumstances, thank you very much! So what if she and Zack had enjoyed a roll in the hay. So damn what! Like, wasn't it *about time* she enjoyed herself a little? Must she always be elbow deep in diaper rashes, sore throats, and ear infections? Must her life always revolve around a hormone-ridden thirteen-year-old?

So she was edgy. Who the hell *wouldn't* be edgy? There was a madman after her; her daughter was making her nutso. She had a root doctor boiling herbs and innards in her kitchen; and a black hen running around in her chicken coop for reasons unbeknownst to her. She had a cage full of rabbits breeding at the speed of light. Just when she thought she had all of them spayed and neutered, she found two or three new ones that looked just like the other ones. She had a goat with crooked eyes in the backyard who could literally eat her out of house and home. She had overhead at work.

And to top it all off, there was a drop-dead gorgeous FBI agent in her house who had seen her naked. And vice versa, she reminded herself with an eye roll. She was going to have to back off, she told herself; otherwise, she wouldn't be able to think straight. No more thinking about his body. No more hot kisses and hot sex. She was sure she could do it. She was a disciplined person.

"Maggie?"

The soft whisper startled her and she almost dropped her bowl of ice cream. Maggie turned and found Zack peering through a crack in her door.

"Huh?" It wasn't the most intelligent thing that had ever come out of her mouth.

He stepped inside and closed the door. "Are you okay?"

"Um." Another single-syllable word. Nobody would have guessed she'd spent a gazillion years in college and medical school.

He slid across the bed next to her. "Is that the famous, one and only, Better than Sex chocolate ice cream I've heard people whispering about?"

"Yep. It's the real enchilada."

He grinned. "May I have a bite?"

"What? You think you can just waltz into my bedroom willy-nilly and eat my ice cream?" she said. She sighed, scooped up a spoonful, and fed it to him. She waited until he tasted and swallowed. "Well?"

"It's good, but it's not *that* good."

She shrugged. "One less person I have to share it with." She noted the thoughtful expression on his face. "What?"

"There were a number of accidents this afternoon on I-20, east of Atlanta. A big pileup due to fog and rain," he added. "An eighteen-wheeler turned over, the gas tank exploded, and a bunch of people were rushed to the hospital."

"What about the driver of the eighteen-wheeler?"

"He's going to live, for what it's worth. I didn't mention any of this because I didn't want you to start *fretting* about something else, but I just found out this guy has been linked to Raymond Boyd, Stanton's buddy."

"Was Carl Lee in the truck?"

"Yeah. He and Boyd were dressed as priests, and caught on camera shortly after the accidents robbing a convenience store. The police have confirmed it. And that's the last they've been seen or heard from."

She didn't try to hide her disappointment.

"I'm sorry, Maggie. I want Stanton caught even more than you do." He gave an impatient sigh. "I feel like I need to be out there working it, you know? Instead of getting information secondhand, this time a little later than I should have," he added.

"All the big guns are on it, but Stanton keeps slipping through their fingers. Back to what I said before, he's either very smart or very lucky."

Maggie set her empty ice-cream bowl on her night table, dragged a pillow from the top of her bed and propped it beneath her chin. They were quiet for a moment, caught up in their own thoughts. "I don't blame you for being frustrated, Zack. You're accustomed to being in the thick of things, not babysitting. I just want you to know that I am glad you're here. Mel and I need you right now."

"I'm not going anywhere. You and Mel are top priority. I'd like to be the one who nabs Stanton. I'd like to come face-to-face with him."

"Why is that so important to you?"

Zack averted his gaze. "He's a cop killer. Cops don't like cop killers."

"Yeah, well, neither do I," she said. "I hate him. I hate him for making my daughter afraid. I've never hated anyone this much."

Maggie touched his arm. "I'm sorry. Could you just hang out with me for a while?" she asked. "I don't want to be alone right now."

Carl Lee opened his eyes and blinked several times as he took in the wooded area through the windshield of Ed's Cadillac.

"Did you sleep okay, Carl Lee?"

"What time is it?"

"Seven A.M."

"Shit!" He sat up quickly. "Why the hell did you let me sleep this long?"

"We're in the homestretch, Carl Lee. Your big day," he added. "I figured you'd want to have a clear head."

"Do me a favor. Don't try to think for me."

"Why are you so grumpy, man? You're going to see her today. After fourteen long years," he said with a grin. "You're going to get your money. I'm going to get paid."

"I've got to *get* to the money first," Carl Lee said.

"What's that supposed to mean?"

"It's in her house. The cops are going to be watching it, remember?"

"You forgot to mention that." Cook looked out his window.

"But first we have to get through the roadblocks. We've been lucky so far, but our luck could run out."

"It doesn't have a damn thing to do with luck," Cook muttered. "What the hell do you think I did for two months? What the hell do you think I did the two weeks I spent in Beaumont? You think I was sitting in my motel room watching HBO? Hell, no. I know every road leading in and out of that place.

"This really pisses me off, Carl Lee. You don't appreciate anything I've done for you. Maybe you've forgotten who helped you escape. I got us fake IDs, a car, and I've paid our way."

Carl Lee glanced in the backseat again. "I

wonder if the old man has anything on him. I'm sick of him anyway."

Cook's expression changed to horror and disbelief. "You're going to kill an old man and take his money? What is it with you? Are you crazy or just mean as hell?"

"Don't you pay attention to the news, stupid? I'm a cold-blooded killer."

Cook reached to the floor and grabbed Ed's travel bag that held his medication. He passed it to Carl Lee. "Open it. There's a flap beneath the prescription bottles."

Carl Lee frowned but did as Cook said. He dumped the plastic bottles in his lap and searched. "Well, now, this is more like it."

"There's two grand in there. The old guy has probably been tucking away what he could spare from his Social Security checks," Cook said, "but I know that doesn't mean a damn thing to you so go ahead and take it. Just leave him alone."

CHAPTER ELEVEN

Maggie opened her eyes and found Mel standing over her, face scrunched in what looked to be confusion and disbelief. "What's wrong?" Maggie asked.

Mel pointed.

Maggie turned and gasped at the sight of Zack sleeping beside her. "Oh, well, I can explain that."

Zack opened his eyes and looked from mother to daughter. "I bet you're wondering what I'm doing in your mom's bed. Am I right?"

"Did you guys have sex?"

Zack looked at Maggie. "Did we?"

Maggie sighed and put her hand to her forehead. "Look at us, Mel. We're fully clothed. Does it *look* like we had sex? We were eating ice cream and talking and I guess we just fell asleep."

"I just wanted to tell you we have company," Mel said.

Maggie heard a noise at the door and saw Queenie and Everest peering in. Queenie wore a wide grin. "Finally!" she said.

"Oh, great," Maggie muttered.

"Look at the lovebirds," Queenie said.

"They claim they didn't have sex," Mel said, eyeing her mother and Zack suspiciously.

"I knew this would happen," Queenie said.

"Yeah?" Maggie shot her a quizzical look. "Mind telling me *how* you knew? Or what part you played in it?"

Queenie looked surprised. "What makes you think I had anything to do with it? I told you Zack was hot for you the first day. And now you're hot for him."

Maggie could feel her daughter's gaze on her. "I am not hot for Zack."

He looked crestfallen. "You're not?" He looked at Mel. "Your mother is one fickle woman."

"This is so dumb," Mel grumbled, scooting past Queenie. She went into her room and closed the door.

Queenie looked at Maggie. "We really need to do something about that girl's hormones."

"It'll pass in about ten years," Maggie said and climbed from the bed. "I need coffee."

"I think it's romantic," Everest said, following the women into the kitchen. "But how are you and Zack going to form a relationship when he works undercover most of the time and doesn't come home?"

"We're not." Maggie poured her coffee, which was timed to go off at six A.M. when she got up for work. Which meant it had been sitting a while. She suddenly noticed they were dressed up. "You two look nice this morning."

"Granny Queenie and I have to be in church in half an hour."

"Would either of you like coffee?" she asked.

Everest shook his head. "No, thank you. I'm in FBI training."

"None for me," Queenie said. "You and Zack were meant for each other."

Maggie shot her a dark look. "If I find out you're working spells, that's it!"

Queenie opened her mouth to answer, but her cell phone rang. "This is Queenie Cloud," she said. "How may I help you?" She listened. "Mm-hmm. Oh, my. Yes, that's bad. Well, you would need a dirt-dauber nest for that. And a lot of spit," she added.

"Oh, geez," Maggie said. "Another day at House of Weird." She sat down at the kitchen table and leaned forward on two elbows.

Zack walked into the room and headed for the coffeepot.

"I'm pretty sure I have one or two dirt-dauber nests in my home office," Queenie went on, "but they're pricey. I have to pay a boy to get them for me, and every time he gets stung he asks for a three-percent rate increase. I can't find a decent dirt-dauber nest from supply stores these days, and I am very particular. Yes, call me when you decide." She hung up and faced Maggie. "My black hen didn't lay an egg. That's why we came by."

"That's too bad," Maggie said. "You could have used it to put a hex on the man who sold her to you."

Queenie looked at her. "Now I know where Mel gets her mouth. But I'm going to let it slide because I know you're tense."

"They say the waiting is the worst," Everest said softly.

Maggie smiled at him because she knew he meant well. But her gut told her there was much worse that could happen.

Carl Lee and Cook sipped their coffee in the front seat of the car outside of a convenience store while Ed went to the bathroom. "I don't know if he bought that story about why we changed clothes," Carl Lee said.

"We're going to have to watch him closely."

"His memory isn't that great," Cook said. "He has probably already forgotten."

"Why do you take up for him all the time?" Carl Lee said. "He's a pain in the ass."

Cook, who'd asked Ed to buy him a Savannah newspaper when he'd sent him in to pay for their gas, mumbled something incoherent as he turned to the next page. "Oh, hell," he said.

Carl Lee glanced over and stared openly at Ed White's picture, beneath the headline ELDERLY MAN VANISHES.

He slammed his fist against the steering wheel. "Now we have to worry about somebody recognizing him too." He made a sound of pure disgust. "It's all crap," he said. "Just one damn thing after another." He started to look away but something caught his eye. "Read the article up above it," he said. "Something about Beaumont and Elvis."

Cook scanned it. "There's an Elvis impersonator convention going on. There are, at last count, two hundred Elvis look-alikes in Beaumont, South Carolina, it says."

The two men looked at each other.

Jamie dragged through the double doors

leading into the *Gazette* and stopped in her tracks at the sight of Vera at her desk. "Isn't today Sunday?"

"Last time I checked."

"Why aren't you in church?"

"I don't have to be there until eleven o'clock."

"What about Sunday school? Sunday school starts at nine-thirty. It's —"

"Eight A.M." Vera gave her a funny look. "What are you, the church police? I don't go to Sunday school anymore. Remember, I stopped going when they made Eileen Denton our teacher."

"Is she a bad teacher?"

"Oh, no, she's one of the best."

"If she's so good why did you stop going?"

"She made that snotty remark about my dress."

"Which dress?"

Vera paused. "I don't remember."

"So what did she say?"

Vera rubbed her jaw. "I don't remember that either. That was six months ago, Jamie. Why are you still carrying on about it? Why are you so crabby? *I'm* the one who should be crabby. Who do you think Mike calls every time he needs something from the pharmacy or feels like complaining, which is all the time? Me, that's who," she said. "What have *you* got to be crabby about?"

Jamie looked at her. Max had inquired about her sour mood as well. "I guess I'm tired of living in an insane asylum!" she said. "I can't walk through a room without tripping over a board or getting wet paint all over me. Men all over the place, yelling, accusing each other of stealing their tools," she added. "And after spending a *fortune* on the master bath, the toilet runs all the time and the faucet drips."

"I hate a leaky faucet," Vera said, "almost as much as I hate the sound of Mike's voice on the other end of the line."

"And it's loud!" Jamie said. "Max sleeps right through it. I should move to a hotel. Or maybe start sleeping in my office."

"Go pour yourself a fresh cup of coffee, and you'll feel better."

"No, thanks. I'm getting to where I don't even like the taste of it anymore."

"Since when?"

Jamie started to answer but was interrupted when Destiny opened the front door and stepped inside. Jamie and Vera stared openly. Destiny wore oversized sunglasses that had been fashionable in the early eighties. One lens was badly scratched, and one stem had been taped in place with a Scooby-Doo Band-Aid. Her long hair was hidden beneath a wrinkled lime-green scarf that matched the blousy, ankle-length shift she wore. A man would have been hard-pressed to find a curve. Paint-splattered sneakers covered her feet.

"Is it okay if I sleep here for a couple of nights?" she asked Jamie. "On your sofa? And maybe grab a nap on it right now?"

"Is that a new dress?" Jamie asked.

Vera frowned and shook her head. "I know she didn't get it at one of those fire sales because they would have burned that one on purpose."

Destiny glanced over her shoulder, turned back to Jamie and pulled off her sunglasses.

"You're not wearing makeup!" Jamie said.

"I'm in disguise."

"Freddy Baylor?" she asked.

"Yeah. He knocked on my door half the night, said he had something very important to talk to me about. I'm hoping he'll see me like this and move on."

"I think you may be right," Vera said. "If that look doesn't send ice water through his loins, nothing will."

"I don't feel so good," Jamie said. "I'm exhausted. I need to lie down. You can use my sofa after I'm done with it, Destiny."

Jamie went into her office and closed the door.

"What's wrong with her?" Destiny asked Vera in a whisper.

"Her bathroom faucet leaks."

"See what I mean?" Destiny said. "You can't even answer a simple question without being sarcastic. It wouldn't kill you to be nice to me."

Lamar Tevis leaned back in his chair, his feet propped on his desk, his phone tucked between his ear and shoulder. "What did you say your name was?"

"Tom Curtis," the man said. "Curtis Promotions," he added. "We talked a few months ago about the Elvis convention and the parade."

"I don't remember," Lamar said, "but go on with what you were saying."

"I just want to make sure we're on target with the time. My boys will be arriving at noon; I assume all the floats will be lined up."

Lamar frowned. "Look, Buddyroe, I don't have one danged clue what you're talking about, and I've never heard of anybody by the name of Tom Curtis. I'm the chief of police; I'm not in the parade business."

"This is a joke, right?" the man said. "I

mean, we're talking about one of the biggest celebrities in Vegas here and he's expecting a parade. We're talking Kenny Preston!"

"I've never heard of him."

The guy on the other end gave a grunt of disgust. "Where have you been, man? He's the *original* Elvis impersonator, not to mention one of the most famous people in the country. Listen up, pal. You *swore* you'd get with this committee and that committee and see that it was all taken care of. Are you telling me it *isn't* going to happen?" he suddenly shouted. "Do you have any idea how much money your town is making on this convention? Does the mayor know you forgot to follow through on your promise? I'm calling our legal department. We'll sue the whole damn town."

Lamar held the phone far from his ear. "Hold on a minute, young man. Don't get yourself into such a snit. I'll ask my dispatcher if she knows anything about it. Delores knows everything about everything. If you don't believe it, just ask her."

Lamar punched the hold button and dialed dispatch. "Delores, can you come back here a minute?" He put the phone down and scratched his head. He searched through his old phone messages, his notepads, and his middle drawer. "I don't see anything about a parade," he mumbled to himself.

Delores opened the door. "Okay, Chief, I'm here. What did you want to tell me that you couldn't tell me over the phone?"

"Um, do you know anything about some kind of Elvis parade we're supposed to be having?"

Delores let out a squeal of joy that rattled the glass on Lamar's desk. "I knew there would be a parade!"

Lamar's eyebrows shot up in surprise. "Really?"

"Of course there will be a parade! This Elvis convention is the biggest thing that ever happened to this town."

"Have you ever heard of anybody named Kenny Preston? Supposed to be some hot-shot Elvis impersonator?"

"I'm sure I have," Delores said. "I'm sure it'll come to me."

Lamar was clearly perplexed. "I wonder how come Abby Bradley didn't mention this parade business when I stopped by for some of that new —" He paused and blushed. "That new chocolate ice cream everybody is raving about. Come to think of it, she didn't say anything to me."

"She has laryngitis."

267

"Oh." He nodded. "Okay, so the people in charge of putting together the parade are working on it?"

"Why wouldn't they be working on it? Of course they're working on it."

"All right, then. Do me a favor. I'll have someone cover dispatch for you. I want you to check and make sure everything is on schedule with the floats and whatnot. We'll need to put a few officers on it too," he added, "although I don't know where we'll get them. Everybody needs to be ready at twelve sharp."

"Twelve sharp, tomorrow?"

"Today."

Delores blinked several times. "I can do that, Chief. I know everybody on every committee."

"I'm sure you do, Delores. Oh, and talk to this Curtis fellow on line two, would you? You'll have to fill him in on the, um, particulars. Tell him I don't have time to fool with a parade on account of I'm looking for a murderer."

"I forgot the egg basket," Zack said to Maggie, standing just outside the kitchen door. "Would you hand it to me so I don't track goat, um, stuff on the floor."

She looked amused. "You stepped in goat poop?"

"Yeah."

"How's she doing in her new pen?"

"Staying busy. Once I fed her I went for the hose to fill her water bowl and discovered she had eaten most of it. We should probably start a list of replacement items."

The words had barely left his mouth before Maggie's expression changed to horror. Zack went for his gun before her scream left her lips. He shoved her inside and spun around, eyes assessing the situation.

"Oh, gross!" Mel said loudly.

Zack glanced over his shoulder. Maggie darted across the room and didn't stop until she'd reached the door leading into the hallway. Her eyes were bright with fear. Zack noted the grimace on Mel's face. He followed her gaze. A homely-looking cat held a dead mouse between his teeth.

Zack sighed and tucked his gun away. "Damn!" he said to Mel. "That's the nastiest-looking thing I've ever seen. That's not *your* cat, is it?"

Mel shot him a "you're so dumb" look.

"I'm sorry I screamed," Maggie said. "That stupid cat is always bringing me dead mice because he knows it freaks me out.

Please get it out of here. I'll be in my bedroom."

"This is getting old," Zack said. "I have to guard the fort, feed the farm animals, bury the mice. Now, how do I do this?" He grabbed the cat by the scruff of the neck and shook him slightly. "Let it go, boy."

"His name is Okra," Mel said.

The cat dropped the mouse and ran.

"Would you hand me some of that newspaper from the trash can?" Zack asked her.

Mel brought several sheets and handed them to him. "I guess you can tell my mother is terrified of mice," she said. "Sometimes she has nightmares."

Zack did not look at all surprised.

Savannah's Best Costumes & Designs was tucked between Bernie's Subs and Mc-Cracken's Bookstore. The man who unlocked the door bearing the CLOSED ON SUNDAY sign was tall, black, and bald and wore a gold loop in his left ear. He held out his palm and Carl Lee slapped a hundred-dollar bill in it. "Welcome to Savannah's Best Costumes," the man said. "We're always willing to open our doors on Sundays to our special friends." He tucked the money in his shirt pocket.

"Do you have what I need?" Carl Lee asked.

The black man led him to a counter where several plastic bags hung from a rack. "You're lucky I still have Elvis costumes left with the convention in Beaumont. Everybody wants to be the King."

"You have the right sizes?"

"The slacks are going to be an inch too long on two of them; same with the sleeves. But it's as close as I can get. Inside each hanging bag, you'll find what you need: a wig, fake sideburns, and gaudy-looking chains. You know, Elvis crap." He shoved a form across the counter. "You'll need to fill this out and show me some identification."

"I'm in a hurry," Carl Lee said.

"Yeah? Well, then, moving right along. How long will you need the costumes?"

"A day or two."

"It'll cost you sixteen hundred, including the deposit."

Carl Lee's gaze turned hard. "Are you messing with me, pal?"

"I got some money in those suits, man, and you don't want to give me an address or ID? I definitely need a sizeable deposit."

Carl Lee stood quietly for several minutes, his gaze unwavering, muscles in his jaw flexing. Finally, he leaned on the counter. The other man's smile faltered. "Here's the way we're going to do it," Carl Lee said. "I'm going to put five hundred dollars on this counter, and then I'm going to walk out that door with the costumes, and you're going to be happy with it."

The other man looked into Carl Lee's eyes and took a step back. "Okay, man, I'm good," he said quickly. "I don't need any trouble. I got my own stuff going on around here, know what I mean? I can't make a living renting stupid Elvis costumes."

Cook watched Carl Lee exit the costume shop with the plastic bags and head toward the car. "Like I said, Ed, it's just a little side trip, and it's for a good cause. It'll be fun. Then we'll head north to Canada as planned."

"What if somebody recognizes me?" Ed said.

Cook laughed. "They'll say, 'Hey, look, it's Elvis!' "

Ed smiled.

Zack opened the back door and stepped aside for Jamie to enter, giving her a friendly smile. "Maggie said you were coming by. Where is Romeo-the-hound?"

"He headed straight for the backyard. I'm pretty sure he's going to ask Butterbean for her hoof in marriage, although I think they're rushing things."

Zack draped his arm around her shoulders and began walking her down the hall. "Jamie, you can't measure love according to time. When it's right, it's right. A couple just knows. I think that may be the case with Fleas and Butterbean."

Jamie studied him. "Are you speaking from experience?"

Zack gave her a funny look as he tapped on Maggie's bedroom door. "Jamie is here," he called out.

"Send her in, Jeeves," Maggie said.

Zack pulled his arm from Jamie's shoulder and winked. "The mistress of the house and I are on a first-name basis." He opened the door, stepped aside so she could enter, and closed the door behind her.

Maggie was staring at her checkbook and wearing a perplexed frown. She held up one finger. "Give me a second, I'm almost done."

"You're getting pretty friendly with your staff," Jamie said. "Have you seen him naked yet?"

Maggie jerked her head up, felt the heat rush to her face. She tried to answer. "Wh . . . uh?"

This time Jamie cocked her head to the

side. "Did you say 'whuh'?"

Maggie was almost sure her ears were scorched. She shrugged.

"Why is your face so red?" Jamie asked. "How come you're not breathing? How come you didn't tell me you and Zack were doing *real* undercover work? And don't give me 'whuh.' "

Maggie just sat there not knowing what to say.

Jamie kicked off her shoes and sat cross-legged on the bed, studying her friend thoughtfully. "You don't *look* any different."

Maggie closed her eyes and sighed.

"He's got it bad for you," Jamie said.

Maggie opened her eyes. "Oh, please."

"I'm serious. I know that look. I've seen it on Fleas when he looks at Butterbean."

"Have you forgotten why Zack is here? Besides, if anything *is* going on between us —" She paused. "No, it's too weird."

"What?"

"I think Queenie has something to do with it. I mean, good grief! Zack and I don't have time for this stuff. Carl Lee Stanton is probably out there right now trying to decide whether to use a knife or a gun on me."

"You don't really believe Queenie would do something like that. You and Zack are just irresistibly drawn to each other."

"I can't think about it right now. It's too much. I have to keep a clear head. I have to protect my daughter. I have to have that talk with her." Maggie stacked her bills and envelopes and put them on the night table. She looked up. "Would you like something to drink?" she asked, purposely changing the subject. "I have lemonade, diet soft drinks, coffee, bottled water," she said.

Jamie shook her head. "I'm fine. Besides, I've given up coffee. It upsets my stomach. And citrus drinks give me heartburn."

"Oh?"

"Yeah. Where is Mel? I don't hear her stereo."

"She's in her room reading *Gulliver's Travels.*"

"Grounded, huh? Dare I ask why?"

Maggie told her.

"I'm sorry you had to go through that," Jamie said. "I'm sorry you have to go through all this," she added sadly. "It makes my problems sound petty."

"Don't be silly. Your problems have never been petty to me. So, talk."

Jamie updated her on the never-ending, nerve-rattling problems going on at her house and repeated her story about the leaky faucet. "It's driving me crazy. I'm tired and out of sorts." Sudden tears filled her eyes. "My marriage is on the rocks," she added.

"No way! Max adores you. If he seems distracted, it's just because he's impatient to get the plant up and running. He's dealing with contractors at the house *and* the office. Now, would you like a little advice?"

"Yes!"

"Okay, Oakleigh Apartments has long- and short-term executive rentals. I've seen them, and they're gorgeous. They're fully stocked, right down to linens and dishes and toilet paper. They have daily maid service. You and Max could have a quiet time together."

"I'd forgotten about Oakleigh. I wonder if there is a vacancy," Jamie mused aloud. "I wonder if they allow pets."

"They're running ads in your newspaper. And I'm sure they'll let you take Fleas. Good grief, you're Max and Jamie Holt. You guys saved the town! You guys are celebrities. You guys —" Maggie paused. "You'll probably have to pay a pet fee."

"That's a great idea," Jamie said. She climbed from the bed and stepped into her shoes. "I'm going to drive over there right now and rent one. Thank you, Maggie." She hurried toward the door.

"Oh, one more thing," Maggie said.

Jamie turned. "Yeah?"

"Take a pregnancy test."

CHAPTER TWELVE

Zack opened the back door just as Jamie reached for the knob. He stepped inside. He wore an old hat with a raccoon's face on the front; the top part of the hat was covered in fur. "Found it in the back of the van," he said at the look Jamie gave him. "Thought maybe I could gross out Mel," he added.

"Yeah, that should work."

"You're not going to believe this," he said. "The goat is gone, and so is your dog."

Jamie blinked several times. "Wh . . . uh?"

Zack gave a slight frown. "Sorry, I didn't get that. Did you just say 'whuh'?"

"Ignore it," Jamie told him. "How long have they been missing?"

"I just now noticed," he said. "Butterbean chewed through her pen. I've been looking for them. They couldn't have gotten very far."

Maggie came up behind Jamie. "What's

wrong? Other than Zack having really bad taste in hats?" she added.

Jamie told her what was going on.

Mel came into the room, still dressed in her pajamas. She looked at Zack and gave a huge sigh. Finally, she opened the refrigerator door, stared inside for a moment and slumped. She proceeded to the cabinet, looked inside, closed the door, and banged her head gently against it. "There's never anything good to eat in this house."

Maggie, deep in thought as to where the animals could have gone, paid scant notice to her daughter's food complaints. "Honey, just try to make do for now," she said. "I think we should drive around and look for them," she told Zack.

He nodded. "I was going to suggest that, but I want you and Mel with me."

Mel had her hands in the potato chip bag. "Who are you looking for?"

"I think Fleas and Butterbean have eloped," Zack said. "Guess they won't need a best man. Guess I won't get to show off my new hat." He grinned at her.

Mel just stared back at him as she stuffed potato chips in her mouth.

Maggie grabbed her purse from the kitchen counter. "Mel, you need to come with us."

"In my pajamas?"

"Run and throw on something quick, okay?" Maggie glanced at her, then gasped. "Why are you eating potato chips for breakfast? I'm a doctor, for Pete's sake! I preach healthy food to my patients' parents every day, and my own daughter eats cold pizza and potato chips for breakfast."

She reached for the bag, but it slipped through her fingers and fell to the floor, scattering potato chips in every direction. Maggie closed her eyes. "I'll clean it up while you change clothes."

Mel looked up from the mess. "Why can't I have a normal childhood?"

"You *do* have a normal childhood," Maggie said, hurrying for the broom and dustpan. "Hurry, now, we have to find a goat who has obviously lost her head over a hound dog. Oh, and I need to leave a note for Queenie in case she comes by for her black hen's egg and decides to paint bat's blood on our front steps or something."

"Maybe I could go to a boarding school," Mel said hopefully as she plodded down the hall to her bedroom.

"We need to take the van," Zack said. "We can put Fleas in the backseat with Mel. Butterbean will fit in the luggage area."

"I don't have any rope," Maggie said. "A

belt, maybe?" She saw Zack wasn't wearing one. "I'll grab one of mine." She raced down the hall.

"I'll drive around and look too," Jamie said to Zack. "I don't like them disappearing so close to town. I hope they don't get hit by a car."

Maggie returned with her belt. "Ready? Where's Mel?"

Mel came through the kitchen door. "I'm here! Geez!"

"Wear this," Zack said, plunking the hat on Maggie's head, "just in case Stanton is out there watching."

"Please tell me you're not really going to wear that in public," Mel said.

Zack backed the van out of the garage a few minutes later. Jimmy Hendrix was blasting through the speakers singing "Purple Haze" and beads swung behind the seat. The raccoon hat all but covered Maggie's eyes. At the end of the driveway, Zack paused to let a car pass, and he began playing an air guitar. Mel lay in the backseat, hands covering her face.

Zack pulled from the driveway. "Okay, keep an eye out, Maggie," he said. "Mel, keep your head low, okay?"

"I'm really nervous," Ed said, his black Elvis

wig falling forward on his head again. "I've never been in front of a crowd. I'm feeling light-headed and dizzy, and I'm having heart palpitations. My whole body is shaking, and my palms are sweating, and I feel sick to my stomach. I have to pee. I wish I had gone to that nursing home."

"Would you shut the hell up!" Carl Lee yelled, so loudly that Ed and Cook both jumped. "We are on a schedule, old man. If I have to stop this damn car one more time I'm going to stuff your wig in your mouth and lock you in the trunk. You got that?"

"I knew you weren't a real priest," Ed said. "I knew you were faking it. You're going to be screwed when the pope finds out."

Carl Lee swerved to the side of the road, slammed on the brakes, and pulled out his gun. He swung around and shoved it against the elderly man's forehead.

Ed's eyes shot open wide. He gasped and wheezed and clutched his chest. His eyes rolled around in his head and he fell sideways on the seat.

"Oh, shit!" Carl Lee said.

Cook gaped and shrank against the passenger door. "Is he?" He gulped. "You killed him, Carl Lee! You killed Ed! I'm outta here." He reached for the door handle.

"Think again." Carl Lee moved the gun

to Cook's left temple.

"You can't shoot me. You'll get blood all over the car, and we're supposed to join that parade in fifteen minutes. You've already got one dead man in the car. What do you plan on doing with two?"

"You're right," Carl Lee said. "I can't shoot you so I think this is the perfect time to play my trump card." He reached beneath the seat, pulled out a photo of a young woman and a blond pigtailed girl playing with a puppy in front of a neat, white frame house. He dropped it in Cook's lap.

Cook's hands shook as he picked it up and held it almost reverently, a recent photo of his daughter and granddaughter. "H-how did you get this?" His voice was strangled.

"You're not the only one I hired, retard. I give the word, and they disappear. My friend needs the money." Carl Lee lowered the gun. "Don't make me prove what I'm capable of, Ray."

Someone knocked on Lamar's door, and a young officer opened it and stuck his head inside. "Chief, we have a little situation."

Lamar Tevis had his phone pressed to his ear. He held up one hand. "Yes, Vera, I've definitely decided it's time I pass the old badge to someone else," he whispered, "and

283

I was thinking you or Jamie would like to interview me. You know, tell people how devoted I've been to my job and all I've accomplished while serving as police chief. And I'd really like it if you'd mention my deep-sea fishing business."

The officer waved. "Um, Chief —"

Lamar held up his hand again. "Just one thing, Vera," he said. "I don't want anyone to know about it until after I get this mess cleaned up with Stanton." Lamar hung up and looked at the officer. "What!"

"Well, the parade is about to start, Chief, and there's this goat running loose on Main Street. And there's an ugly hound dog with the goat, and he won't let anybody close to the goat. Starts growling and snarling like he's going to eat us alive. He looks pretty dangerous."

Lamar yanked off his cap and threw it on the floor. "Do I look like Animal Control? Do I look like a parade organizer? Don't people realize that I'm trying to catch a dad-burned killer?"

"Is that Kenny Preston?" Delores from dispatch asked Carl Lee, as she and two other women tied helium balloons to the door handles and hung banners on either side of the Cadillac. She stared at the newly deceased Ed in his sunglasses and rhinestone-laden jumpsuit, propped between Carl Lee and the back door of the car, his pillow tucked beneath his head. "He looks really old," Delores added. "Is he okay?"

In the front seat, Cook gripped the steering wheel tightly, but remained silent.

"He's asleep," Carl Lee said. "And yeah, he's old. He's the oldest and most famous of all the rest of us Elvis impersonators. I'll wake him up when the parade starts. Doesn't look like much of a parade," he added.

"I'm sorry it's small," Delores said, "but there seemed to be a big mix-up. I only found one float. It's our Thanksgiving float. It has an enormous turkey on it, but we took off the HAPPY THANKSGIVING banner." She fidgeted with her hands and spoke in rapid-fire sentences. "And we couldn't put together a marching band, but my aunt's friend has a daughter who is married to a musician so we —"

"I think I get the message," Carl Lee said, giving her a tight smile.

"But we provided the police escort you asked for," she said, motioning to the squad car in front of them, "so the fans won't try to rush Mr. Preston, but —" She glanced down Main Street where only a few people lingered and looked about curiously. "I don't think we'll have a problem with crowd control."

"Are we about ready?" Carl Lee was clearly impatient to begin.

"There's a goat and a bloodhound in the road. We're just waiting for the police to catch them. Um, we're honored to have Mr. Preston with us today," Delores said. "On behalf of the town of Beaumont, let me welcome you." She hurried away.

Carl Lee chuckled. "So what do you think, Ray? Not only have we made it past the roadblock, we have a police escort."

"Yeah, you're a genius, Carl Lee," Cook said as he continued to stare straight ahead, his tone flat. "Now you need to figure out what we're going to do with Ed after the parade."

"What's going on?" Maggie asked when she saw the large turkey towering above the cars ahead of them. "That's our Thanksgiving float. I didn't know we were having a parade. Mel, do you know anything about a parade?" she asked, glancing over her shoulder.

"How could I?" the girl said. "I'm grounded. I'm not allowed contact with the outside world."

"There's Butterbean and Fleas!" Zack said, motioning toward the other side of the street where police were in pursuit of the pair. He pulled off the road and cut the engine. "Wait here."

Zack climbed from the van and ran in the direction of the scurrying animals. He heard someone call out to him and glanced over his shoulder. Jamie was trying to catch up.

"Are they getting ready to have a parade?" Zack asked as they hurried toward the dog and the goat.

"I just found out it was some last-minute thing they threw together to welcome a famous Elvis impersonator to town so it's obviously tied to the convention. Oh, no, did you see that? Fleas just tried to bite a policeman!"

Several minutes later they had their animals in tow and a furious Jamie was giving Fleas a stern lecture. Every once in a while he looked back mournfully at Butterbean; Zack was leading her in the opposite direction toward the van. He opened the back door and hefted the little pygmy in and closed the door, just as a loudspeaker screeched in the background, causing a number of people to wince and cover their ears.

"We'd better get out of here fast," Zack said, turning on the ignition.

"Yeah, we don't want to get stuck behind a parade," Maggie said.

Zack shook his head. "I'm more worried that loudspeaker will go off again." He eased forward, waiting for several cars to pass.

"Zack, my man!" a male voice called out.

"It's your friend Lonnie Renfro," Maggie said. "Get a load of that outfit."

Mel moaned in the backseat. "Could we please leave now?"

Zack glanced out his window as Lonnie crossed the street, bedecked in a fire-engine-red satin jumpsuit and matching cape. Rhinestones formed streaks of lightning across his chest and down the back of his cape. "Wow," Zack said. "I don't think I've ever seen anything like that. I hope nobody lights a match close to him."

Lonnie waved wildly and hurried toward them, hand on his head as though afraid his Elvis wig would fly off. "Dude!" He reached inside the window and punched Zack on his left arm. "How's it going, my man?" He nodded at Maggie and glanced in the backseat at Mel. "Is your daughter sick?"

"Just a cold from being in the night air," Maggie said.

Lonnie's blackened brows arched high.

"Whoa, mama, you've got a goat in the back of your van."

"Our new pet," Zack said.

"That is too cool. Did you come to see the parade?" He didn't wait for an answer. "It's to honor Kenny Preston, the very first Elvis impersonator. He must be pretty important because the cops wouldn't let me get his autograph." Lonnie leaned closer. "The officer said he heard from someone *in the know* who heard from an *unknown source* who got it straight from the *horse's mouth* that the rhinestones on Mr. Preston's outfit are real diamonds." Lonnie gave a huge eye roll. "Can you e-magine what that sucker must be worth?" he added, almost whispering. "I'll bet they have to haul it to the dry cleaners in a Brinks truck."

Lonnie suddenly shoved one hand forward. "Hey, buddy, I might not see you and the wife again on account of I'm leaving tomorrow. Take care of that arm," he said, nodding at the cast. He glanced over the seat. "I hope you feel better real soon, young lady," he told Mel before hurrying away.

"What do you think?" Jamie asked Max once they'd gone through the three-bedroom apartment at Oakleigh. The leasing agent had gone back to her office, leav-

289

ing them to decide. Maggie had been right; the place was beautiful and more than large enough. Even Fleas seemed to appreciate it, despite being forlorn and missing his girl-friend. He'd found a sunny spot in the room at the back that was lined with windows and looked out over the marsh, favored by stately white egrets that added to the beauty of the landscape.

Max slipped his arms around her waist and kissed her forehead. "I'm thinking it's great, Swifty," he said, using the nickname he'd given her shortly after they'd met. He kissed her. "So when do we move in?"

Jamie grinned. "I've already put a deposit on it, Bubba."

"I like a woman who knows her own mind," he said.

They parked beside the newspaper office shortly before three o'clock. They walked toward the front door, hands linked, grin-ning like a couple of sixteen-year-olds on their first date. Jamie's outlook on life had vastly improved now that she and Max were moving out of Hell House until it was habit-able again.

Jamie smelled garlic even before they opened the front doors. She gave an enor-mous grimace as they stepped inside the lobby. "Holy crap!" she said.

"Wow," Max said. "I feel like I've just been bitch-slapped by an Italian chef."

It grew increasingly worse as they neared Jamie's office, where Destiny lay curled on the sofa beneath the oversized afghan that Jamie kept on hand. Destiny opened her eyes and stretched. "I thought I heard voices. Hi, guys." She sat up, yawned, and rubbed her eyes.

Max's eyes widened. "Destiny? Is that you?"

"Uh-huh. I'm posing as an ugly person."

"This place stinks," Jamie said. "Has somebody been cooking garlic in the kitchen? Like maybe a truckload of it?"

"It's my temporary perfume," Destiny said. "I rubbed fresh garlic behind my ears and on my wrists hoping it would keep Freddie Baylor away."

"I think it would chase off a hungry bear," Max said.

"One good thing, I got rid of that pain-in-the-butt Earl G. Potts." When Max arched one brow in question, she explained. "Another dead guy following me around. He caught one whiff and shot off like a bottle rocket toward the light. Unfortunately, he was wearing my favorite dress, and my brand-new silk stockings," she added, clearly annoyed. "I don't know why a *normal* dead person doesn't latch on to me once in a while."

"Excuse me?"

All three turned at the sound of a male voice. The handsome blond man standing in the doorway was impeccably dressed. Jamie could tell he'd spent big bucks on his Italian suit; it was of the quality Max wore. He looked very familiar, but she couldn't quite place him. "May I help you?"

He sniffed. "I don't mean to be rude, but this place smells terrible." He looked about as though trying to figure out the source. He gave a slight frown at the sight of the woman on the sofa.

"We're trying to keep evil spirits away," Jamie said. "Do I know you?"

He smiled. "It's me, Freddy Baylor."

Jamie and Destiny gasped and gaped. Destiny fell back on the sofa and covered her face with the afghan. "I didn't recognize you!" Jamie said.

He grinned. "I clean up well."

Max held out his hand. "I'm —"

"I know who you are," Freddy said, and shook his hand. "We've met before. At the Four Seasons in New York. A charitable function, I think."

"Wait a minute," Max said. "You're Theodore Frederick Baylor of Baylor Electronics. What brings you to Beaumont?"

"I got burned out on the corporate world and bought a bait shop." He laughed at Max's look of astonishment. "Hey, I was going through an early midlife crisis so I became a bum for a couple of months. Have you guys seen Destiny?"

"Oh, she's —" Max saw the look on Jamie's face and swallowed the rest of his sentence.

"Destiny left," Jamie said quickly. "She wasn't feeling well."

"Yeah," Max said. "She wasn't herself today."

"I went by her house first. She's probably mad at me for knocking on her door so many times last night. I sort of lost my head over her. I'll just have to live with the embarrassing memories." His cell phone rang, and he glanced at the number. "Uh-oh, it's my pilot. He has already filed a flight plan. I should have been there by now." He pushed a button. "Fifteen minutes," he said and hung up.

"I have to go," he said. "I wanted to apologize to Destiny. I was hoping to make it up to her by taking her to New York for a few days. A little wining and dining," he added. "I think she and I could have had something, but I probably turned her off with my good-old-boy routine. I sort of went over the top, I think."

"Wait!" Destiny threw off the afghan and bolted from the sofa. "Freddy —"

"Destiny? Good grief, what happened to you!" He sniffed, took a step back, and held up one hand.

She stopped at a respectful distance. "Oh, um, I'm not Destiny," she said. "I'm her, uh, ugly twin. I'm uh —" She shot Jamie a frantic look.

"Desmeralda," Jamie said quickly, then shrugged at the odd look Destiny and Max shot her.

"But I know where to find my sister," Destiny said quickly, "and I know she would be thrilled to go to New York with you."

Freddy just stood there looking horrified. He clearly saw through the act. He checked his wristwatch. "Oh, boy, I'm really late," he said. "I've got your number," he told Destiny. "I'll give you a call." He was gone.

"I should probably go after him," Destiny said.

"No!" Max and Jamie said in unison.

Vera came through the front door a few minutes later. "Holy Hades!" she cried. "This place smells like a garlic breeding ground." She stepped into Jamie's office. "Are we trying to get rid of vampires or something?" She shot Destiny a quick look. "What's wrong with Ugly?" she asked Jamie, cutting her eyes at Destiny once more.

"Freddy Baylor has lost interest in me," Destiny said, giving a huge sniff. A lone tear ran down her cheek. "He wants nothing to do with me."

Vera was clearly dumbfounded. Finally, she squared her shoulders. "Okay, we have to stick together," she said. "I don't care if Destiny *is* a loose screw in slutwear; we can't let word of this get out. If anyone learns that scraggly-looking bait shop owner *Freddy Baylor* rejected her, no man will ever want her." She pretended to zip her mouth.

"I fold," Zack said to Mel, laying down his cards. "You've got most of the chips anyway. I think you lied when you said you didn't know how to play poker. I think you're hustling me, kid."

"Sore loser," Mel said, raking her chips across her bedroom floor.

"I'm sore, all right," he said, stretching his long legs. "Hard for an old man to sit on a floor," he added.

"Don't complain to me," Mel said. "Tell the evil doctor."

"Hey, at least she let you play poker. I

wish you guys could clear the air."

"Don't you *get it?*" Mel said, leaning forward. "She called Travis and lectured him. Like he *forced* me to meet him," she added. "Like I'm three years old and don't know how to make my own decisions."

"If that were true you wouldn't be spending most of your time in this room reading *Gulliver's Travels*," he said. "She's holding you accountable."

"It figures you'd take her side."

"No way," he said. "I'm sort of playing devil's advocate."

"Like I'm supposed to know what you're talking about?" she said.

"It's where you oppose someone's argument, even though you don't *really* oppose it; you're just looking at it from different angles. To test its, um, accuracy," he added. "To see if it's a valid argument."

"Why?"

"I have no idea. Maybe because my stepdad used to drive me crazy doing it to me," he said. Zack leaned against one of her beds, propped his elbows on his knees and linked his fingers.

"Maybe you should be testing this out on my mom," Mel said, examining one of the chips. "Find out why she expects me to be the perfect daughter. She wasn't so perfect.

It's like a major sin that I stood outside the movies talking to a boy. Look what mom did." Her eyes misted. "Look what *she* did!"

"I'm looking," he said.

Lydia Green was clearly annoyed as she quickly tossed aside the grimy blouse and slacks she'd worn helping Ben put up the clothesline, and then pulling weeds from the flower beds and putting out fresh pine straw as he'd mowed the grass. Without taking time to shower first, she slipped into a clean outfit.

In the den, Ben snored in his recliner. She looked past him, through the window, where a truck from Southland Phone Company was parked in front of her neighbor's house. She hurried into the kitchen and scribbled a note. Her hands shook.

Ben:
Gone to pick up your insulin at Bi-Lo pharmacy. I'll grab your juice while I'm there.

Back soon. L.

She taped the note on a cabinet door in plain view and went for her purse. She dug for her keys and started for the door. She opened it and as she stepped outside a man in a blue uniform approached the back of her house. He stared down at a clipboard he held and whistled the Johnny Cash song "I Walk the Line." He wore the Southland Phone Company insignia on his uniform, and beneath it, the name Joe.

"May I help you," Lydia said as he neared her steps.

He jumped, obviously startled. He covered his heart and rolled his eyes. "Lady, you just scared the meanness right out of me," he said loudly. "I didn't see you standing there."

Lydia put one finger to her lips. "My husband is resting."

"Oh, sorry," he said, lowering his voice as he put a finger to the bill of his cap in a polite gesture. His teeth were pronounced, even more so when he smiled.

"I didn't mean to scare you," Lydia said, fitting her key in the lock and jiggling it several times before it finally turned and locked. "I'm in a hurry. What can I do for you?"

"I'll be lickety-quick," he said, still smiling as he shoved his glasses higher on his nose and blinked several times through the thick lenses. "Some of your neighbors are having problems with their phones. Just checking to see if you've still got service," he added.

Lydia's brow puckered. "You look familiar. Do I know you?"

"Been living here all my life," he said. "Do you know Joe and Doris Frazier? They're my parents. I was named after my dad, of course," he added, pointing to the patch where his name had been sewn. "They attend the big Baptist church in town. I go with them now and then when they shame me into it."

Lydia shook her head. "I'm Methodist." She checked her wristwatch. "My telephone is fine. The pharmacy called not more than twenty minutes ago. I need to get there before they close. My husband is diabetic and insulin-dependent."

"Then I will just mark your name off of my list and be on my way," he said, pretending to draw a great big *X* on the page. "You have any problems you call and ask for Joe." Once again, he touched his cap, then turned to leave.

"Hold on a sec," Lydia said with a loud sigh before he reached the steps. "You've got me all worried now."

"Sorry."

She put her key in the lock, hands still shaking. She struggled with the key. "This thing is so hateful."

"Let me have a shot at it," the man said,

taking the key from her. He paused. "What happens if he forgets his injection?"

"He gets sick," she said flatly.

"Could he die?"

"Yes!" She covered her mouth because she had spoken too loud. "Yes, he could," she said quietly.

"What would you do if that happened? I mean, if he died? Maybe even died at home?"

Lydia just looked at the man. "Well, I —" She frowned. "Oh, good grief!" she said, waving off the remark. "That's a terrible thing to ask someone. I have to go. Are you going to open my door or do I have to ring the bell and wake my husband?"

"Sorry," he said, putting the key into the lock and turning it slowly. He jiggled it like she had. "I was just thinking how terrible it would be if somebody I loved died right in front of me." The lock finally clicked. He opened the door, stood back, and grinned. "There you go."

Lydia didn't return his smile. She looked deeply troubled, anxious. She took her keys from him, crossed the room, and lifted the receiver from the wall phone. She waited a few seconds and tapped the receiver. "I'm not getting a dial tone. The line is dead. What do you suppose —" A hand covered her mouth before she could finish her sentence. She looked up, straight into the barrel of a gun.

He leaned close. "Tell me, Lydia," he whispered as softly as the breath that fell against her cheek. "What are you willing to do to keep your husband alive?"

CHAPTER THIRTEEN

Maggie opened her eyes and found the living room dark and herself half sprawled on the living room sofa. She blinked several times. She was groggy and disoriented and still tired, even though it felt as though she'd slept a long time. Someone had covered her with a blanket. She touched the tiny button on her wristwatch, and the face lit up so she could read it. It was after eight P.M.! She had slept for three hours! She quickly threw off the blanket and bolted from the sofa.

Anxiety spurred her into the kitchen. Dark and empty. She stepped into the hallway. She heard Mel's voice coming from her room and felt dizzy with relief. She followed the soft light and found Zack leaning against Mel's bed studying one of her sketches with the help of a fat candle. Mel sat nearby, pointing to something on the drawing. They glanced up. Maggie's eyes lingered on Zack's face. She realized she had already memorized it.

He smiled. "Welcome back." The smiled faded slightly. "What's wrong?"

"I just —" Maggie paused. She had been on the verge of blurting out how much she hated that her daughter was forced to sit in the near-dark. She wanted to rant and rave and maybe kick something; she wanted to yell from her rooftop how unfair it was. She wanted an answer as to why Carl Lee had not been found and how many more days they would have to sit around and wonder when he'd show up. She wanted to turn on all the lights, yank the drapes off their rods, peel the tacky aluminum foil off the kitchen window, and do something really immature and totally stupid like yell out to Carl Lee and dare him to do something about it. It would almost be worth getting shot. Only problem, it wouldn't be worth leaving Mel orphaned. The expression in Zack's eyes told her he knew what she was feeling.

"I didn't mean to sleep so long," she said. "I didn't know I was so tired. You guys are probably starved."

"We made a sandwich," he said, "and napping isn't a bad thing. It's not even illegal in most states now. By the way, Queenie called, mostly to check in, but she didn't want me to wake you. She said she hasn't had a chance to come by to see if her hen laid an egg yet because she's been bogged down with appointments."

"Sunday is a busy day for her. People come from all over for her, um, *services*."

They were quiet. As if sensing the tension, Zack grinned. "Your daughter kicked my behind in poker," he said. "She felt so sorry for me she agreed to let me see her artwork. This girl is *good*." He looked at Mel. "This is your calling, kiddo. Your mission. Your reason for being. Your key to limos, and a penthouse in New York."

Maggie smiled proudly. "Mel's teacher says she finds beauty in simple things, and she makes simple things beautiful." Even in the dim light Maggie could see the bright flush on her daughter's face, and she was surprised the girl had shown Zack her work.

"Zack, I hate to ask this, but I really do need to go back to the grocery store," Maggie said. "This time with my list," she added. She could see that he wasn't thrilled with the announcement.

"Isn't there anyone you could ask to do it for you?" he said. "Maybe Queenie?"

"I need to go," Maggie said. "I'm really particular about what I buy. I can't use scented soap, certain shampoos, or hair conditioners because they give me a rash.

Same goes for facial and toilet tissue. I only buy laundry detergent that has a bleach alternative, and I steer clear of foods with additives. Also, when I shop for beef I only use certain cuts that contain less fat content, and I prefer organically grown vegetables."

Zack looked at Mel, whose eyes had already climbed heavenward. "Well, damn, Maggie. I guess we're going to the grocery store."

She hurried into her bedroom, slipped on fresh clothes, and ran a brush through her hair. She found Mel and Zack in the kitchen; he was talking on a police radio.

"Okay, here's the deal," he said, when he got off. "I double-checked with the guys in the area and nobody has seen anything unusual so we're good to go. Even so, I've asked for an escort in and out of here. Now that it's dark, I'm going to move the van inside the garage so we'll be driving your car."

"Thank you, God!" Mel said.

"I've decided to have a patrolman take the two of you to the office tomorrow, but I won't be far behind. Also —" He looked at Maggie. "Just so you're not surprised, I put a couple of patrol cars at the entrance of your subdivision last night, knowing Carl Lee will expect it. He's probably planning on it. Otherwise, he's going to be looking more closely for unmarked cars."

Someone tapped on the door and identified himself. Zack checked the curtain and disarmed the alarm system. "We need a couple of minutes to look around and get the van in the garage." He sighed. "I need to make sure the goat is still in her newly secured pen, although I think she's still exhausted from her busy day. I'll come back for you." Zack reached for the raccoon hat and put it on Maggie's head. "And you'll need to wear your disguise."

Mel looked at him. "She doesn't have to wear it in the store, right?" she said.

Twenty minutes later, Zack parked Maggie's car in front of the Bi-Lo store. A sedan with a plainclothes officer named Bill pulled up beside them. He followed the three of them into the store, carefully maintaining a distance. Zack had wanted him to stay back and watch the people around them.

Maggie grabbed a cart and started through the store as Zack and Mel made their way toward a table where free cookie samples were being offered. Maggie felt Bill's eyes on her from time to time and knew he wasn't far.

The white-haired woman at the table

looked like a typical grandmother except she was unsmiling. When Zack and Mel approached the table she held out her tray, one frizzy eyebrow arched in question. "Cookie?" Her voice was flat.

"Sure," Zack said, waiting for Mel to grab one of the fat chocolate chip cookies before taking one for himself. "Thanks," he said.

"Here's your coupon." She handed it to him. "You get fifty cents off if you buy a bag."

"That's a great deal," he said. He and Mel stepped back as a mother with four children approached her.

They ate in silence. "She isn't very nice," Mel said, her voice just above a whisper, once she'd finished off her cookie. "I don't think she likes her job. I don't think she wants to be here. I don't think she's going to give us another cookie."

"You want another one?" Zack asked. "I can get us one because I'm charming and women can't resist me."

Mel gave an eye roll as Zack went back to the display table and gave the woman a big smile. "Did you bake these cookies yourself?" he asked.

The woman looked at him as though she thought it was the dumbest question she'd ever been asked. She pulled the tray closer as though guarding it. "No."

"Those sugar cookies look great," he said.

"You only get one cookie and one coupon. You've already had both."

"Oh." He paused. "If you didn't bake them how come your name tag says Baker and the brand name on the packages say Mrs. Baker's cookies?"

"It's a coincidence," she said. "Plus, they misspelled my name. Mine has two letter *k*s in it."

"I see." He lingered, shot a quick glance at Mel, who looked hopeful. "So the two names aren't even pronounced the same. Your name is pronounced Backer."

"No it's not," she replied sharply. "They are pronounced exactly the same. You're not getting another cookie."

"We should go," Mel said.

"But we didn't try the peanut butter."

"You had your choice just like everyone else. The rules are, I'm only allowed to give one cookie to each customer who comes through the door."

"What if we leave and come back?" he asked.

The woman's face tightened in annoyance. "It doesn't work that way," she said, raising her voice and drawing looks from several customers standing nearby. "If you want another cookie you can use your coupon and *buy* some. Now, back off!"

"Grandma, is this man bothering you?" a young security guard asked; the name Bakker was stitched to his uniform.

"Yes! You should use your club on him. You should have him arrested for being a public nuisance. And trying to steal cookies," she added.

The guard turned and scowled at Zack. "You just bought yourself a whole lotta trouble, mister."

Maggie scanned the selection of cakes in the bakery, spied the double-fudge chocolate, and snatched it up before anyone else could claim it, and hoped Bill hadn't noticed. She didn't read the ingredients as she did on everything else. Her rules about healthy foods became null and void when it came to chocolate. She turned to her cart and spied Lydia Green in the deli and hurried over. "Hi, Lydia," she said, coming up beside the woman.

Lydia jumped. One hand flew to her chest as though she feared it would leap right into the cold cuts bin. "Good Lord, Maggie, you scared the daylights out of me! Don't *ever* sneak up on me like that again."

Maggie was surprised by Lydia's harsh

tone. "I'm so sorry," she said, as her friend seemed to struggle to pull herself together. Maggie had never seen her so ridden with anxiety. She raised her hand to touch Lydia's arm, but she didn't feel it would be welcome at the moment. Instead, she pretended to push her hair back. "You're buying a lot of groceries," she said lightly, trying to ease the tension. She didn't want to just hurry away when Lydia looked so troubled. "Are you having a dinner party?" She smiled. "How come I didn't get my invitation?"

Lydia stared at her for a moment. She opened her mouth, then closed it.

Maggie saw the panic in her eyes. "Lydia, what is it? What's wrong? Where is Ben?"

The woman blinked rapidly. "He's resting. He's not feeling well."

"You mean you're alone! You're in no shape to drive home. You need to pay for your groceries, and I'll drive you."

"No!"

This time Maggie did touch her. She took Lydia's hand. It was icy. "Take a deep breath."

Lydia did as she was told. "I'm okay," she said, even as tears glistened in her eyes. "I'm just upset with Ben. I'm furious. I saw his empty insulin vial in the bathroom trash earlier. He missed his morning dose, but do you think he bothered to tell me? Do you think he called his doctor and asked for a refill?"

"Oh, no. Is he in ketoacidosis?" Maggie asked quickly. "Shouldn't he go to the ER?"

"I have his prescription now," she said. "I got here about two seconds before the pharmacy closed. I'll give him his injection the minute I get home."

Maggie looked at the woman's cart. Why on earth was she grocery-shopping when Ben needed his medication? She felt her jaw drop at the sight of sweet rolls, a pie, and a box of cookies. Lydia did not keep sweets in the house. Had she lost her mind! "I'll get Zack to go through the checkout for you and drive you home like I said." She was already scanning the store.

"I am perfectly capable of taking care of my own husband!" Lydia snapped. "Why don't you mind your own business?"

Maggie was so stunned she didn't speak for several seconds. "I was just trying to help."

"I don't *need* your help, and I don't have time to stand here arguing with you. Please, just —" She shook her head. "I have to go."

Maggie stepped back as Lydia pushed her cart away. Maggie almost didn't see the case of beer on the metal shelf beneath Lydia's basket. Beer! Very few people knew that Ben was a recovering alcoholic, and an active member of AA for some thirty years. They didn't keep alcohol in their home. Maggie could not imagine Ben having a relapse after all this time, but it would certainly explain Lydia's behavior. Maybe the woman had lied about Ben's missed injection, maybe she was embarrassed. Maybe that's why she wanted Maggie to stay out of it.

Maggie reminded herself that Ben had gone out in the dead of night many times when a fellow alcoholic needed help. Lydia would know to call someone. She would know better than Maggie what to do. Maybe the poor woman was trying to work through shock and disappointment. Maggie pressed her hand against her forehead. Her brain felt like scrambled eggs.

She had only put a few things in her cart when Zack and Mel showed up. She was unable to focus; she only vaguely remembered where items were kept in the store.

Mel seemed to appear out of nowhere. "Will this take very long?" the girl asked, looking disappointed at the near-empty basket.

"Is something wrong?" Maggie asked, wondering how it was possible that anything else could go wrong in their lives at the moment.

"Zack almost got arrested for bothering an old lady." Mel looked up at the ceiling.

"What!" Maggie looked at Zack.

"I was only teasing her," he said. "I didn't know she had *issues.*"

Mel's eyes were still at the top of her head. "I'm never coming back in this store as long as I live. I wish I were in Egypt with Grandma and Papa. I wish I *lived* in Egypt."

"Yeah," Maggie said, thinking Egypt would be a nice place to visit about now. She and Mel could hide out in a tomb until the police caught up with Carl Lee. "Why don't you and Zack grab a cart and help me," Maggie said, "and we'll be out of here in no time. You know what I buy." She tore the list in half and handed it to her daughter. The look on Mel's face was the same as when the dentist announced she needed braces.

Max and Jamie sat at a small table in Donnie Maynard's sandwich shop, sampling his new brie and turkey wrap, as he waited breathlessly for their verdict. Every few minutes he darted a look at the front door, which had been locked and the shade pulled low. The turkey wrap had not yet been announced to the public. It was top secret. Max and Jamie had been forced to take an oath of silence until Donnie was ready to unveil his creation in the food section of the *Gazette.*

Jamie made a production of tasting his new sandwich and making notes in her purse-sized tablet as Max looked on in amusement.

"So, what do you think?" Donnie whispered. "Think folks will like it as much as Maynard's Famous Meatloaf?"

Jamie touched her lips with the cloth napkin that Donnie had provided for their taste-testing pleasure, as well as actual dinner plates and wine goblets filled with iced tea. "Donnie, I think people will like your wraps even better than Maynard's Famous Meatloaf," she pronounced.

Donnie looked at Max who was smiling broadly and nodding his approval. "Very tasty," Max said.

"Magnificent," Jamie added. "The brie that you chose as an accompaniment to your turkey is subtle, yet has a distinct flavor that creates a unique coupling. The strawberry jam and butter spread enhance the culinary marriage, and the grapes and avocado slices on the side give your presentation a certain —" She paused and held her head to the side in thought. "Panache and sophistication," she added.

"You wowed her, Donnie," Max said.

"Holy mackerel!" Donnie staggered back, obviously dazed by Jamie's high appraisal. He shook his head hard. "Can you remember to say all that in your food review?"

Jamie pointed to her tablet. "I've got it all down on paper."

Donnie grinned. "It was worth it," he said. "All those hours I put into it, trying to find the perfect ingredients to go into my jam and butter spread. Not to mention what I use to baste the turkey itself, all of which is a secret, of course. It's all up here," he added, pointing to his head.

"I want this thing to be big," Donnie said. "I'm going to present it to the town next Saturday. I'm going to have free helium balloons and cookies. I've already set most of it up. I hired this lady, Mrs. Bakker, who hands out cookies at Bi-Lo, so she's going to take care of dessert, and then I hired the musician from the parade today. Gave him some money up front so he could fix his speaker," he added.

"So you want me to print the review on Friday?" Jamie asked, "and announce the little party you're planning for the following day?"

"Yes, indeedy," Donnie said. "Let me get these plates out of your way."

"Oh, what do you plan to call this grand new addition to your menu?" Jamie asked.

He grinned. "That's simple. I'm going to call it 'Maynard's Famous Turkey Wrap.' "

Jamie nodded as he hurried away. She looked at Max. "I knew that."

He leaned close and took her hand. "You're beautiful. I'm glad I married you. If I hadn't married you I wouldn't get the inside scoop on all this top secret stuff." He paused and looked around. "I wouldn't get all these free meals."

Jamie nodded. "You just have to know the right people, Holt."

He looked about the small restaurant. "Remember the first time we came here?" She nodded and he squeezed her hand again. "I was already hot for you."

"No!"

"Oh, yeah. I knew you would be the one. I have great memories of this place."

"Really?" she said softly. "How would you like to make a new memory?"

He pondered it briefly. "You know, I think it would be great, sweetheart, but I'm afraid Donnie might walk in on us."

"We're going to have a baby, Max."

Lydia pulled into her driveway and pressed the button attached to her visor. The garage door lifted slowly, and she pulled inside, pressed the button once more and waited for it to close. She had followed her instructions to a T.

"Bastard," she muttered. Without wasting a second, she grabbed the pharmacy bag and went inside. The house was quiet. In the master bath, she took one of Ben's syringes, a foil pack containing an alcohol swab, and went in search of her husband. The first floor was empty.

She started upstairs, paused and took a deep breath, and continued on. She gasped when she found Ben bound and gagged in one of the guest rooms. "Oh, my —" Her eyes filled with horror. She raced forward and yanked the cloth from his mouth. "Are you okay?" she whispered frantically.

"You don't need to be up here."

"Where is he?"

"I don't know. Just give me the injection and go."

"Any symptoms?"

"I'm thirsty. Lydia, please."

She cleaned the rubber tip at the top of

the vial. Her hands shook so violently it slipped from her fingers. She bent to retrieve it, swayed, grabbed Ben's arm to keep from falling.

"Sweetheart, you need to calm down," he whispered.

"I saw Maggie." She choked on her tears. "I should have warned her, Ben. I should have said something. He's going to hurt her, I just know it." The words tumbled from her mouth rapidly and in no order. "I'm not thinking straight. I almost ran off the road several times. He's pulled the drapes. Nobody will be able to get to him. He'll kill you if he suspects someone is out there." Her cheeks were wet. "Tell me what to do! Please —"

"Give me the injection."

Lydia swabbed both the rubber tip and his arms with alcohol. She drew insulin into the syringe and put the vial in her pocket. She raised the needle. Ben's expression changed. She turned.

Carl Lee Stanton stood in the doorway. "Why are you up here?" His voice was low but as threatening as the gun in his hand.

"My husband needs his insulin."

"Step away from him."

"What!"

Carl Lee pulled back the hammer on his gun.

"Do as he says," Ben told his wife.

Lydia moved aside. "Mr. Stanton —"

"Shut up," Carl Lee said and walked over to her. He took the syringe. She frowned.

"Where is the vial of insulin?" he asked.

"What?" She stared at him for a full minute. "The pharmacy was closed when I got there. I had to use what little was left in the old vial."

"You're lying."

"Look in the bathroom trash. I just threw it away. I need to go back out. I need to call his doctor. The Wal-Mart pharmacy will still be open."

"You're not going anywhere."

"You don't understand," she said.

"No, Lydia, *you* don't understand." He pressed the syringe, and the insulin spurted out.

Zack parked Maggie's car as close to the back door as he could. "Hold tight for a few seconds," he said, hitting the master lock as he climbed out. He and Bill searched the area.

In the backseat of the car, Mel sighed. "This is so dumb."

Maggie did not try to mask her annoyance. "It's not dumb. What's dumb is that I didn't *make* you go to Charleston. I should have hauled you right up there and *forced* you to do as I said instead of letting you talk me into staying here. *That's* what is dumb, Mel. And tomorrow, I am going to take you to Charleston if I have to drag you every step of the way."

"What!"

"I'm calling Cheryl tonight and arrange it. You *will* do as I say or you will face serious consequences." Maggie had to stop and suck in oxygen. It had happened. Her daughter had driven her over the edge.

"I *hate* living with you! I wish I could live anywhere but here."

Maggie twisted around in her seat. "That is great news," she said loudly, "because you are going to be living with Cheryl for a while. And then when you get home you can live in your room for a while. And I have even better news. By the time I let you out you'll be old enough to date."

The locks on the doors clicked, and Maggie jumped. Tension knotted her stomach. Zack opened the door and stuck his head in. "Hello, ladies," he said, giving them a smile even as they glared out their windows into the darkness. "You know, Bill and I were just saying what a great thing it is that a mother and daughter are able to communicate so freely."

"Is it safe for us to get out of the car now?" Mel grumbled.

"Probably safer than it is for the two of you to remain inside with each other."

Zack had already disabled the alarm; he and Bill saw that Maggie and Mel were safely inside the house before the two men headed back out to unload groceries. Mel crossed the kitchen toward the hall.

"I'll need your help putting away the groceries," Maggie said, trying to sound calm even though she wasn't sure she remembered what it was like. She had been *insane* to keep Mel there, to put her own child at risk. She should have yanked the kid out of school the minute Jamie told her the news. She should have put the girl, kicking and screaming, in the car and driven her straight to Cheryl's. What had she been thinking? What *had* she been thinking!

She and Mel were quiet as they put the food away, using the light over the stove and a large candle. In the living room, Zack was in the middle of a phone conversation, his voice so soft she couldn't make out the words.

"Is it okay if I go to my room now?" Mel asked once they were done.

"After you set the table," Maggie said.

"You're going to cook *now?*" Mel said.

"Yes." Maggie was determined to put a hot meal on the table even though it was well past the dinner hour.

"I'm not hungry," Mel said.

"Then you can provide interesting dinner conversation while Zack and I eat. But set a plate for yourself in case you change your mind." Maggie gave her best smile. As though everything were perfectly fine, even though they could have been a poster family for dysfunctional homes.

Mel stared at her for several seconds. Finally, she went to the cabinet and pulled out plates and salad bowls. She quickly set them out, along with the flatware and salad dressing, and without a word went to her room.

Maggie put a large pan of water on the stove to boil, grabbed a bag of chopped broccoli from the freezer and stuck it in the microwave to thaw while she gathered the ingredients for a broccoli casserole: fat-free cheese, reduced-fat cream of mushroom soup, and light mayonnaise. She mixed it all together, and slid the casserole dish into the oven that had been set on a high temperature.

Zack came into the room as she was tossing a salad. "You're cooking?"

Maggie smiled and nodded. "Mel looked surprised too," she said, "but I'm tired of sandwiches. It won't take long. I picked up a rotisserie chicken at the grocery store."

"Is Mel in her room?"

"Yes. She's in the process of making a list of reasons to hate me. Or maybe she's on the phone with the Department of Social Services."

"Why does she hate you?"

"Other than the fact I'm mean and don't want her to have any fun? Because I'm sending her to Charleston in the morning, even if I have to request a patrol car and have her handcuffed. I'm furious at myself for waiting so long."

"You're too hard on yourself, Maggie," he said, coming up behind her and massaging her shoulders. "I know why you didn't send her away. You wanted to keep a close eye on her. In case I haven't told you, you're a pretty awesome mom. And —" He paused and grinned. "Mel is a pretty awesome kid."

"She can be," Maggie said softly. "Mel and I have never had this much trouble between us, and I don't think she takes this situation with Carl Lee seriously. Maybe because of all the waiting and nothing happening," she added.

Zack stepped closer and worked his fingers up her neck, pausing at the base of her skull, his thumbs pressing gently, drawing small circles. "Things will settle down once this is over. Wow, you're tense."

Maggie almost groaned in pleasure as he kneaded the tight muscles in her neck. "I should write myself a prescription for Valium. I should start drinking. Oh, crap, I should start exercising again."

They became silent. "I've been thinking about last night a lot, Maggie," he said softly. "And no, it wasn't all about the sex part."

Maggie had been thinking about it too, and she had to admit she *had* thought a lot about the sex part. But sex with Zack was the last thing she needed to be thinking about. "I'm surprised you haven't tried to escape this place," she said, trying to make a joke because talking about their lovemaking made her head spin and her stomach flutter. Obviously, it made the muscles in her neck tense too.

"I was thinking maybe when this is over I could visit you and Mel once in a while. Maybe you guys could come to Virginia."

"The water is boiling," Maggie said, stepping away from him. She pulled fresh corn on the cob from the refrigerator and gently dropped it into the pot.

"What do you think?" he asked.

"That's a great thought, Zack, but you'll probably have an assignment waiting when you return to Virginia, and there's no telling where you'll be or how long you'll be away."

"Not until I'm on the mend," he said. "I could show you and Mel a great time in Virginia."

Maggie checked the casserole, found it bubbling and took it from the oven. She pulled the still warm rotisserie chicken from the carton. "It really does sound nice, Zack, but I have a practice to run, and Mel's in school all week, during which time she plans her weekend to the nth of a second. Plus, I'm on call every other weekend."

"Is that a maybe?"

Maggie looked at him. He was smiling, but she was not. She could feel the frown between her eyebrows. "I can't think about that right now. Good grief, I can't even think about five minutes from now." She searched his face. "You're accustomed to dealing with dangerous people, but Mel and I aren't. We're just average citizens, Zack."

"You and Mel are anything but average," he said with a chuckle. "The two of you are pretty special, Maggie."

She avoided looking at him because she

knew she was wearing a wimpy expression. "Would you please tell Mel dinner is ready?" she said, trying to keep her voice light.

Mel dipped half a tablespoon of the casserole onto her plate and refused Maggie's offer of baked chicken or corn on the cob. Maggie gave Zack a look that told him to ignore it.

"Did you check to see if Butterbean was okay?" Mel asked Zack. "Or if she's even here?"

"She's sleeping like a baby," he said. "It'll probably take her a couple of days to catch up on her rest."

"I feel sorry for her," Mel went on, "that she can't be around Jamie's dog. Nobody cares or takes it seriously because they're animals. But dogs and goats have feelings too." She picked at her broccoli. "I don't blame them for running away."

Maggie saw that Mel was itching for a fight. She wanted to send her evil-witch-dictator mother on a first-class, all-expenses-paid guilt trip. Only Maggie wasn't buying. She had to stop getting wrapped up in Mel's *stuff.* Her thirteen-year-old hormone-induced dramas would drive Maggie nuts if she let it. She gave a mental sigh. If thirteen was going to be like this, fourteen and fifteen was going to be hell on wheels and kick Maggie's butt.

Maggie was going to protect her butt. She looked up and smiled at her daughter. "More broccoli casserole or are you full?"

Maggie lounged on the sofa reading her *People* magazine by candlelight while Zack napped in the big overstuffed chair nearby. The house was quiet. Mel had been in bed for a couple of hours. Maggie had showered and put on her favorite Victoria's Secret signature pajamas, pink satin with black piping. Understated elegance, the caption had read. She decided that look was perfect for a single mother and doctor who hadn't had a man in her bed since long before the warranty on her mattress had expired.

Maggie closed her magazine, her weekly update of who was sleeping with whom in Hollywood. There was a whole lot more sex going on in Hollywood and New York than in Beaumont, South Carolina. Not many people in Beaumont had affairs. There was only one really seedy motel, and Abby Bradley passed it on her way to and from the ice-cream parlor each day so fooling around was risky.

Maggie sighed. She was restless and wide-eyed awake. Three-hour naps had a way of doing that to a person, she thought. She wanted to move around. She wanted to go outside and breathe in the night air and feel it on her skin. She wanted to walk barefoot through the cool grass and gaze at the stars. Even jogging sounded palatable at the moment.

She did not want to sit in a dark living room and think about the sad state her life was in.

She needed to throw off the crap that was dragging her down. She needed to be positive. She needed, um, cake! She tossed her magazine aside and started to get up.

"Maggie?"

She turned to Zack, still sprawled in the chair, head back, eyes closed. "I thought you were asleep," she said quietly.

"FBI guys don't sleep. We take short breathers."

"You slept last night," she said. "I heard you snoring."

"I don't snore."

"You snore."

"You're bored, aren't you?" He grinned.

"How can you tell?"

"You sigh a lot when you're bored."

"Really?" Maggie hadn't realized. Her mother sighed a lot. Mel sighed a lot. And all three of them muttered under their breath when they were annoyed, and they had this eye-rolling thing going on. Their gene pool had to be one weird swimming hole.

"You want to play strip poker by candle-light?"

She looked at him and tried not to sigh.

"You want to sit in my lap?"

"Excuse me?"

He gave her a sexy, lazy-as-a-river smile. "Stop playing hard to get," he said. "You wouldn't have worn those slutty pajamas if you didn't want me."

Maggie found comfort in his casual, laid-back demeanor. He didn't appear worried or afraid. He wore his confidence on his wide, squared shoulders and in his stance and how he held his head.

"Don't make me beg," he said. "All I have left is my pride."

Maggie suddenly realized that the one place she really wanted to be was in Zack Madden's lap. She rose and walked over to him. He held out his arms, and she sank against him. He felt warm and solid beneath her. Maggie swung her legs over the side of the chair and leaned against his chest. He wrapped his arms around her and pressed his lips into her hair.

"You always smell good," he said. "How come you smell good when you're allergic to everything that smells good?"

"What you smell is chocolate oozing from my pores." Maggie tipped her face back to look at him. He took it as an invitation to kiss her. His lips barely grazed hers, light as dandelion fluff. It reached inside and touched her heart.

Zack leaned back, and they simply gazed into each other's faces in the semidark. Maggie saw the longing. She touched his cheek, explored his face with her fingertips. She leaned forward and touched his lips with hers. His mouth was warm and firm and responsive. Maggie got lost in it. Zack stroked her bare arm, and she wondered how he managed to make her skin feel so good.

Maggie was self-consciously aware of her breathing, ragged and unsteady. Then she realized Zack seemed to be having the same problem. She could feel his heart thumping in time with hers. They kissed and touched until Maggie felt achy all over but in a good way.

She wasn't sure how they made it upstairs, only that she had forgotten the fifth step creaked. In the quiet house it seemed to cut the air like a siren. They waited. As they headed upstairs once more, Maggie swore she would never again become annoyed with Mel for being a sound sleeper.

"Maggie!"

The roar of her name was so loud it yanked Maggie from her dream the next morning. Her feet hit the floor before her brain became fully awake, before Zack bellowed her name a second time. She skidded into the kitchen. Anger knotted his forehead. "What!" she cried.

"Did you touch this alarm system?"

"No!"

"Well, *somebody* did. The damn thing is disarmed. Mel, wake up," he shouted, already making his way down the hall. "Mel, get out here!"

Maggie winced. "Good grief! Would you stop yelling?"

Zack didn't wait for Mel to open her door. He knocked loudly. "I'm coming in," he warned. He opened the door and looked inside. "Where the hell is she?"

"What do you mean where *is* she?" Maggie said, pushing him aside and entering her daughter's bedroom. No sign of Mel, only a sheet of paper on the bed.

Zack reached it first. "Dammit!" he shouted. "She's gone! She's run away from home!"

"What!" Maggie shrieked the word. She

yanked the note from him and scanned it as Zack turned and raced down the hall. He flung open the back door and hurried out. Maggie's heart pounded as she ran behind him.

Outside, Maggie called her daughter's name as she and Zack searched the property. They found Mel's bicycle lying on the ground behind the shed, her school back pack nearby. Maggie simply stared in stunned silence as she tried to take it in. She caught Zack's gaze, followed it, and drew in a sharp breath when she spied a bracelet of beads that Mel often wore, the twine broken so that many of the beads had scattered across the grass. "Oh, my God!" she cried. "He has her!" She reached for the bracelet.

"Don't touch it," Zack said.

Maggie yanked her head up, and saw the expression in his eyes that told her they were thinking the same thing. Her world came crashing down around her.

CHAPTER FOURTEEN

Lamar Tevis and one of his deputies, disguised in full fishing regalia, including wading boots, stood near the bicycle as Bud from the crime lab, dressed in white, paint-splattered overalls and carrying his crime-scene gear in a large paint bucket, dusted for fingerprints. The two officers assisting him were similarly dressed so they looked like a painting crew. Lamar stared openly at the little goat busily chewing on a garden hose. Fleas was curled beside her.

"Whose goat is that?" Lamar asked.

Zack and Max looked up from the map they were studying.

"Somebody gave it to Maggie," Zack said.

"Oh, gur-reat," Lamar said. "Dr. Davenport knows she's not supposed to have a goat inside the city limits. How do you think I'm going to feel having to ticket her at a time like this?"

"Like a jerk?" Bud replied.

"Chief, do I really have to stand here holding this fishing pole?" the young officer beside him asked. He had recently joined the force, and Lamar had insisted on personally showing him how things were done. "Anybody who sees this fish dangling from my line is going to know it's a fake. This fish is *posing*. And my waders won't stay up." He'd barely gotten the words out of his mouth before the left one slid down and clumped at his ankle.

"They're props," Lamar said, "I told you I want everybody in *disguise*. Why do you think we're riding around in a rust bucket pickup truck, pulling a fishing boat that would sink in a bathtub? We don't know that our kidnapper isn't watching us right at this very moment." Lamar raised his binoculars to his eyes and scanned the property once more.

"Why would the kidnapper hang around if he's got the girl?" the rookie asked.

" 'Cause some criminals are sick in the head, and they get their kicks watching folks suffer." Lamar lowered his binoculars. "Hey, Zack, what's in that building at the back of the property?" he asked.

Zack and Max were combing a map of Beaumont, and Max was marking wooded and isolated areas. Zack looked up. "That's where Maggie keeps her chickens."

"Chickens!" Lamar slapped one hand against his forehead. "It's like a zoo back here."

"That looks like the same goat that interrupted the parade yesterday," the young cop said. "Same dog, too. He almost bit me."

"Oh, good grief," Lamar said. "I don't need this right now. I got enough stress, what with the girl missing and all. Now, I got farm animals inside the city limits, and I find out that goat and that dangerous dog obstructed our parade. That's at least four or five offenses."

"How can it be an offense to obstruct a parade when it wasn't even a real parade?" the other cop asked, reaching to pull up one of his waders again.

"Doesn't matter if it was a fake parade or not," Lamar said. "That dog is a menace."

Zack glanced up. "What do you mean by *fake* parade?"

Lamar threw up his hands. "Just one more piece of nonsense I've had to deal with since Stanton's escape," he said. "Some phony-baloney practical joker thought it would be real *cute* to pose as a famous Elvis impersonator just so the town would give him a parade. Said it was all part of the convention, only later we found out the guys running the convention didn't know a dang thing about it and said this so-called *famous impersonator* didn't exist. The whole thing was a big fat hoax."

Zack was clearly stunned. "So now we know how Carl Lee Stanton got through the road blocks. I'm surprised you didn't offer him a police escort."

Lamar started to say something; instead, he closed his mouth and looked at the ground, red-faced. Delores from dispatch spoke from the radio, and he answered. He pulled his small notebook from his pocket. "Can you give me an update on Operation Find Kidnapped Girl and Catch Dangerous Sicko Guy?" he asked, having named the case.

Standing a short distance away, Zack gave an impatient sigh and looked at Max.

"Lamar is retiring soon," Max said quietly. "I know it doesn't feel like it, but he's moving pretty quickly on this. It has only been an hour since Mel was discovered missing."

"It's not just Lamar," Zack said. "I didn't do my job. I got *involved* with Maggie and lost my damn head. Now her daughter has been abducted. There's no excuse for my actions."

Max put his hands on Zack's shoulder. "Hey, wait a minute. You've given Maggie and Mel around-the-clock protection. You put in a top-notch alarm system. It was installed to stop someone from getting in, not out."

Zack didn't respond. He joined Lamar and waited for him to get off his radio. "Where do we stand?"

Lamar glanced down at his notebook containing Zack's instructions as well as his own notes. "The posters will be ready to hit the street in an hour," he said. "The local media has alerted the public to the girl's kidnapping and asked for volunteers to join search parties. They've already started streaming into the armory building, and a number of my men are on hand to brief them. None of Dr. Davenport's neighbors noticed anything out of the ordinary."

"And the search warrants?" Zack asked.

"We're working on it. The judge is on standby."

"What about the search and rescue dogs?" He handed Lamar the map. "We need to get dogs to these areas as soon as we can."

"We're, um, working on that, too," Lamar said, "but we sorta ran into a little snag on account of most of the dogs are in Atlanta where they're holding some kind of appreciation ceremony for the hard work these dogs and their trainers have done."

Zack frowned. "Are you saying there are no dogs available to search for Dr. Davenport's daughter?"

"We have a couple, but one is ready to have puppies, and the other one is lame. I put in a few calls to Charleston, but they've got dogs searching for an elderly lady who wandered away from some old folks' home, and then a couple of teenagers were out hiking and obviously got lost 'cause they didn't return to camp."

"I don't need all the details," Zack said, obviously growing frustrated by the moment.

"I'm thinking maybe I could send some coon dogs out," Lamar said.

"Maggie, they are going to find Mel," Jamie said. "Practically the whole town is searching for her."

"Yes, but what condition will she be in?" Maggie said. "We already know what Carl Lee is capable of." She covered her face with both hands. "This is my fault. I *ran* her off. My own child," she added, "because I was unreasonable and demanding." Her voice broke, and tears filled her eyes once again. She dropped her hands to her lap. "And would you like to know what I was doing as my daughter slipped out?" She didn't wait for an answer. "I was upstairs, in bed with Zack!"

Maggie heard a sound, looked up, and found Everest standing in front of her holding a cup, his mouth slightly agape. She was too upset to blush.

"I made fresh coffee for the men, Dr. D." Everest said, having appointed himself host, "and I set out that box of doughnuts and I sliced the cake and put it on a nice plate and —"

"You cut my chocolate cake!"

He covered his mouth with one hand. "Uh-oh." It came out muffled. He removed his hand. "Uh-oh."

"Never mind," she said miserably. She took the cup and patted his hand. "The way I feel right now I would probably eat the whole thing and blow up like a hot air balloon. Did you check in with Queenie?"

He nodded. "She's still at the office rescheduling your appointments," he said. "She phoned Dr. Gray like you said, and he's going to follow up on the boy in the hospital."

"Jimmy Sanders," Maggie said. "That's good." Queenie had shown up to see if her black hen had finally laid an egg, only minutes after Maggie and Zack had discovered Mel was missing. That the hen had still not produced the egg Queenie claimed she needed desperately in order to stop Carl Lee only added to her distress. Maggie had sent her to the office to cancel her appointments for the next few days.

Everest looked at Jamie. "Would you like coffee?"

"I don't drink coffee."

Maggie looked at her. "Are you, um — ?"

"Yes." Jamie smiled.

"That's great, Jamie." Maggie took her hand and squeezed it. "I'm really happy for you and Max." She forced herself to smile, just as she had forced herself to remain as calm as possible while Zack, Max, and Lamar discussed strategy. She was afraid if she let her guard down she would loose it completely. She knew police and volunteers were sweeping the town looking for her daughter, but it did not stop her from imagining the worst.

Carl Lee followed a tray-laden Lydia up the flight of stairs to the second floor and to the guest bedroom that had looked out over the backyard until Carl Lee had nailed a sheet of plywood over the window. He held his pistol in one hand, a key in the other. He unlocked the door, pushed it open, and Lydia carried the tray inside. She set it on the night table.

Mel was awake. Her wrists and ankles had been bound and joined behind her, her mouth covered with duct tape. Her eyes climbed to Carl Lee's face, her gaze sharp and assessing and unwavering.

Lydia looked up at Carl Lee and he nodded. She leaned over the bed and very gently peeled the tape from Mel's mouth. The girl sucked in air. "I'm going to give you something to drink, sweetie," Lydia said, offering a tremulous smile. She reached for a glass of orange juice in which a bendable straw had been placed. Her hands shook as she helped Mel raise her head, then put the straw to her lips. Mel sucked greedily. "I have a sweet roll for you too," Lydia said.

"She doesn't even resemble her mother," Carl Lee said.

Mel's green eyes flickered and filled with contempt.

"Oh, I think she does," Lydia said softly.

"Where's Ben?" Mel asked.

"He's in the next room, dear."

Mel looked at Carl Lee. "I want to be in the same room with Ben. I don't want to be in this dumb Barbie room." Lydia looked hurt. "I'm sorry, but I've never really been a big Barbie fan," Mel said.

"Who are those people with your mother?" Carl Lee said. "They're dressed in fishing clothes."

Mel gave him her "you're so dumb" look. "Fishermen?"

"You've got a smart-ass mouth, kid, you know that?"

"Why did you grab me last night?" she said.

His smile was more of a smirk. "Because it was so easy. That's what happens to little girls who sneak out at night."

"You're not going to get away with this," Mel said. "They'll find you."

"Tape her mouth shut," Carl Lee told Lydia.

"She hasn't eaten."

"When she gets hungry enough she'll answer my questions," Carl Lee said.

Lydia hesitated.

"My mother told me all about you," Mel said.

Carl Lee looked at her. "Yeah, what did she say?"

"She told me what you did. Why did you shoot those men?"

He shrugged. "Because I could," he said. "Put the tape back on the kid's big mouth and let's go," he told Lydia once again.

Tears filled Lydia's eyes as she gently

placed the tape over Mel's mouth. Carl Lee motioned the woman toward the door. He looked at Mel and smiled. "By the way, did your mother ever tell you about the time I played a little joke on her?" he asked and laughed. "I put her in the trunk of my car and locked her in. It was funny as hell." He laughed again. "But here's the really funny part. Right after I put her in, I shook this bag over her and all these field mice fell right on top of her. The look on her face was priceless, especially since I'd bound and gagged her, and she couldn't do anything about it. Funniest damn thing I'd ever seen."

Jamie had needed something to fill her time once Maggie had gone into her bedroom to be alone for a while, so she had grabbed a cloth and beeswax and begun polishing the antique pieces Maggie had restored and loved so well. Her cell phone rang, and Jamie grabbed it from her purse. She answered and received an enormous sneeze in response.

"Hi, Destiny," she said. Jamie would recognize that sneeze anywhere.

"Sorry, I didn't mean to do that in your ear," Destiny said. "I haven't slept all night for sneezing —" She paused and sneezed again. "I had this vision last night, and I keep seeing it over and over in my head. A little girl, tied up, with something covering her mouth. I couldn't see her face or the color of her hair, and I couldn't tell how old she was, but her wrists and ankles were tied together. I didn't really *see* that her ankles were tied together because somebody had covered her in a bedspread with doll faces on it. I just sort of knew in my vision that they were tied, you know?"

Jamie could feel the tension building inside as she considered what Destiny was telling her.

"I didn't think anything about it until I stopped by the Full Scoop ice-cream parlor," Destiny said. "Abby Bradley has a little coffee area now. She told me Maggie's daughter had run away. So I got to thinking maybe there's a connection or I wouldn't be sneezing like this. You know I sneeze when my visions are true."

Maggie lay very still on her bed with a wet cloth over her face. She had suffered through a case of dry heaves that had left her weak and trembling. Her phone rang, and she almost dreaded answering it in case it was another friend or neighbor asking if there had been any word on Mel. But she had refused Jamie's offer to catch the phone calls in case her daughter called.

Her voice croaked when she spoke into the phone.

"Dr. Davenport, is that you?"

Maggie sat up quickly at the sound of McKelvey's voice. "Yes, I'm here," she said, her heart already beating hard.

"He called me."

Maggie took a deep shaky breath. "And?"

"He was angry. I told him I wanted to help him, and that I had kept my promise about not calling the police. I offered to meet with him. I even gave him my cell phone number so he could reach me at any time." McKelvey paused. "I'm on my way to Beaumont, Dr. Davenport. I'm calling from the Atlanta airport. I'll be flying in to Savannah where I'll rent a car and head your way. I want to help you and your daughter. Please take down my cell phone number in case you need to reach me before I get there."

He called it out to Maggie, and she scribbled it down. "What do you plan to do?" she asked.

"When Carl Lee makes an appearance I want to be there. I can talk to him. I can try to convince him to —"

"You said *when*," Maggie said.

Silence.

"He's already in Beaumont, isn't he," she said. "He called you so he could tell you he's already here."

"In so many words, yes."

"What words, Dr. McKelvey?"

The man took a deep breath. "He called me and told me to get a message to you. He told me to tell you that he's closer than you think."

CHAPTER FIFTEEN

Zack stopped outside Maggie's bedroom door and tapped lightly. He found her sitting on the edge of her bed, her eyes red and swollen. He closed the door. "How are you holding up, pretty lady?" he asked as he sat beside her and placed his hand on her knee.

She looked at him. "I need to be out there searching for my daughter, Zack. I'll go mad if I have to just sit here and wait."

"Babe, you need to be here in case you get a phone call."

She wanted to tell him she had *already* received a phone call, but she hesitated. She didn't know if McKelvey would be able to help or not, didn't know if the man was even competent or if Carl Lee would listen or sooner kill him than anyone. But the police had given her nothing, *nothing,* and now her daughter was missing, and Maggie was frozen with fear. She couldn't think or make the slightest decision. It was like trying to find the shallow end of a pool and discovering both ends were deep and well over her head. She pressed her fists against her head as though it would push aside the mental pictures, all worst-case scenarios that her daughter might be experiencing at this very moment.

"Maggie, we're going to find her," he said. "I won't stop looking until we do."

She swung her gaze in his direction. She tried to read his expression. Sorrow? Dread? Pity? "What if it's too late?"

"Maggie, you have to trust me. I care about Mel, too. I will do whatever it takes."

Maggie's eyes were suddenly hard. "I know you will, Zack, but there's something else I want you to do for me. Once you find Mel, I want Carl Lee dead."

Zack disabled the alarm for Queenie. She looked weary as she came through the back door. In one hand she grasped her purse and a plastic bag emblazoned with the Full Scoop name, beneath it a strawberry ice cream cone dusted with colorful candy sprinkles. In the other hand she gripped a worn and faded gift bag announcing someone was fifty and over-the-hill. "Reinforcement," she said, putting the bag of ice cream in the freezer. "If Abby Bradley didn't have our favorite flavor I would never set foot in her place again."

Maggie sat at the kitchen table in the chair nearest the telephone. Waiting. Checking her caller ID each time it rang, avoiding calls from the well-wishers and the concerned. Lamar and his men had cleared off the property, but they weren't far away. Zack's rifle sat at the bottom of the stairs.

Max walked into the room. "Okay, sorry it took so long, but the phones are up. The calls are routed to my computer where they'll be scanned immediately. We'll be able to check numbers that are otherwise unavailable. Jamie's still lying down?"

Maggie nodded. Jamie had felt queasy so Maggie had insisted she lie down in Mel's room. "I gave her a couple of magazines. She'll be fine."

Max and Zack returned to the living room. Queenie stared at photos clipped to a magnet on the freezer door. Maggie and Mel had taken pictures of each other during Mel's spring break when they'd gone to Disney World in Orlando. Queenie's face drooped, Maggie noticed, and the light had gone out of her eyes. And Maggie was unable to comfort her because she had nothing left inside.

"You should have seen Abby Bradley holding court with the women customers in her new Gourmet Coffee Parlor, as she calls it. You would have thought the Queen of England had personally flown over and crowned that woman Duchess of Blabberville. And there's poor Travis, just getting out of school and working like a one-armed paper hanger trying to keep up with customers. You'd better believe Abby shut her face when I walked through the door, let me tell you. Next time I give her laryngitis I'm going to make sure I —" Queenie winced, but the words were already out. She averted her gaze.

"Make sure it lasts longer?" Maggie said dully.

"That stupid bird hasn't laid egg one." Queenie sighed. "I've been hexed by a hexing hen." She set her purse and birthday bag down on the table and joined Maggie. They sat there for a moment, thinking their own thoughts.

Maggie could hear Zack on his cell phone in the living room. Agents had searched every house on Zack's list and found nothing, and Maggie's hopes had plummeted to new depths.

Queenie reached into her bag. "I ran by the house and put together a few things," she said. "Oops, I almost forgot, I brought Zack some smart weed. Snake weed would have done just as well, but I didn't have any on hand." She set a small homemade pouch on the table. "He needs to carry it in his pocket. Clears the mind," she added. "It also attracts money, so that's an added feature." She reached into the pocket of her blouse and unfolded a square of tissue. "Silver dime," she said. "You need to put this in your shoe to keep you safe. I brought a bunch of stuff," she said, rummaging through the sack. "Always be prepared, I say."

For once Maggie didn't comment on Queenie's practices. She could see that the woman was upset but doing her best to hide it.

"And look, I brought goofer dust. I always keep it in this can because it's so powerful. You want to lay a good jinx on some old mean person, this will surely do the trick." She paused and rubbed one eye. "I remember when we lived in Charleston and Mel got her hands on my goofer dust and flushed it down the toilet. Do you remember that?"

Maggie nodded. "I remember the plumbing bill."

"That toilet never worked the same after that. I told that girl then if she belonged to me she would have gone down that toilet right behind my goofer dust on account of it takes forever to make a batch."

"Queenie?"

Maggie propped one elbow on the table and leaned against her fist. She knew Queenie talked a lot when she was nervous or upset. Like the night Maggie had gone into labor, the time Mel had fallen from her bicycle and needed stitches. "Are you going to go on like this much longer?" she asked. "You're going to end up with laryngitis like Abby did."

Queenie looked at her. Her black eyes were moist. "I'm going to beat that girl into next week when she gets home." She waited. Hesitated. "I don't guess you've heard anything."

Maggie shook her head. "You know, I've been sitting here thinking." Maggie said. "Mel should have a little Halloween party this year. Not a kiddie party like in the past, something a little more, um —"

"Age appropriate," Queenie supplied. "Meaning no tequila shooters."

"Right. And since you and I would be here acting as chaperones, I don't think parents would have a problem with boys attending. And I think it would be okay if Mel and Travis got together once in a while, like on

Saturday. They could play putt-putt or go to the library. I would drive them, of course."

"Travis is really worried about Mel," Queenie said. "He wants to get a bunch of his friends together on bicycles and look for her. I told him you'd call him if you wanted him to set it up. I hate I had to lie to him about Zack being gone. He's such a nice boy. On the honor roll too," she added.

"Yes, he's very polite," Maggie said, remembering how respectful he'd been when she'd called and taken him to task for slipping out of the theater with Mel.

"Of course, Mel is going to have to realize that if she wants to have a little more freedom, she has to earn it," Maggie continued. "She'll have to take on more responsibility around here, and improve her attitude."

"Amen to that," Queenie said.

"And she has to regain my trust."

"Are you going to ground her when she comes home?"

"Damn right I am. She's going to read *David Copperfield.*" Maggie gave a tremulous smile. "This is too hard, Queenie," she whispered.

Queenie took one of her hands and held it tightly. "Hold on, Maggie. I'm not going to let you fall."

Carl Lee sipped his beer on Lydia's sofa in
silence while she sat across from him and
glared. He had been drinking for two hours,
his mood becoming progressively worse.
"Does Maggie still have that old trunk that
belonged to her grandma or her great-
grandma or somebody or other?"

Lydia tapped her fingers impatiently on
the arm of the chair. "I don't know what
you're talking about."

"It's sort of grayish-brown and has leather
straps on it."

"Oh. She keeps it in her living room.
Why?"

"I just remember it being in Maggie's
parents' barn. A friend of mine had one just
like it." He took another sip of his beer and
wiped his mouth. "Does she have a boyfriend?"

Lydia gave an enormous sigh of disgust.
"I don't know, and it's none of my business. The woman is trying to build a practice
and raise her child as best she can. Why
can't you just leave her alone? And why
would you take an innocent child who has
never done one thing to you?"

"You need to shut up, Lydia," he said,
waving the gun at her. "I don't think you

know what I'm capable of."

"Well, if you think I'm going to let a child and an old man lie upstairs without food and water you'd better think again. I'd rather be shot than watch suffering."

She stood and squared her shoulders.

Carl Lee immediately straightened. "What the hell do you think you're doing?"

"I just told you."

Lydia turned and started toward the kitchen, her fingers touching the pocket that held Ben's syringe. She jumped when she heard Carl Lee pull back the hammer on his gun. Lydia closed her eyes and took a deep breath. And waited.

Carl Lee laughed.

Zack walked into the room with his coffee cup, and his gaze immediately sought out Maggie. "How are you doing?" She shrugged and looked away because her tears were too near the surface, and her eyes already ached from crying.

Queenie reached for the small pouch and handed it to Zack. "Keep this in your pocket," she said. "It'll help you find Mel."

"Really?" He looked it over. "Is it some kind of tracking device?"

"You don't really want to get on my bad side right now," she said.

He grinned and stuffed it into the pocket of his jeans, then filled his coffee cup and returned to the living room.

Max walked down the hall, obviously to check on Jamie.

"Excuse me for a minute, Queenie," Maggie said and joined Zack in the living room. She took in the makeshift office, which had started out with Zack's laptop and had turned into a conglomeration of complicated-looking equipment with Max's arrival. Several telephones had been connected to various blinking apparatuses, and cords sprouted from every direction and coiled like snakes on the wooden floor. She wasn't sure what they were doing, but she knew they were doing everything they could to find her daughter. That was enough.

"Didn't mean to mess up your living room," Zack said, reaching out to her. She joined him on the sofa, and he took her hand and held it for a moment. He turned it over and traced the lines inside her palm.

His touch made her stomach quiver. "I appreciate all your hard work," she said. "Max's, too," she added. "I'm sure you had to lean on Lamar to get things moving so quickly." She suspected he felt as guilty as she did that Mel had slipped from the house unnoticed.

Zack gazed into her light blue eyes. "You're one of the bravest people I've ever met."

Maggie shook her head. "No I'm not. My guts feel like they've been crammed into a washing machine and turned to the spin cycle. I'm hanging by a very thin thread, Zack."

Queenie shouted to them from the kitchen. "Hurry, come look at this!"

The small countertop TV was on, turned to CNN. "It's too early for Paula," Zack said, as he and Maggie entered the room.

"Da-um!" Queenie said, as a dog food commercial came on. "You missed it! But it's coming back on so they'll have more."

"More what?" Maggie said.

"That man that was with Carl Lee," she began quickly. "Not the one that got shot, the other one. Ray or Roy —"

"Ray Boyd," Zack said.

"Okay, well, guess what? Ray and Carl Lee stole a car with a dead man in it!"

Maggie frowned. "Huh?"

"This old guy named Ed White left Alabama because his daughter was going to put him in a nursing home, right? He was gone for a couple of days; it was on the news and in the papers. Anyway, Carl Lee and Roy —"

"Ray," Zack said.

"Okay, *Ray.* Somehow they ended up with Ed's car."

"And he was in it, *dead?*" Maggie asked.

"Nobody knows yet when he actually died. But this is where it gets *weird.*"

"I think what you just told us is pretty weird," Maggie said.

Queenie went on. "Ed's daughter looked out the window this morning, saw her daddy's car in the driveway, ran out to it, and you won't believe what she found!"

"What!" Zack and Maggie said in unison.

"She found her daddy propped in the backseat wearing an Elvis costume and sunglasses! And he was dead! And guess what? Ray Boyd left a note. Said her father died of natural causes and did not suffer."

Max and Jamie came into the room. "Hold on," Queenie said, "it's coming back on."

"They're doing a story on Carl Lee and Ray Boyd," Zack said.

Queenie waved her hands in the air "Quiet!"

Max and Jamie came up beside them, pretending to tiptoe and zip their lips.

"Who is that *ugly* woman taking Paula's place?" Zack said.

Queenie glared at him and turned up the volume.

In a follow-up to our story, police and FBI are still searching for convicted killer Carl Lee Stanton who escaped outside of a hospital near Texas Federal Prison in Houston after complaining of severe chest pains. Roy Boyd —

"Ray!" Zack and Queenie shouted in unison.

Excuse me, that was Ray Boyd. Boyd and another ex-convict named Luis Perez assisted in the escape as Stanton was being led by authorities to the emergency room. Gunfire was exchanged and several guards shot, but all are recuperating. Perez suffered a fatal injury, and his body was later discovered near Birmingham, Alabama. Stanton was serving a life sentence at Texas Federal for robbing and shooting an ATM driver, as well as the shooting death of FBI Agent Robert Hamilton, shown here in a family photo shortly before he was gunned down in the parking lot of a motel in Richmond, Virginia . . .

Maggie and the others leaned in to see the photo. "Da-um," Queenie said. "That agent's son looks like you, Zack."

Agent Hamilton's stepson, also FBI, has worked undercover for ten years and recently put a Colombian cartel out of business, after arresting a dozen key players and confiscating two thousand pounds of cocaine. Paula Zahn will air an interview with this agent in days to come.

Max and Jamie exchanged looks as Maggie and Queenie stared at Zack in disbelief. Queenie reached over and turned down the volume.

"Why didn't you tell me?" Maggie asked, trying to make sense of what she'd just heard.

"That's what I'd like to know," Queenie said. "Do you have any idea what I would give to meet Paula Zahn? Why, I love her almost as much as I love —" She paused and her voice became hushed, reverent. "Oprah."

"It was a long time ago, Maggie," Zack said. "I didn't think it was important —"

Max led Jamie quietly from the room.

"Wait." Maggie pressed her hand against her forehead where everything seemed to be swirling about in all directions. "Your stepfather was the agent that Carl Lee Stanton killed in Virginia fourteen years ago."

"Yes."

"And the FBI assigned you to work this case? To bring in your stepfather's killer?" she asked.

"Unofficially," he said.

"And you didn't think it worth *mentioning* to me? Why is that, Zack?"

"Uh-oh," Queenie said, slipping past them and joining Max and Jamie on the front porch. "I don't want to be in there," she whispered, "when this place blows." Her eyes widened as she looked into Jamie's face. "You're pregnant!"

"Yes," she said, sharing a private smile with Max. "I have my first doctor's appointment the end of the week, but I passed seven in-home pregnancy tests," she said proudly, "and I've already started having morning sickness."

In the kitchen, Zack tried to explain his position. "I didn't feel it was a good time to discuss my stepfather with you."

"That makes me feel pretty dumb since I shared *everything* with you." Maggie suddenly felt very sad, and it showed on her face. "But then, you already knew my secrets when you signed on for this job."

Maggie marched to her bedroom, picked

up her phone and dialed the number she'd left on her bedside table. She suspected McKelvey was en route to Savannah, but she could leave him a message. She was surprised when he picked up.

"Bad news," he said. "The plane has been delayed due to some kind of problem with the electrical system. I may have to take a flight into Charlotte, North Carolina, and fly to Savannah from there. I'm so sorry."

"I understand," Maggie said.

Maggie stepped out on the front porch a few minutes later. Max and Jamie shared the porch swing; Queenie sat nearby in an old rocking chair, one foot pushing it back and forth as though she were priming it to shoot right off the porch. They were quiet.

Maggie put her hands on the porch rail and leaned forward. She closed her eyes and sucked in fresh air. "Sorry 'bout that, guys," she said.

Max grinned. "I'll go in and stitch his wounds." He went inside, leaving the women on the porch. Jamie's phone rang. She grabbed it from her purse and answered it. "Hello, Vera. Yes, we watched CNN. Saw the whole thing." She paused and listened. "You're not serious!" Jamie shook her head. "I'll explain it when I see you."

"What was all that about?" Maggie asked.

"Destiny is in love, might not be coming back. Abby Bradley has already applied for a job as a gossip columnist to fill Destiny's place."

All three women just shook their heads, and Maggie was reminded that no matter how badly somebody was hurting, life went on around them.

She looked out onto the quiet street of her neighborhood. "I've always felt safe here," she said. "Even as a little girl." She knew the bus would have been by already, but she didn't see any of the neighborhood kids playing. She wondered if parents were keeping them inside because of Carl Lee Stanton.

She glanced across the street at Ben and Lydia's house and was surprised to see the drapes closed and the morning newspaper still in their yard. "I don't like the looks of that," she said.

Queenie followed her gaze. "Ben and Lydia's place? They must be out of town."

"Ben's not well," Maggie said. "I can't imagine Lydia taking off or putting him in the hospital without telling me. And I can't believe she hasn't called to see how I am. The police knocked on everybody's door this morning. She has to know. Something strange is going on over there. I'm very worried, but Lydia doesn't want me to *interfere*."

"That doesn't sound like Lydia," Queenie said. "She and Ben are like family."

Maggie nodded sadly. "They're like a second set of grandparents to Mel," she told Jamie. "When their little granddaughter visits, Mel acts like the big sister, and when Lydia wanted to decorate the small guest room for the girl, Mel and I pitched in. We decorated the room in Barbie. Everything is Barbie, right down to the drapes, sheets and bedspread, and rugs."

"The bedspread?" Jamie asked.

"Yes. Barbie faces all over it."

Jamie felt a chill run through her as she stared at the cloaked windows and thought about what Maggie had just said. She looked at Maggie. "I know where Mel is!"

"It's too dangerous," Zack said.

"It's my choice," Maggie told him. "I have no idea what my daughter is going through over there, I don't know if she's hurt, I don't even know if she's alive. Bob and Lydia could be dead. I'll do it with or without your help."

"I'll need time to get things in place," he said sharply.

"I suggest you move quickly."

"There is no phone service going into that house," Max said, "and Southland Phone Company can't find a problem, which means —"

"Stanton cut the phone lines," Zack finished for him, as Maggie grabbed her address book, searching frantically for Lydia's cell phone number.

"I've got it." She picked up her telephone and dialed.

Lydia had just come downstairs with the tray when her cell phone rang. Carl Lee had guarded it carefully by putting it in his pocket. "Only a few people have my cell number," Lydia said.

Carl Lee pulled it from the pocket of his jeans and read the number on the caller ID. "How interesting," he said, his words slurred. "Maggie Davenport." He pointed his gun and handed Lydia the phone. "One wrong word and you're dead."

Lydia pressed the button. "Hello, Maggie," she said, her voice surprisingly calm. She put her hand over the mouthpiece and looked at Carl Lee. "It's for you."

The seconds ticked by slowly as Maggie

waited and wondered if Carl Lee would answer. Her heart pounded so loudly that she feared she wouldn't be able to hear him. She didn't seem to be getting enough air; she felt as though she were living the nightmare all over again, locked in the trunk of his car. Finally, he spoke, and Maggie steeled herself. Her anger was enough.

"You have my daughter." Her tone was cold. "I want her back. Now."

Silence. "Why would I do that, Maggie?" he finally asked. "The longer you feel pain, the better *I* feel."

She could tell he had been drinking, and she didn't know if that was good or bad. "If you want revenge, take it out on me. She doesn't deserve it."

"I didn't deserve what you did to me," he shouted. "I've spent fourteen years thinking about it and wanting to kill you, but that's too easy. There are worse things than death, Maggie. Don't you agree?"

Maggie felt as if she were going to be sick. Her jaw muscles ached; she tried to swallow back the urge to throw up. She weighed her options.

"She's your daughter."

"You're a lying bitch."

"Look at her closely, Carl Lee. Then tell me you don't see her resemblance to Kathleen. It's too obvious to miss."

"But here's the thing, Maggie. I don't care if she's my kid or not, you got it? I don't *care*."

"I can get you out of here alive," Maggie said. "Otherwise you don't stand a chance." Max grabbed the notepad she kept by the phone and scribbled on it. "I will go with you," she added. "I'll be your damn hostage! I'll do anything."

"I love it when you beg, Maggie."

Max shoved the slip of paper in front of her. She read it quickly. "I have a friend here, Carl Lee. His name is Max Holt. He has a special car that we can use. It's bulletproof."

Carl Lee laughed.

"Ask Lydia and Ben about him," Maggie said.

"I'm done talking, Maggie. You send one cop to this door, I'll shoot him on the spot, and I won't stop shooting until everybody in this house is dead, you got that?"

Maggie jumped at the loud click in her ear. She looked up at the anxious group waiting to hear. "He doesn't care," she said, as her stomach lurched. She covered her mouth and ran to the hall bathroom.

Carl Lee shoved the cell phone into his

pocket and pointed his gun at Lydia. Her eyes were sunken from fatigue. "What do you know about a guy named Max Holt and his wonder car?"

Lydia recounted everything she'd heard about Max.

"Upstairs," Carl Lee said. "And don't give me any trouble. Everybody knows I'm here so gunshots no longer matter."

Lydia hesitated. "I heard what you said on the phone. You can't kill your own daughter."

"Really?" He looked amused. "I sat in a courtroom fourteen years ago and listened as a psychiatrist testified that I had no conscience. I think he may have been right."

Upstairs, Mel flinched as Carl Lee yanked the tape from her mouth. He grabbed her jaw, turned her face toward him. "Well, now, aren't you something?" he said, his tone mocking. "Your mother is right. You look just like my sister. I don't know how I missed that." He pulled his hand away.

Mel looked at Lydia, her expression confused.

"Why don't you tell Mel the good news, Lydia?" Carl Lee said.

Lydia gave a shaky sigh as she pulled the Barbie bedspread to the girl's shoulders and patted her gently. "Honey —" She paused and blinked back tears. "This man is your father."

Mel swung her gaze in Carl Lee's direction. "That's a lie!"

He laughed as he nudged Lydia out the door.

Maggie sat on the edge of the tub, massaging her stomach muscles. There had been nothing inside of her to throw up, but it hadn't stopped the violent heaving. Fear shook her. It swallowed her. She covered her face with her hands. She didn't bother to look up when someone tapped on the door.

Zack stepped inside the room and wet a washcloth. He put down the toilet lid, sat down, and reached for Maggie's hand. She pulled away.

"Listen to me, Maggie," he said softly. "Stanton is bluffing." She looked up. Her eyes were filled with pain. Zack tried to choke back his emotion. "Maggie, I would *gladly* take on your pain if I could. I would do *anything* if I could just take —" He paused. "I can't hide in this house anymore. I'm going after Stanton." He stood.

Maggie bolted from the tub. "Oh, hell no, you're not! Carl Lee will kill you the minute you step out this front door," she said, "and then he'll kill everybody in his path, including my daughter. You're all I've got, Zack, my only hope of ending this nightmare and saving Mel's life. Carl Lee can't know you're here."

He turned away and raked his hands through his hair.

"I am begging you," she said. She jumped when the phone rang in the kitchen, and she blindly pushed her way past Zack and ran. She answered on the second ring.

"Okay, Maggie," Carl Lee said. "I think we can make a deal. But first I have a little job for you."

Zack cleared the top of the trunk, moving the laptop and everything else to Maggie's sofa. She emptied it of books and magazines and old newspapers. While the others looked on, Maggie and Zack ran their hands along the old satin lining. "I don't see or feel anything," Zack said.

Maggie hurried from the room. She returned with scissors, chisel, and hammer. "If it's there, I'll find it." The group watched quietly as Maggie cut the lining and ripped it out. When she saw nothing to indicate a false bottom, she slammed the chisel into the wood and pounded with the hammer. Together she and Zack freed the boards and answered the fourteen-year-old question as to where Carl Lee had hidden the robbery money.

"I don't like this one damn bit," Queenie said as Zack helped Maggie adjust the Kevlar vest in her bedroom. "What if he decides to shoot her in the head? Then what?"

"Let's try to think positively," Maggie said, knowing Zack was a breath away from scrapping her plan. She shrugged on her blouse and buttoned it. He and Maggie made their way into the kitchen, Queenie following close behind. Jamie and Max leaned against the kitchen counter. Jamie was clearly upset.

Zack's cell phone rang. He yanked it from his pocket impatiently. "Yeah, what?" he said. His eyes registered surprise. "Um, Miss Zahn, you've caught me at a really bad time," he said as Maggie sighed and gave a major eye roll. "May I call you back?"

"Okay," Zack said to Maggie a few minutes later. "Remember what I told you. I'll be watching every move through the scope. Everybody is on standby."

Maggie nodded. "You're positive the street and sidewalks are clear?"

"Yes. Once it's done, that place will be surrounded. Ambulances too," he added.

"And don't forget, you'll need to —"

"I know what to do, Zack," she said.

His gaze lingered a few seconds before he started for the stairs. Maggie swallowed and dialed Lydia's number as Queenie and Jamie walked into Mel's bedroom and closed the door. Only Max remained.

Carl Lee answered. "Did you find the money?" he asked. "Is it in good shape?"

"Yes, the plastic bags protected it."

"Where is your friend's car? Lydia has already moved hers from the garage. She's waiting so she can close the garage door once it's inside."

"After I speak with Mel."

"Watch what you say, Maggie."

Maggie took a deep breath.

"Mom?"

Tears spurted from Maggie's eyes. She struggled to find her voice. "Oh, honey," she said. "I've missed you so much. Are you okay?"

"Uh-huh. I think Ben is sick. Lydia is very upset."

"I'm sorry to hear that, Mel." Maggie swiped at a tear. "Do you know what to do?"

"Yes, but why are you coming over here?"

"I'm giving Mr. Stanton his money. But you are to walk across the street and go straight inside the house. Queenie and Jamie will be waiting for you."

"Are you going to be okay, Mom?" Mel sounded afraid.

"As long as you do as you're told."

"Okay, but I have something very important I want to ask you later."

Carl Lee took the phone. "I'm waiting on the car."

Maggie turned to Max who walked out the door. "It will be inside the garage in two minutes," she said. "I'll be carrying a black suitcase with me. I will cross the street as Mel crosses." She paused. "I want to be able to give her a hug."

He hung up.

Maggie waited until Max returned through the back door. "Be careful, Maggie."

Maggie waited on her front porch. Across the street, Lydia and Ben's door opened and Mel appeared on the threshold. Maggie's heart soared at the sight of her daughter. On the outside she appeared unharmed. Maggie would do what was necessary to help her with any wounds on the inside, and she took great comfort knowing how strong and determined Mel was. Finally, she nodded at the girl, and they began to walk across the opposite lawns. They met in the center of the street and hugged. Tears streamed down Maggie's cheeks. "You know you're grounded again, right?" Maggie said with a grin.

"Duh. Is Carl Lee Stanton my father?"

"Yes. I'm sorry you had to find it out this way."

"Well, I hate him. If he goes back to prison I don't have to visit him, do I? I mean, a judge can't order it, right?"

"No." Maggie kissed her forehead. "Go to the house, honey. Arm the alarm system. Do not come back out until I get there." She saw the question in Mel's eyes. "You have to trust me."

"Don't forget about Ben."

Maggie stood straight and walked toward the Greens' house. The door was open and empty. She stopped at the bottom of the steps. And stared into the barrel of a gun.

"Let me see what's in the suitcase," Carl Lee said.

Maggie set the suitcase on the ground, flipped the locks, and opened the lid. The money was stacked neatly inside.

"Toss one of the stacks to me," he said.

She did as she was told. It landed inches from the door. "Sorry. Do you want me to try again?"

"Close the suitcase and come forward

slowly."

From Maggie's upstairs guest room, Zack held the rifle steady and looked through the scope, his target fixed on the front door across the street. The window was open, a breeze fluttered the curtain, but Zack was careful to keep the barrel out of sight. "Come out, you mean bastard."

Maggie walked up the steps slowly. She paused at the edge of the porch. She could see Carl Lee's hand on the gun. "Don't point that thing at me."

"Come forward, Maggie."

She sniffed. "I hate guns. Stop pointing it at me."

He pulled the hammer back.

"Okay, I'm coming," she said quickly. She stopped several feet in front of the door. "Could you stop pointing it at my head now? I'm not coming any closer with that gun at my head." She sniffed again.

"Shut up and follow the plan!"

She started to cry. "I'm scared!" She stepped a foot closer. "Stop pointing that gun at my face. What if it goes off accidentally?"

"I'm going to count to three, Maggie," Carl Lee yelled, "and you'd better have your ass inside this door or you won't have a face left."

The words floated to the window where Zack stood, gaze and rifle steady, face dark with hatred.

Maggie hesitated. She didn't fear death; she feared leaving her child motherless.

"One —"

She inched forward.

"Two —"

Maggie cried louder. The suitcase slipped from her hands, hit the porch and fell open, tossing stacks of bills in every direction.

"Shit!" Carl Lee shouted a list of obscenities.

"It's not my fault. This suitcase is crap," Maggie said.

All at once, Carl Lee grabbed a handful of her hair. She yelped and tried to pull free.

"Three!" he said.

Suddenly a look of outright shock and disbelief hit his face, and he went slack. The gun fell just inside the door, and Maggie yanked her hair free. She couldn't tear her eyes from his dazed expression, even as she wondered what was happening.

He suddenly lurched forward as though propelled by a strong wind.

"What the hell?" Zack said, finger poised

on the trigger as he watched Carl Lee stagger forward, unarmed.

Maggie rolled away only seconds before Carl Lee slumped and folded on the threshold. She saw the large knife buried in the back of his neck; her doctor's mind quickly told her the wound was lethal. She looked up at Lydia. Her face ravaged, the woman stepped over Carl Lee's body and offered Maggie her hand. Maggie grasped it tightly. They sobbed in each other's arms. "Ben?" Maggie managed to ask.

"He's holding on," Lydia said.

"Mom!"

Lydia released her, and Maggie turned and smiled as Mel flew out the front door of their house. Not wanting her daughter to see Carl Lee's body, Maggie quickly cleared the steps and porch and met her near the street. Mel threw herself into Maggie's open arms, and they clung together tightly. Maggie drank in her scent as the first siren wailed.

Maggie was jolted from her sleep, her heart pounding hard and erratically, stomach twisting. She bolted upright on the sofa, looked about the room, and her mind quickly flashed a rerun of Carl Lee Stanton's draped body lying in Ben and Lydia's doorway. Carl Lee was dead. She went slack with relief.

It was over. She and Mel were safe. Safe!

She took pleasure in turning on the table lamp. They could stop hiding behind closed drapes and stumbling about in the dark. Life would be normal again. They could go back to their old routine, and Maggie would never again complain about feeling as if she were in a rut. She couldn't wait for her next rut. She looked forward to Mel complaining about how bored she was.

Maggie looked at the clock on the fireplace mantel. Eight P.M. Once she and Mel had pulled themselves together, answered questions put to them by the police, and said good-bye to everyone, they'd slogged to the nearest horizontal location and dropped.

Now, Maggie felt numb. She was grateful that her ordeal and the exhaustion that had followed left her senses dulled. It would make things more bearable over the next few days. Like remembering the regret in Zack's eyes as he'd hugged Mel and promised to keep up with her via e-mail. And watching him drive away, heading back to his life and a career that left little room for anything else. Maggie felt the ache tug the fringes of her heart and dreaded that moment when everything became clear and she had to face the enormous loss.

Zack had made Mel and her laugh. He'd lifted them and comforted them and done all he could to make them safe. That he had personally given Maggie multiple orgasms was an added bonus.

Okay, so she was going to feel like shit for a while.

Maggie heard a car turn into her driveway, and she waited a breathless moment before pulling one drape aside and peering through the small slit. She did not recognize the man who climbed from the car and started up her front walk. She disarmed the alarm system and opened her door, but made certain the storm door was locked. She watched through the glass as the man hurried up the front walk and climbed her front steps. His yellowish-gray hair was mussed, and his navy suit looked as though he'd slept in it.

He gave a sad smile and shrugged helplessly when he saw her looking through the glass. "I know I'm too late, Dr. Davenport. I heard the news in the car on the way over."

Maggie recognized his voice. "Dr. McKelvey?"

He nodded. "James."

■ ■ ■ ■

Zack tried Maggie's number again, and it rang endlessly. "Dammit, Maggie, stop looking at your caller ID and pick up the phone!" He hung up and spouted a foul word. After driving around for more than an hour and missing her so bad his gut ached. Not only that, something was wrong. He felt it. It had begun as a nagging doubt when he'd slipped into Maggie's bedroom with a brief note. He needed time to think, he'd written. He'd reached to put the note on her night table when he'd spied James McKelvey's name and number. He wished now that he'd asked Maggie about it.

He was probably being paranoid, but McKelvey was a drunk who'd been accused of professional misconduct by one of his female patients. Instinct told Zack there was probably more to it or McKelvey would not have closed a lucrative practice or taken a job in a prison, a huge step down professionally. He punched in Max's number. "It's me, Zack," he said, the minute Max answered. "Just how good is that damn computer of yours?"

Maggie unlatched the storm door and

opened it. In all the commotion she had completely forgotten about the man. "Please come in." She closed the door behind him.

"I'm so sorry, Dr. Davenport," he said. "I won't waste your time giving you the dismal details of what I went through to get here. I tried calling you several times on the drive from Savannah."

"I unplugged the phone," she said. "It was literally ringing off the hook, and my daughter and I were just too tired to deal with all the calls." She smiled. "I'm Maggie, by the way." She offered her hand, and they shook. Maggie guessed him to be about fifty years old. He had the ruddy red look and tiny broken veins on either side of his nose that suggested he might indeed be an alcoholic.

"I have reservations at a hotel in town, but I had to come by and make sure you and your little girl were okay. Did I wake you?"

Maggie realized her clothes were badly wrinkled, and she had no idea how her hair looked. She smoothed it back. "I was already awake when you pulled up," she said. "My daughter and I pretty much zonked out once everybody left. Please sit down."

He looked surprised as he took a seat on the sofa. "You're alone?" he asked. "Wouldn't you feel better having a friend or family member with you?"

"We're fine," she said. "Really." She started to sit. "Could I get you a cup of coffee or soft drink?"

"No, thank you."

He slid close to the edge of the sofa, leaned forward, and clasped his hands in front of him. "I heard your daughter was, um, taken hostage. How is she?"

"Shaken but better than most girls her age would be after that kind of experience. Carl Lee did not hurt her in any way," she added. "I think by the time she wakes up, probably a couple of days from now, she'll be even better."

McKelvey studied her. "You're a lot prettier than the grainy newspaper clipping Carl Lee and I have."

Maggie wasn't certain she'd heard him right. "Excuse me?"

He reached for his wallet. "Carl Lee asked me to get him a photo of you. All I was able to get was this newspaper clipping." He pulled it out and unfolded it. "You're much prettier in person."

"I don't understand," she said. "Why do *you* have a clipping of me?"

He looked at her. "I felt —" He paused. "I felt I knew you. You were all he talked about, Maggie. In session after session," he added. "How you followed in your grandfather's footsteps and became a doctor. I'll bet you're a good pediatrician. You have a very gentle and loving nature about you. No wonder Carl Lee couldn't exorcise you from his thoughts," he added. "I imagine it would be difficult for any man."

Maggie heard the warning signs in her mind. "Dr. McKelvey, I'm very tired," she said. "Perhaps we could visit tomorrow." She stood.

He carefully slipped the clipping inside his wallet, which he tucked away. "Obsession is a scary thing, you know. A person can become so fixated with something or someone that he or she will go to any lengths to have it. To possess it," he added, almost in a whisper. "It's crippling, actually. Have you ever wanted anything that badly, Maggie?" He stood slowly.

"Thank you for coming, James." She led him to the door. She did not see the knife until it was at her throat.

"Be very quiet, Maggie," he whispered. "You do not want to wake your daughter. She has been through enough."

Maggie waited for the stark fear to pass. "Why are you doing this? What do you want?"

"I want *you*, Maggie," he said softly. "I've

wanted you for a long time. To possess you. To be inside you. Carl Lee painted very vivid descriptions of what you were like."

"I thought you came here to help me. I thought you were going to try to convince Carl Lee to turn himself in."

"I made sure he was good and dead before I arrived, Maggie. I didn't even like him, although I will be forever in his debt for his gifts. For giving me you," he added, his voice at her ear.

"I can help you, James," she said softly, wondering how his mind had become so twisted.

"Don't talk. Show me to your bedroom. I want to consume you, Maggie."

She took a deep calming breath as she considered her options, which were nil at the moment. Think, she told herself. "Okay," she said her voice calm and even. "Toward the hall, turn left, last door on the left."

They moved slowly and awkwardly in the dark toward her room. Maggie felt her stomach jump when she noted Mel's door was partially open. She had closed it when she headed for bed, telling Maggie she didn't want anybody to bother her for maybe a month.

Maggie's gaze slid about frantically, but

the light from the living room did not reach to the back of the hall. Had Mel gotten up to go to the bathroom and forgotten to close her bedroom door?

"This is my bedroom door," she said.

"Turn the doorknob," he whispered.

She hesitated. Felt a shift in the air. Sensed a presence.

"Do what I said, Maggie."

Maggie reached for the doorknob. She barely had time to open the door before the guest bathroom light flashed on behind them. McKelvey jumped and turned just as the bat came down on his head. He stumbled but remained standing, his eyes fixed on the girl in the pajamas. "You little bitch," he said, and reached for her. Fists clamped tightly into a ball, Maggie swung hard, aimed for the kidney area. He cried out and turned, his eyes dazed with pain but obviously determined to do harm. The bat came down a second time, and he slumped to the floor.

Zack cursed when he found the alarm system disarmed. He shoved the door open. "Maggie! Where are you?"

Leaning against the wall opposite her daughter, Maggie glanced up sharply. "Zack? We're back here," she called out.

"Who the hell disarmed the alarm system?" he shouted. "And whose car is that out front?" He stepped into the hall, blindly searching for the light switch. He flipped it on, his gaze sweeping the scene. "Is that McKelvey?"

Maggie nodded wearily.

"He was going to rape Mom," Mel said, "so I hit him with my baseball bat. Twice."

"Your grandfather lied," Zack said. "You don't swing like a girl."

"Why are you here?" Maggie asked, dazed.

"I told you I needed to think. Didn't you get my note?"

"What note?"

"The note that said I need to think about us and my job and how I really wanted to spend the rest of my life. And I decided I wanted to spend it with the two of you."

"You figured all that out in two hours?" Maggie asked.

"I sort of already suspected." He stepped across McKelvey's prostrate body and pulled Maggie into his arms. "There are times, Maggie, when you just know it's right. This is definitely right."

McKelvey moaned but remained motionless. Zack turned to Mel. "You are one awesome young lady. Why don't you pass me the bat and call 911 for me?"

Mel saluted.

Zack waited until the girl walked away. "I want to marry you, Maggie," Zack said, eyes darting to McKelvey. "I want to be a good husband to you and a great stepdad to Mel."

She stared at him in shock. "Marry me? When?"

"Well, first I have to find a job."

"You quit your job!" she said. "You left the bureau?"

"About five minues ago. I got to thinking about it, and I don't want to go back to that kind of life. It doesn't do for me what it did in the past, and I don't want to worry about people breaking my arms and legs or shooting me in the kneecaps. I need to step back and give the younger men a chance at being a hero like me."

"You guys could get married at Christmas," Mel said, coming back down the hall. "Or Valentine's Day," she added.

"Come here, kid," Zack said, pulling Mel against him and hugging them both. He grinned. "I can't promise you a normal childhood."

"I know."

"But I can promise you one thing. This is going to be fun."

EPILOGUE

Two Weeks Later

Zack walked into Maggie's kitchen, his fingers fumbling with the knot on his tie. He paused. "Do you think we have enough time to, uh, you know, before Queenie arrives with Mel and Travis?"

She turned. She wore an apron over the new robin's-egg-blue silk suit she had bought for the occasion. "After all the time I spent on my makeup and hair? Have you lost your mind?"

"You should have figured that out when I agreed to take Lamar Tevis's place as police chief." He yanked his tie in place. "How do I look?" he said. "I wish my arm weren't in a cast so I could wear a nice suit."

Maggie smiled and carried yet another plate of food to the kitchen table where a spread had already been laid out. "Paula Zahn is going to think you're hot."

"Yeah?" He looked delighted at the prospect. "Um, Maggie? When Paula gets here would you not mention that we're, you know, *engaged?*"

Maggie crossed her arms and tried to look stern.

"And did you ask your mother to try and remember that my name is Zack and not Jack?"

"Give her time, Madden. She and my dad are still dealing with what happened while they were in Egypt." Maggie had kept a few details from them, but they had still taken it hard.

Ben and Lydia, armed with food, knocked on the front door, and Maggie hurried to let them in. A weeklong stint in the hospital had pulled Ben through, and even though the two were smiling, Maggie knew it would take time before they were back to their old selves. "We brought a chocolate cake, and picked up your favorite ice cream at the Full Scoop," Lydia said.

"Uh-oh," Zack said, taking the cake and bag of ice cream and carrying it into the kitchen.

Maggie hugged them as Queenie pulled into the driveway, Everest beside her, Mel and Travis in the backseat. Mel had suffered a few nightmares after her ordeal, but she and Maggie had spent a lot of evenings sitting on Maggie's bed eating Better than Sex chocolate ice cream and talking things out, including the secret Maggie had guarded so long. Mel had been hurt, although she seemed to be taking it in stride, and she had no desire to share the information with the world. She looked forward to having Zack as her stepdad, and she was thrilled to have her first real boyfriend.

Queenie came through the door first, holding up a Full Scoop bag. "I don't guess I have to tell you what's in here."

Everest came in behind her. "Where's Zack?" he said, not waiting for an answer. "I want to show him what two weeks at the gym can do to a man." He held up his shirt. "Look at this washboard-stomach thing I've got going. And guess what? I take my FBI exam next month. If I get accepted I'll have to teach you how to do Mel's hair." He glanced around. "Have to find my main man, Zack." He hurried away.

Maggie greeted Travis and hugged her daughter as Max and Jamie pulled up, followed by Vera and Abby Bradley, the *Gazette*'s new gossip columnist. The column was called "Gab from Abby" and Vera took great pleasure in helping her get the latest scoop.

"Is that a maternity dress?" Maggie asked Jamie, who blushed.

"I know I'm not far along, but I wanted to practice."

Zack came up beside them and shook Max's hand. "How is your new goat?" he said grinning. Max and Jamie had taken Butterbean and put her in the pasture behind the house that was being renovated.

"She and Fleas are enjoying the small barn I had built for them," Max said. "It's a good thing he moved out because no way is Jamie going to share the butter pecan ice cream." He grinned at Zack. "You're looking good, buddy. What time will Paula be here?"

Zack checked his wristwatch. "Any minute now. Notice my new haircut?" he said, showing off his now trimmer hair.

Maggie laughed. "He's waiting with bated breath."

Abby came through the door holding a bag from her ice cream shop. She handed it to Maggie. "Your favorite," she said.

Maggie and Zack stepped back as the house began to fill with guests: Mike Henderson with the cute nurse he'd met at the pharmacy while buying more itch cream for his chicken pox; Lamar Tevis sans wading boots; and finally Destiny and Freddy, who'd flown in to pack up her apartment. It was hard to say what stunned the guests most — Freddy's new look or Destiny's gigantic engagement ring.

Once Vera stopped gaping at the groom-to-be, she studied the ring. Finally, she gave a grunt and looked at Destiny. "Won't this be husband number six for you?"

"Like they say, Vera. Sometimes you have to kiss a lot of frogs before you meet your prince."

"I wish you hadn't said that," Vera told her. "I was just getting my sanity back."

Maggie's parents arrived, her father bearing something tall wrapped in aluminum foil.

"Jack!" the woman said, giving Zack a hug. "You look so handsome. You and Maggie are going to give us beautiful grandchildren."

"Oh, gross," Mel said, giving Travis an eye roll as Maggie kissed her father on the cheek.

"It's okay," Travis said. "My family embarrasses me too." They linked hands and walked out onto the front porch while Maggie's mother proudly displayed the chocolate fudge cake she'd baked in the shape of a pyramid.

Mel rushed through the front door a few

minutes later. "Everybody quiet!" she said. "A limo just pulled up out front. Let's try to act natural so Miss Zahn doesn't think we're a bunch of nutcases."

"Paula Zahn!" Queenie cried, and raced through the door as the house emptied out behind her, women reaching into their purses for pads of paper to get Paula's autograph.

"Oh, gur-reat," Mel said. "We're going to look like a bunch of idiots."

"Well?" Maggie asked Zack, straightening his tie. "Aren't you going to greet our new guest?"

"Okay, but don't get jealous if she can't take her eyes off me," he said.

The group parted as Zack made his way toward the limo. The chauffeur opened the door, and a middle-aged woman with frizzy blond hair, an enormous nose, and clunky glasses stepped out. A man bearing a camera joined her.

Abby nudged Vera. "Get a load of *that,* would you? That Paula Zahn doesn't look a bit like she does on TV. Goes to show you what make up artists and good lighting can do for a person."

Zack gaped at the woman. "Who are you?" he said. "Where is Miss Zahn?"

"Paula couldn't make it," the woman said.

"She's interviewing Oprah today."

"Oprah," Queenie said with a heartfelt sigh.

"I'm her assistant, Pam, and you must be Jack. I don't have a lot of time so if we could just get started. You'll need some sort of disguise, since you worked undercover. Maybe a hat and sunglasses," she added.

"I've got just the hat," Zack said.

In the background, Mel moaned aloud.

Zack saw the last of the guests off, including Queenie, who was driving Mel and Travis to the putt-putt course. "Maggie?" he called out.

He walked down the hall, tapped on her door and opened it. He arched both brows at the sight of his fiancée lying on her side, naked, across the bed. One arm was curled around a half gallon of Better than Sex chocolate ice cream.

Zack looked long and hard at her slim body as she spooned a large scoop of ice cream into her mouth and closed her eyes. "I should have guessed," he said.

She smiled and held up a second spoon.

"Oh, babe." Zack grinned and joined her on the bed.